One Traveler

One Traveler

ALISON TREAT

AVENTURA
PRESS

Cover painting by Sue Hand
www.suehand.com

ISBN-13: 978-1-936936-04-5

Published by
Avventura Press
133 Handley St.
Eynon PA 18403-1305
www.avventurapress.com

First printing February 2013
Printed in the United States of America

For Todd,
my only one

The Road Not Taken

TWO roads diverged in a yellow wood,
And sorry I could not travel both
And be one traveler, long I stood
And looked down one as far as I could
To where it bent in the undergrowth;

Then took the other, as just as fair,
And having perhaps the better claim,
Because it was grassy and wanted wear;
Though as for that the passing there
Had worn them really about the same,

And both that morning equally lay
In leaves no step had trodden black.
Oh, I kept the first for another day!
Yet knowing how way leads on to way,
I doubted if I should ever come back.

I shall be telling this with a sigh
Somewhere ages and ages hence:
Two roads diverged in a wood, and I—
I took the one less traveled by,
And that has made all the difference.

Robert Frost (1874–1963). *Mountain Interval.* 1920.

one

THE sun was setting by the time Sidney Judson reached home on that April day. He was surprised when Chloe told him his parents still hadn't returned from Atlanta. Sid felt he ought to wait up for them, so he took tea in the drawing room and sat by the fire trying to read the volume of Shakespeare sonnets Catherine had given him for his birthday a few months before. The words began to run together around Sonnet Number 21.

The Grandfather clock in the foyer woke him. He sat up with a start and counted four strikes, but the mantel clock above the dying embers of the fire told him it was midnight. Chloe had cleared his dishes away. His parents must have gone to bed, not wanting to wake him. He would have to talk with them in the morning. Surely they could all come to an agreement. They had to understand that he was a grown man now.

Sidney yawned as he went to the staircase in the foyer. He stopped short at the sight of the corner stand that normally housed his mother's parasol and his father's cane. The stand was empty.

Sid opened the front door and went out onto the porch. The night was clear, with a full moon lighting the yard. His heart pounding, he headed towards the stables. The pony was in his stall for the night, but the horses' stalls were empty. They were not home.

Sid broke into a run. By the time he got back into the house, to Chloe's little room next to the pantry, he was soaked with cold sweat. He knocked furiously. The minutes seemed like hours before she opened the door.

"Massa Sidney? What on earth?"

"Mother and Father aren't home yet. It's after midnight!"

"Oh, my lands! Where they at?" She wrapped a shawl around her small frame. "I'll wake George. Don't you worry, Massa Sidney. We gonna find out what's going on."

Sid's heart stopped racing while Chloe and George determined what to do. Instead, a great, hollow feeling began to settle inside, one that would become familiar in the days ahead of him. It stuck in the pit of his stomach sometime around dawn—the same time George and Lem found his parents at the bottom of the ravine just a mile down the road. It consumed him when he sat before the two caskets as the minister delivered the homily. Somehow he did not feel so grown up anymore. He didn't feel much of anything, in fact. And that is the state he was in when he came home from the funeral and discovered the letter from his aunt and uncle on the table in the foyer.

Sid's best friend Drew tried to dissuade him from going. But it was too late. Sid only told Drew of his plans after he'd written accepting the invitation. He stood on Drew's front porch, scrutinizing his friend's expression as he sat in a ladder-back chair. Drew stared past Sid. His face, busy with the big chaw of tobacco in his mouth, gave no sign of his thoughts.

"What did you expect me to do?" Sidney pressed his spine against one of the porch's large white columns.

"Exactly what you were fixing to do last month." Drew got up, walked across the porch and spat into the tulip bed. "You don't have to change your whole life, Sid."

"Yes, I do." Sidney ran his fingers through his hair in the manner he'd unwittingly picked up from his father. "I can't ride past that bend in the road anymore."

"Up North everything's different," Drew spat again before returning to his chair. "All the darkies are free and everyone else is poor white trash."

"Have you even been up North?" Sid asked. "My aunt and uncle are fine people."

"After a while you'll be a Yankee," Drew continued.

"I won't become a Yankee," Sidney said. "If war breaks out I'll come right back here and fight for the Cause."

Sid was tall for his seventeen years. He crossed his arms over his chest, his dark brows furrowed over brown eyes. Their darkness contrasted with his sandy-colored hair.

"Look, Sid," Drew leaned forward. "I'm not saying it's easy to lose your parents. I sure don't know what it's like. But going up North will not make it any better."

"You don't know that."

"If I were you, I would stay at Tall Pine. Your father left you a fine position at the Mills. You have everything you need right here in Roswell."

"I already told them I'd come." Sid bent down to tighten his boot laces.

"I wish you would've talked it over with me first."

"I don't have to talk things over with you." Sid scuffed the back of his heel against the porch pillar, scowling. "You're not my father."

"You need to relax." Drew said. "Want to go fishing on the river?"

Sid shook his head. "I have to go see Catherine now."

"Does she know you're going?"

"She knows I've been thinking about it," Sid said.

"Good luck!" Drew rose as Sidney turned to walk out to the road.

※

Before the death of his parents, Sidney had fully participated in Catherine Cartland's admiration of herself. When he arrived at her house and observed her sitting in the parlor gazing into a mirror, a forgotten needlepoint in her lap, he would have some words of praise for her deep blue eyes or porcelain skin. Of course, his motivation was the favor it might afford him. He was the one who enjoyed the benefits of her beauty—to the extent she was willing to bestow them. His fixation on this was almost entirely responsible for his determination to marry Catherine as soon as possible.

Today, though, he only offered her a brief kiss when she swept over to him.

"You're so distracted lately, Sid," she said.

Sidney wandered to the pianoforte and tapped middle C. "Perhaps I am."

Catherine settled herself on the sofa. "You don't truly look at me anymore."

He sat stiffly, his hands on his knees. "Remember when I told you that my aunt wrote and asked me to visit?"

She straightened suddenly. "You're not going to go!"

"I am." Sid nodded. "I've already written accepting the invitation."

"But, Sidney!" Tears started to her eyes. "Pennsylvania is so far away! You can't go!"

"This doesn't change anything between you and me. It's just for a little while."

"And with a war coming!" She rose and stalked to the window, arms crossed. "How could you do this to me?"

"I'll come back when war breaks out. And I will marry you—just as I promised."

"How long will you be gone?"

"I'm not entirely sure." Sid got up and stood beside her. "I hate to leave you. But I think it will do me some good to spend time with my father's people. Can't you understand that?"

"No." Catherine drew her full lips into a pout.

"It's been years since I've seen them." Sid took her hand. "They're my family."

"You'd better not stay away for long!"

"How could I?" Sidney pulled her close and whispered in her

ear. "The memory of your kiss will draw me back before you even notice I'm gone."

"Oh, Sid." She breathed.

⚜

The next morning before Sidney had finished breakfast, Chloe had most of his clothing packed in a big trunk. He came into his bedroom as she folded his black wool overcoat on top.

"I won't need that, Chloe," Sid said. "I'll be back before autumn."

"Just in case, Mr. Sidney. It gets chilly up North." She smoothed the pile of clothing. "I've got everything you'll need in the way of clothing in here. Your satchel has a few books and a sack lunch for you. Make sure you take some money, so's you can buy dinner an' such."

"Thank you, Chloe," he said. "I took some from the safe last night."

"I don't know how we going to get along without you, Mr. Sidney." Chloe put her hand to Sid's cheek, shaking her head.

"You'll be all right." Sid cleared his throat. "Attorney Cardwell will look after anything that needs attention. If you have any problems, contact him and he'll get in touch with me."

Chloe was silent—she was a small woman, with skin only two shades darker than Sidney's own. She looked up at Sid.

"That's all well and good," she said. "But I lost the only mistress I ever known just two weeks ago. And now I'm going to lose the boy I nursed from babyhood as well."

Sid swallowed, trying to dislodge the lump in his throat. He put his arms around Chloe. His voice came in a whisper. "I won't be gone long."

"Don't forget your homeland, now. That's all." Chloe gently pushed away. "George'll be up for your trunk any minute. I can't have him see me blubbering."

Sid smiled at the familiar way she briskly closed the trunk

and locked it. He picked up the satchel and looked around at his brass bed, at the wainscoting and pinstripe wallpaper. He would see it all again soon.

Since the carriage had been destroyed in the accident, George borrowed the Cartlands' rig to drive Sidney to the Atlanta train station. Drew and Catherine rode along with them so they could see him off. All the way, Catherine clung to Sid's arm. He felt her gaze on him and every time he glanced at her, she sniffed or dabbed at her eyes with a handkerchief. He squeezed her hand in response. Drew made no attempt at conversation until they reached the outskirts of Atlanta.

Then he said, "You can still change your mind, you know."

"I'm not going to." Sid shrugged.

Catherine whimpered.

Catherine and Drew went to the platform to wait with Sid. Two of their other comrades, Jimmy and Sam Richardson, arrived just as Sidney was about to board the train, dispelling the somber mood a bit.

"We heard you're turning Yankee!" Jimmy said, punching him playfully.

"Get outta here!" Sam slapped him on the back.

Sidney grinned at them. "Thanks for coming, fellows."

"We wouldn't miss this!" Jimmy said. "I'd chase you all the way to Mason's and Dixon's line if I had a rig!"

Sid shook his head. "I'll be home before you know it."

Drew shook Sid's hand. "I'll miss you, brother. Hurry back."

Sid kissed Catherine, ignoring her wet handkerchief, and stepped aboard the train. He'd barely found a seat before the train lurched into motion.

The low mountains began slipping by. He craned his neck, looking back at the platform to find his group of friends. Without warning, his vision blurred. He turned from the window, pushing the feelings away. The emptiness crept back into his core.

Before the day was gone, Sidney lost track of how many stops they'd made, and his resolve had been shaken more than once. He kept telling himself that he would feel better once he was with his kin. He closed his eyes, trying to sleep, and pictured Uncle Daniel and his father laughing together. Their faces were vivid—at least he would see one of them soon. As dusk fell around the moving train and the other passengers nodded off, Sidney stayed wide-awake. When he arrived in Philadelphia at dawn, he took his satchel and boarded the Lehigh and Susquehanna Railroad. On this, the last leg of his journey, he finally dozed.

❧

"Wilkes-Barre!" called the conductor, jolting Sidney awake. He rubbed sleep from his eyes, found his bag, and slowly made his way off the train.

A middle-aged couple stood at the other end of the platform, scanning the train cars. The man wore a frock coat and held his top hat in his hand. He was stouter than Sidney's father had been and had a sterner expression on his bearded face. The woman's skirt and bodice were respectable but not ostentatious. Her tawny hair was graying around the temples, yet she stood comfortably erect and held her head high.

"Aunt Sarah!" He started towards them.

The woman turned towards him, shielding the sun from her eyes.

"Sidney!" A smile overtook her face as he reached them. She swept him into an excited embrace. "Just look at you! I knew you would grow up, but I still half expected a little blond boy to meet us here!"

"It has been a long time." Uncle Daniel shook Sid's hand. "Welcome to Wilkes-Barre."

"Thank you, sir," Sidney replied. "I appreciate your inviting me to visit."

"It's no trouble," Uncle Daniel said.

15

"We're glad to have you." Aunt Sarah said.

"Is this yours?" Daniel headed off towards Sid's trunk, still sitting on the platform.

"Yes, sir." Sid looked around for someone to carry the trunk.

He raised his eyebrows as Uncle Daniel grabbed the trunk by both handles and lifted it. Was he expected to help? His mother's careful training hadn't prepared him for this situation.

He took a deep breath. "Need a hand, Uncle Daniel?"

Daniel nodded. Sid took one of the handles, while Daniel held the other. Still, no servant appeared to assist them. Aunt Sarah led the way to a double buggy hitched to two Morgans. Sid and Daniel hoisted the trunk up onto the back.

Sid watched as Daniel strapped his trunk to the buggy. "Can I help?"

"That's all right." Daniel grunted. "Just about finished."

Sidney went to Aunt Sarah and helped her into the back seat. Then took his seat next to her.

"Sidney." Aunt Sarah put a hand on his arm. "I'm so sorry about your parents."

Sidney shrugged and swallowed. "These things happen, ma'am."

"So sad. So untimely." Sarah shook her head. "It's hard to believe they're gone."

Uncle Daniel finished with the trunk and climbed into the front seat. He clucked to the team and they started trotting towards town.

Before long, he turned the buggy into a drive next to a sage Italianate-style house sheltered by large oak trees. Daniel pulled up the horses just before the carriage house.

"I see you've moved since I was here last," Sidney said.

"Oh, yes!" Aunt Sarah said. "I forgot we were still in the apartment over the Mercantile then."

"It's a lovely house." Sid helped Aunt Sarah down from the buggy.

"Thank you," Aunt Sarah said. "It's a lot to take care of."

"Do you have any help?" Sid asked.

"We have a maid—Rhoda. She... she's almost like family, really," Sarah said.

"Well, if I can do anything to help while I'm here, please let me know," Sidney said.

"Oh, it will be good just to have your company," Aunt Sarah said.

Uncle Daniel went to the back of the buggy to unstrap the trunk. "You could help out at the store while you're in town."

Sid nodded. "I'd be glad to." He'd always enjoyed visiting Uncle Daniel's mercantile when he was a boy.

"Daniel," Aunt Sarah said. "Don't put the boy to work right away!"

"Well, not today," Daniel said. "After he gets settled."

"Aunt Sarah, I don't mind," Sid said. "I don't want to sit around twiddling my thumbs."

"Well, there's no hurry. You can do all the thumb-twiddling you want," Sarah said. "I'm going to help Rhoda finish dinner." She went into the house ahead of them.

Sid and Daniel carried the trunk across the porch and through the front door. The oak floors and staircase shone. Sidney looked up to a railing hemming the upstairs hall. They climbed the staircase.

"The first door is our bedroom." Daniel led Sidney through the upper hallway, pointing out two other doors. "This one is a spare room and the other is Aunt Sarah's quilting room. This room will be yours."

Uncle Daniel opened the fourth, and last, door. The room was smaller than his bedroom at home, but the four-poster bed looked comfortable. It was spread with a colorful quilt. He went to one of the windows and looked out on the river common. A woman walked along a path, leading her child by the hand. The other two windows had a view of the side yard by the carriage house.

Sidney turned to look at Uncle Daniel. "Pretty view of the river." He shifted his weight and put his hands in his pockets.

"Do you need help getting unpacked?" Daniel asked. "I can send Rhoda up."

"No, thank you, sir. I can manage."

"Dinner should be served soon. You're welcome to come down as soon as you're ready. Make yourself at home."

"Thank you, sir."

He was gone and Sidney shifted his weight once more.

Had Daniel's offer to send Rhoda up been sincere? Sarah had said she was like family. How did a maid get to be like family? The house slaves at Tall Pine were almost an extension of the family in a way—still, they knew their place. Maybe Rhoda wasn't a darky, but even so. He'd forgotten how different things were in the North. Sid heaved a deep sigh and busied himself for the very first time with the task of unpacking his own belongings.

✤

The dining room was paneled with pine. Sunlight from the front window gave it a cheerful glow. Sidney found the room, adjacent to the front hall, as Daniel and Sarah came in for dinner. Daniel seated Sarah across from the doorway.

She smiled at Sid. "Did you get your things unpacked?"

"Yes, ma'am." Sid stood behind his chair, waiting for Uncle Daniel to sit.

The door to the kitchen opened and a buxom black woman, dressed in light blue calico, came into the dining room, carrying a big bowl of stewed vegetables. She set it down at the head of the table, where Uncle Daniel stood. Her skin was smooth and dark like cocoa powder. Her tight, black curls were wound into short braids, close to her scalp. She looked at Sidney and took him in with a warm smile.

"You must be Mista Sidney!" she said.

"Yes," Sidney said.

"I'm Rhoda." The woman made her way to the foot of the table and took a seat.

Sidney stared in disbelief. Realizing that Daniel had taken

his seat, Sid grabbed his own chair by the top rung and pulled. It slipped from his hand and went sailing. Sid caught it just before it hit the floor.

"I'm sorry." He struggled to right the chair, seating himself carefully so he wouldn't upset it again. He stayed completely still during the blessing, afraid of moving his suddenly awkward limbs.

Sarah filled Sidney's plate with chicken pie as Rhoda passed the vegetables around the table.

"Oh, Rhoda!" Sarah spoke up. "This reminds me of the last time you made chicken pie. Remember?"

"I remember, ma'am!" Rhoda chuckled.

Sarah looked at Sidney. "The minister and his wife stopped by unexpectedly right before dinner."

"We was in the midst of spring cleaning that day," Rhoda said. "So the missus hadn't much in mind for dinner. We just thought we'd have leftover roast chicken and eat it cold."

"That would never do for company, though," Aunt Sarah said.

"Miss Sarah asked me to do what I could while she visited with them in the parlor," Rhoda said. "So I just whipped up this pie and you should have seen her eyes when I served dinner."

"It was as if we'd been planning it all week!" Sarah laughed. "I just couldn't get along without you, could I, Rhoda?"

"I daresay ya couldn't, Ma'am." Rhoda laughed in return.

"You wouldn't dare—" Sidney stopped himself.

The laughter ceased. Two pairs of eyes turned to Sidney. Rhoda looked down.

"What were you saying?" Daniel asked, his voice level.

Sidney shook his head. "Never mind. I'm sorry, sir. I'm just unaccustomed to..." he trailed off, with a glance at Rhoda.

"You'll have to get accustomed to it," Daniel said.

"We want you to feel welcome here, Sidney," Sarah said. "But this is also Rhoda's home."

"Yes, of course." But he didn't understand. "I'm terribly sorry to have made you all uncomfortable. It was very rude of me."

"It's all right, Sidney," Sarah said. "We're bound to have some misunderstandings."

"Forgive me," Sidney said. He looked from face to face around the dinner table, ashamed at his rudeness, but still aghast that Rhoda could sit there as though she were one of the family. She still did not look up.

Daniel began eating again, the deep lines around his eyes evident.

Sarah cleared her throat and attempted a smile. "How is your meal, Sidney?"

Sid swallowed hard. "Very good, ma'am."

"We'll try to make some dishes you like," Sarah said. "What's your favorite meal?"

"Oh... I like just about anything. You can't go wrong with chicken pie and vegetables." He took another bite.

Sarah smiled. "Well, I'm sure you're used to different types of food in the South. Rhoda and I might like to learn something new."

Rhoda ate silently. Sidney glanced around the table. Sarah looked at him, waiting for an answer. He struggled to chew and swallow the pie. It had no taste to him now.

Then he said, "There's nothing like Chloe's cornbread."

"Rhoda makes cornbread," Sarah said. "I don't know if it's the same as your Chloe's, though."

"I'm sure it's very good," Sid nodded.

After dinner, Sarah urged Sidney to take a nap. Exhausted from his sleepless night on the train, he agreed. Daniel would be heading back to the mercantile for the rest of the day and he'd rather not navigate the afternoon with two women—one of whom he had perhaps deeply offended. At the top of the stairs he paused for a moment, his hand resting on the railing. Voices floated up to him from the dining room.

"He's used to the ways of the South, Daniel. What do you expect?"

"He's just like his father."

"I don't believe so. It's been eight years since he was here last, and I'm sure his parents didn't remind him what the North was like. Give him some time."

"It's too dangerous, Sarah."

Their voices lowered and Sidney went quietly to his room. He began a letter to Drew.

Dear Drew,

I've arrived safely in Wilkes-Barre. I wish I could tell you everything is splendid, but it's so different here and I have made a fool of myself. My mother and father would be ashamed! In Roswell everything was so clear. I knew what to do in any situation. Now I don't know what to expect—nor what's expected of me. They have one servant, but she doesn't behave at all like the darkies at Tall Pine.

I am distraught. My parents are dead and it's my fault. I can only get through the day by forcing the thought from my mind.

Sidney lifted his pen. What was he doing? He couldn't say this to Drew. He read over the letter. It was too much to tell even his best friend. He balled it up quickly, stopping the deluge of feelings. He lit a match and held the crumpled paper to it with a shaking hand. Then he dropped the blazing ball into the fireplace and lay down to sleep.

two

WHEN Sidney woke, the sun was low in the sky on the other side of the River. He opened his door, planning to ascertain what was happening downstairs. Instead, Rhoda came into the hallway from the spare room and nodded to him.

"Afternoon, Mr. Sidney," she said. "I'se just cleaning up here a bit. I can make your bed for you, if you like."

"Certainly," Sid said, stepping aside.

As she deftly snapped the sheets into place, Sidney stood by the doorway and took a deep breath. "Perhaps I should apologize for my rudeness at dinner."

"No need for that, Mr. Sidney." Rhoda shook her head. "I've had worse done to me. I just hope you can get used to treating me proper now. That's how your aunt and uncle do things."

"Of course," Sidney said. He had always treated Chloe properly. Then he said, "Rhoda, have you always lived in Pennsylvania? You sound just like the darkies where I come from."

"I ain't always lived in Pennsylvania, no sir!" Rhoda smoothed the quilt over his bed and straightened. "But I sho' don't come from Georgia, neither."

"It's not a bad place to come from," Sid said.

"Not if you're white." She took a duster from her apron and began running it over the furniture.

Sid shifted his weight and cleared his throat. "All right, then. Good afternoon."

"Good afternoon, sir."

He left the room and headed downstairs as Aunt Sarah opened the front door. "Rachel, come in. I'm just about ready for you."

"Am I early, ma'am?" A girl stepped inside and Aunt Sarah shut the door behind her.

"No, no… I'm just running a little behind today. Our nephew arrived this morning."

"Oh, yes." The girl looked past Sarah, right at Sidney, who had stopped on the bottom step. Her green eyes met his.

Aunt Sarah turned. "There you are Sidney! This is Rachel White, a friend of the family."

"How do you do?" Sidney stepped forward and shook her hand.

"Why don't you two get acquainted while I prepare the sewing room for our lesson," Aunt Sarah said.

Rachel was dressed simply in a light-green calico dress and an emerald coat, her chestnut hair pulled back into a snood at the nape of her neck. A few tendrils of hair had escaped her snood and wisped about her temples. A straw bonnet hung from its cord around her neck as though she had pushed it off her head carelessly. The corners of her mouth twitched in amusement as she watched Aunt Sarah hurry up the stairs.

"Your aunt has been talking about your arrival for a week straight!" Rachel said. "I'm sure you can tell she's happy to have you."

Sid nodded. "I suppose."

"You suppose?" Rachel removed her coat and hat and handed them to Sidney. "It's a fact, let me tell you. Mrs. Judson is thrilled you've come."

Sidney hid his lack of enthusiasm by busily hanging Rachel's things on the clothes tree. He couldn't tell her that Aunt Sarah might not be so thrilled after the scene at dinner.

"I'm so sorry, though." Rachel stood in the foyer, winding her purse strings around her hand. "... about your parents."

Sid nodded. "Thank you."

"My father says your father was a good man."

Sid put his hands in his pockets. "They knew each other?"

"That's what I'm told."

Sid watched as she unwound the strings from her hand. "My aunt is teaching you to sew?"

"She's an excellent seamstress," Rachel said. She wrapped the strings around her other hand. "My mother has taught me the basics, but she wants me to learn to sew elaborate dresses. I have little sisters and the sewing is a lot of work, so Mother thinks I need to help out more."

"Oh." Sid nodded. "Do you enjoy it?"

Rachel sighed. "No. I hate it, actually."

She laughed then. Sid laughed, too.

"But I love your aunt," she said. "So it's bearable."

"I'm sorry it's such a chore," Sid smiled. "Would you like to have a seat?" He wasn't sure when Aunt Sarah was planning to come back.

"Thank you, but I'm sure your aunt will be ready to start soon. Were you on your way out?"

"I was thinking of visiting the Mercantile."

"Oh, good! I know Mr. Judson could use some help there."

Sid nodded. "Yes, he mentioned that."

"Rachel, dear!" Aunt Sarah's voice came from upstairs. "Whenever you're ready."

Sid looked up to see her peeking over the railing at them.

"It was nice to meet you," Rachel said. "I'll see you again soon."

She breezed passed him and pranced up the stairs. Sidney left the house and walked down River Street. Rachel's manner made him uneasy. The girls in Roswell were more self-conscious and affected. He'd never met a young woman with the natural confidence Rachel possessed.

The sun felt warm on Sid's face, a light breeze from the Susquehanna River at his back. As Sidney made the short walk to his uncle's store, he nodded to a couple headed the other direction. They greeted him, pulling three young children along by their hands. A middle-aged man wearing a linen work frock lifted a hand as he drove by in a rig. Sid waved in return. Uncle Daniel's store was a block away from the River, on the corner of Market and Franklin Streets. Two young women stood chatting in front of the store, baskets on their arms. As Sidney walked up to the shop door, he looked through the window and noticed three men leaning on the counter, talking to his uncle. When he opened the door, they turned, suddenly silent. The familiar scent of the place struck Sidney. The goods mingled together to create a comforting aroma, with overtones of leather, sawdust, and peppermint.

"Hello, Sidney." Daniel straightened behind the counter. "Men, this is my nephew—David's son."

A tall, sinewy man, in denim trousers, a worn shirt and suspenders, turned and offered his hand. He had a warm smile and a kind, suntanned face.

"Pleased to meet you. I'm Atticus White. Your father was a good friend of mine. I'm sorry to hear of his death."

"Thank you, Mr. White." Sid shook the offered hand, wondering if he might be Rachel's father.

"Travis Walker." Another man offered his hand. "I have only heard about your father."

"I'm William Gildersleeve." The third man was short and heavyset. "I remember your father well."

Sidney shook his hand.

To his uncle he said, "I just came to look around the store a bit."

"Of course." Daniel waved his hand in a gesture that swept the room with its clapboard walls and plank floor.

Barrels of oats, barley and other grains lined one wall. Bolts of fabric covered the shelves of another. Jars of stick candy stood on the counter, near the register. All around the room, merchandise enticed shoppers in appealing displays.

One by one, the three men left the store.

Sid turned to Uncle Daniel. "Did I interrupt something?"

Daniel was dusting the glass countertop with a cloth and did not meet Sid's eyes. "Men come into the Mercantile to talk about town business from time to time. How do you like the store? It's been a while since you were here."

"I've always loved this store." Sid stood in the middle of the floor and crossed his arms over his chest as he looked around. "I'd come running in with my Daddy and you always handed me a peppermint stick."

"That's right," Daniel chuckled. "Peppermint was your favorite."

"The store is a little smaller than I remembered, but other than that it's the same—everything your heart could desire right here."

"Well, not quite everything," Daniel said. "We're only about an hour from closing time, but you can get acquainted with it before we go home."

"Yes, sir," Sidney said.

"My right hand man moved on a few weeks ago. He started his own store across the river, so I could really use your help." Daniel began straightening the boxes of baking powder on the shelves behind the counter. "I'll need you to stock shelves, take inventory, and keep things clean. I'd also want you to help take care of customers when things are busy. You can start tomorrow, if you're ready."

"I'm ready," Sidney said. "I have to keep busy. I can't even think of facing a whole day in the house."

Daniel chuckled.

"No disrespect, sir," Sidney added quickly. "Rhoda and Aunt Sarah are fine... I mean, I love Aunt Sarah, of course."

"Everybody does," Daniel said with a smile.

The bell on the door jingled and in walked one of the girls Sid had noticed outside. She had fair skin and reddish-blonde hair and looked about Sidney's own age.

"Afternoon, Eliza," Uncle Daniel said. "How can I help you today?"

"Oh, Mr. Judson, wouldn't you know it, when Mother was here this morning she plumb forgot the sugar! She needs brown sugar to make her applesauce cake and we're having company tomorrow night, so she just has to bake it tonight. She won't have any time to do it tomorrow what with the sewing circle meeting."

"Brown sugar," Uncle Daniel said. "How much do you need?"

"I'd better pick up five pounds just so we'll have it," Eliza said. "Mother likes to have it on hand. I think that's why she forgot this morning. We usually have some in the pantry."

The girl turned to Sidney. "I saw you outside and I just knew you must be Mr. Judson's nephew. I'm right, aren't I?"

"Yes," Sid said. "I'm—"

"Sidney, right?" she said. "I'm Eliza Jane Holloway. I don't know if you've met Rachel White yet."

Sid nodded. "Yes."

"We're best friends. We've been friends ever since we were babies, so she's stuck with me."

"Your sugar, Eliza," Uncle Daniel interrupted her.

She stepped to the cash register and paid Daniel, still talking. "But I'm so glad to finally meet you. Sorry about your parents, though. That's horrible luck. Listen to me, the minister's daughter, talking about luck. He'd be so ashamed. Don't you tell him, Mr. Judson."

Uncle Daniel shook his head.

"Well, I really must be going. I hate to run out only just having met you, Mr. Judson, umm... Sidney."

Sid nodded. "Call me Sidney. We don't need two Mr. Judsons in the store."

"You're right," she laughed. "And you call me Eliza. Mother needs the sugar right away and I stood outside talking to Ruth so long, she'll string me up for sure. She knows my weakness for a good chat. I'll see you soon—Sunday, at least."

She swept out the door. Sidney turned to Daniel. They both laughed.

"She's our most talkative customer," Daniel said.

"Glad to hear it." Sid shook his head.

Sidney spent the next hour looking around the store and watching Daniel at work. The customers greeted him like an old friend, obviously loyal with their business.

After tea that evening, Sidney sat in the parlor with Uncle Daniel, browsing his book of sonnets. Rhoda and Aunt Sarah came in after they were finished with the dishes. Rhoda picked up some books from the table and replaced them in the bookcase before she nodded good night to them.

"Rhoda is such a help to me," Sarah said, picking up a needle-point in a wooden hoop.

"Yes," Sid said. "You must like to sew."

"Oh, I do!" She nodded. "I love working on the machine upstairs, but then in the evening I find it relaxing to work on my needle-point. This is part of a quilt we're working on tomorrow in sewing circle."

Sid tapped his book lightly against his thigh. "Well, I'm worn out. I guess I'll head up to bed now."

"All right, Sidney," Sarah smiled. "Have a good night."

"Good night," Daniel said from behind the evening paper.

After climbing the steps, Sid stopped for a moment, leaning on the windowsill to breathe in some of the cool night air. The breeze whispered through the oak trees outside and made the curtains dance softly. Sidney could hear voices in the parlor. His uncle's tone caught his ear.

"He might seem like a boy to you, Sarah, but he must be set in his ways. He's lived in the South all his life."

"I hate thinking of that, especially with the possibility of war."

"I'm more concerned about our own safety, should he find out."

"Well, that's the risk we take for the Underground—"

"Shhh—"

Sidney stood up straight, his heart racing. He suddenly recalled a moment, just a few months before, when his father had been reading the newspaper in the formal room and grunted in dismay.

"What is it, Darling?" his mother looked up from pouring her tea.

"Those Yankees." His father set down his pipe and held up the paper so his wife could see the headline. "They think they can run the country. There are more escaped slaves than ever and they're getting harder to catch because of that Underground Railroad. The fugitive slave law didn't stop the abolitionists. Don't they know how they're hurting business down here?"

"Now, David." Sidney's mother's gentle voice soothed her husband's irritation. "The Yankees have such small farms and businesses. They don't understand our way of life. Look at your brother, for instance. He means us no harm, but he has 'views' on slavery. I wouldn't be surprised if he were actually involved in the 'Railroad' as they call it."

"I'd prefer to leave my brother out of it." He had turned back to the newspaper.

Aunt Sarah said no more. Quietly, Sidney slipped into his bedroom. As he lay in bed, the four walls of the room seemed awfully close. The quilt was unbearably heavy on his chest. He threw it back, but the weight persisted.

The next morning after breakfast, Sidney went with Daniel to the store. He tried to appear cheerful in spite of the troubling thoughts in his mind. Fortunately, the store was busy and required all of his concentration. Before noon, Rachel came in with a basket of eggs.

"Hello," she greeted Sidney, pushing her hat back from her glistening hair. A bead of perspiration trickled down from her temple, tracing the graceful line of her jaw. "Your uncle is taking care of another customer. Do you know what to do with the eggs?"

"Yes. Uncle Daniel taught me how to do almost everything yesterday." Sidney led Rachel over to the end of the counter and began counting the eggs from the basket into a wooden box.

"Are you coming to church tomorrow?" Rachel asked.

"I assume so," Sid said.

"Good." Rachel unbuttoned her top coat button. "I'll introduce you to my friends."

"I've already met your best friend." Sid smirked.

"You have?" Rachel said.

"I'm surprised she didn't tell you already. Her gift with words is... how shall I put it? Breathtaking."

"Oh, Eliza." Rachel laughed, liltingly. "Yes, she's quite the conversationalist."

Sid had lost count. He began again.

"You think she's breathtaking?" Rachel repeated.

"That's not quite what I said." Sid looked up.

Rachel had a cameo brooch at her throat. Her gaze shifted to the door as a bell signaled its opening.

"Here's someone else you should meet!" she exclaimed. "Or perhaps you already have."

A young man in his early twenties came up to the counter next to Rachel. He was thin and tan, with a mop of dirty-blond hair.

"No, we haven't met," he said, extending his hand. "I'm Jake Samuels."

"My pleasure." Sidney shook his hand. "My uncle said you live above the store."

"That's right." Jake flashed a bright smile.

"He works for my father on our farm," Rachel explained as Jake went to Uncle Daniel for assistance.

Sid nodded and began counting the eggs a third time. Rachel was quiet, her eyes darting around the store as she buttoned her coat again. Sidney felt like an eternity had passed before he finished with the eggs and paid her.

"Thank you," she said. "I'll see you tomorrow."

"'Bye." He turned to the next customer, relieved to have a burly farmer take his mind off his uneasiness around Rachel.

During the noon hour, fewer customers came into the store. Sidney worked in the back room, unpacking crates of nails and tools and taking inventory. He heard the door slam and the voice of one of the men he had met the day before.

"Good afternoon, Daniel."

"Afternoon, Bill," his uncle answered.

"I have some business to discuss with you." The man's voice lowered.

Sidney jerked his head up, listening.

"Now is not a good time."

"It is of utmost importance." He paused, lowering his voice even more. "Cargo arrives tonight."

"You know I can't take it—not now."

Sid held his breath, trying to hear Gildersleeve's next words.

"The other stations are full."

Daniel sighed heavily. "All right, if there's no other way."

Sidney was shaking. How can I live with people who break the law this way? Drew was right. I never should have come here.

Sidney threw the sacks of flour and oats against the wall as he organized them. The burlap bags were sturdy enough to withstand his emotion. By the time he'd finished, his nerves had settled a bit. He walked back into the front room. Mr. Gildersleeve was still there.

"Uncle Daniel." Sidney kept his voice steady. "Do you mind if I go for a walk? I thought I might go home for a bite to eat."

Daniel cleared his throat. "Go ahead. I'll be able to hold things down here for a little while."

Sid took off down the street toward the river at a brisk pace. He didn't know how long he sat on the big rock on the riverbank with countless confused thoughts rushing through his mind. What would Drew say? What would his father think? Sid raked his fingers through his thick, sand-colored hair. He couldn't betray his own flesh and blood—but his uncle was an outlaw. Didn't he have a duty to his country? Perhaps he could persuade Uncle Daniel to abide by the law. He would just have to wait for an opportunity.

Sidney slowly walked back to the store. Though he attempted to act as though nothing had happened, making small talk with his uncle, he worried Daniel would sense something was wrong. He breathed a sigh of relief when it was time to close up and go home for tea.

వ

It was a warm night. Sid lay under a single sheet on his bed. All four windows were open and still only an occasional breeze blew through the room. The homes in Georgia were designed to create cool cross-breezes, but Northern houses were built to keep the heat in. Sid tried to sleep, attempting to put the conversation at the store out of his mind.

There was a sound, not more than a whisper, in the carriage yard. Sidney got up and silently went to one of the side windows. Two lanterns bobbed in the yard. Sid thought he recognized Mr. Gildersleeve's stout figure. He heard his uncle's lowered voice but couldn't make out the words. His heart began to pound. Light from one of the lanterns showed briefly on two black faces. Without planning his next move, he pulled on his pants and shirt. Wiping his sweaty hands on his pant legs, he opened his door.

The house was dark and quiet. Silently, he crept through the hallway and down the stairs. He slipped out the front door without a sound and stood on the porch, his back against the house, hoping the shadows would hide him.

The lights were in the carriage house now. He made his way to the porch steps, but with a glance at the carriage house, he saw a figure standing in the doorway. Sid hurried back into the shadows. Then he dodged over the railing and dropped into the rhododendron bushes. He half stood up and began to sneak out of the bushes. His foot caught on a root and he fell headlong on the ground with a thud.

He scrambled to his feet. Uncle Daniel was standing over him. "Sir—"

"Where are you going?" Daniel asked, his voice grave.

"Uh...." Sid ran his fingers through his hair. "Actually, you know, it's very warm up in that room. I decided to come out here to sleep on the porch."

"On the porch or in the bushes?" Daniel crossed his arms and surveyed his nephew.

"The— the porch, sir. But when I got to the porch I saw the lights and wondered what you were doing." Sid shifted his weight and stuck his damp palms into his pockets, digging for excuses.

"So you jumped into the bushes?"

"Uh—" Sid shook his head. "I fell, sir...."

Daniel scowled at Sidney.

"Don't play games with me, boy." Daniel's voice was furious, but controlled. "I know where you were going. You would betray your own family and send runaways back to the horrors of slavery."

Sidney's voice was small. "No, Uncle Daniel. I wasn't going to do that. I just—"

Daniel took the boy roughly by the arm and dragged him through the back yard. Mr. Gildersleeve appeared in the door of the carriage house and quickly ran to help Daniel.

Sid let out a cry and Daniel's hand clamped down over his mouth. "Quiet!"

Mr. Gildersleeve grabbed his kicking feet and the two men carried him toward the root cellar. When Daniel let go of his mouth to open the door, Sid tried to explain.

"I wasn't going to betray you. Please, Uncle Daniel—"

"I don't have time for this now," Daniel said. "I'll deal with you in the morning,"

The men dropped him into the root cellar and slammed the door. Sid tumbled down a short flight of stairs, landing on the hard-packed dirt floor. He staggered to his feet and bumped his head on the low ceiling. The darkness reeled about him and he sat down quickly. When his head cleared, he carefully picked his way up the stairs to the door. It was locked. He sat with his back against the wooden doorframe, determined not to fall asleep.

One Traveler

three

S IDNEY was startled awake by Uncle Daniel's voice, coming from the direction of the house.

"I'm not finished!"

Sidney guessed he was on the porch.

"He's not like David," Aunt Sarah said. "I don't believe it."

"You don't remember my brother the way I do." Daniel's voice was stern. "He was rebellious and defiant. He had the same look in his eyes."

"I do remember him," Sarah said. "You may see David when you look at Sidney, but I choose to see a boy who's lost his parents and needs love."

Sid was wide-awake. He was sure he could hear muffled sobs. His uncle spoke again, his voice kind.

"Go back inside. I'll take care of the boy."

Sidney scrambled up. Before he had a chance to smooth his wrinkled clothing, the lock clicked and Uncle Daniel opened the door.

Sidney stalked out into the sunshine. "Good morning, sir." He crossed his arms over his chest and looked at Uncle Daniel with steady eyes.

Daniel nodded to him. "How was your night?"

"Not very good."

"No?" Daniel shut and locked the root cellar door again. "Then why didn't you stay in your bedroom?"

"I wasn't given instructions to stay in my bedroom, sir. I'm not a little boy."

"Still, I expect you to be respectful," Daniel said. "You're a guest in our home."

"I see!" Sid shook his head with a chuckle. "I'm not acquainted with the custom of throwing one's guests into the root cellar."

Daniel stuffed his hands into the pockets of his coat. "Locking you in the root cellar last night was a necessity. I'm sorry it had to happen, but there was no other way for me to protect myself—and those in my care."

"You're kin, sir. Do you really think I'd turn you over to the authorities?"

"I don't know."

"Well, I wouldn't." Sidney clenched his teeth. "I've never been treated with such indignity in my life."

Daniel sniffed. "I'd like to say it will never happen again."

Sid chewed on his lip. A thousand fresh retorts spun through his mind. But he couldn't say them, not to an elder, no matter how he had wronged him.

Daniel grunted. "Go inside and get cleaned up for church."

Sid set his jaw and turned towards the house. When he reached his bedroom, Sarah was there, pouring water from the pitcher into the basin on his dresser. She had a towel in her hand.

"You're all dusty," she said. "You poor thing."

"I'm all right." He glanced into the mirror, noticing a scrape across his cheek from the bushes. He looked over his bare arms and found a cut above his elbow from the rough wooden steps in the cellar.

"I'll help you clean up, but I don't think you'll be ready in time for church," Sarah said. "We have to leave in a few minutes."

Sidney sat quietly as she washed his cuts. For the first time he noticed the regal shape of her face. He knew she had been a beautiful woman in her day, but he had thought that day had passed. Now he saw the strength of her high cheekbones, the unwearied tilt of her pretty head. She looked up and saw him watching her.

She smiled. "What is it?"

"Uncle Daniel's a lucky man." Sid reddened and looked away. "Does he often speak to you that way?"

"What way?"

"I heard him before he opened the door. He was angry. He made you cry."

"He didn't make me cry." Sarah shook her head. "A great deal of things make your uncle angry. Slavery, for one. Your father. These are the same things over which I weep."

"My father?"

Sarah took up the basin. "Daniel and I need to leave for church."

Sidney ignored her. "Because he was a slave owner?"

"That's not even half of it. They used to be very close."

"Then what?" Sid pinned his eyes on hers.

"People change."

"But—"

"Some things are better left in the past, Sidney." She turned to go. "You need to dress. We'll be going to the Whites' for dinner this afternoon. Daniel and I need to leave for church now. We'll pick you up after the service." Sarah tousled his hair and left him with his questions.

Although he was bruised and stiff from his adventure the night before, the talk with Sarah left Sidney determined to stay. Uncle Daniel was hiding much more than runaway slaves. Sidney might not be able to do anything about the slaves in good conscience, but he could certainly find out about his father while he was here.

At a quarter till noon, Uncle Daniel and Aunt Sarah stopped at the house to pick up Sidney. The Whites lived at the edge of town in a farmhouse surrounded by a white rail fence. Atticus's wife Melinda met them at the door.

"I'm so glad you could come, Sarah, Daniel." She shook hands with them warmly but her smile faded as she turned to Sidney. "And you are David's boy."

Her hand was limp and cold in his grasp. He was suddenly nervous.

"Please, come in and meet the rest of my family." Her iciness succumbed to forced good manners. "You've already met my daughter, Rachel, and my husband, Atticus."

As they entered the house, the aroma of roast beef greeted them. Mrs. White led them into a dining room to the right of the front hall. The polished cherry table and sideboard lent an air of formality to the room, unexpected on a small farm.

Rachel was putting the finishing touches on the table. She wore a cotton dress—light blue with lace at the collar. A vase of yellow daffodils embellished the white table linens. A little boy came running into the room.

"This is Charles," Mrs. White said.

"I'm Sidney." Sid squatted down to address him. "How old are you?"

The boy smiled and retreated behind his mother, clinging to her skirts.

"He's seven," Rachel said. "He's shy with strangers."

Atticus came into the dining room, followed by Rachel's younger sisters, Caroline and Maude. Ruth, the eldest of the four girls, came in with Jake Samuels.

Everyone sat at the table and Mr. White asked the blessing. Sidney had never heard a more beautiful prayer. Mr. White spoke as though God were right there with them. He thanked Him for providing food, family and friends and added special thanks for bringing Sidney to Wilkes-Barre, expressing his hope that Sidney would soon become a close friend like his aunt and uncle. Sid smiled gratefully at Mr. White as they began to eat. The feast reminded him of the many dinner parties his parents had given back home at Tall Pine. The darkies had served those dinners, however.

After the meal, the young people went out to the front porch.

"Are you planning to go to school here?" Jake asked Sidney, as he joined Ruth on the porch swing.

Sidney noticed the color creep into Ruth's cheeks as Jake put his arm around her. He felt a twinge of loneliness for Catherine.

"I haven't decided yet." Sid sat in a rocking chair across from the swing. "I went to school in the South but a lot has changed since my parents died. I may just work with Uncle Daniel while I'm here."

"You ought to come to school," Rachel said, taking the remaining chair while the younger children settled on the porch steps. "Of course, you'd be in the boys' school so I wouldn't really know much about that, but our friend Tom likes it."

"Tom is a bookworm," Ruth interrupted. "Sidney might not be comfortable in a Northern school."

"Actually, the term is almost over anyway," Caroline spoke up from her spot on the steps. "How long are you planning to stay?"

"For a while." Sid smiled. "I won't still be here for the fall term, though. Well, I guess it all depends on what happens with our country..."

"You mean if war breaks out?" Rachel asked. "What will you do then?"

Sid shifted uncomfortably. "I'm planning on fighting for the South."

"Oh," Rachel said. "Of course."

They were silent for a few moments.

Maude placed a hand over her eyes to shield them from the sun and peered down the road.

"Who is that?" she asked.

"Someone's coming?" Caroline looked down the road. "Oh, it's just Tom."

"I completely forgot." Rachel got up and waved to the figure. "I told him to stop by to meet you. I hope you don't mind."

"Not at all." Sidney smiled, relieved at the change of subject.

"I'm glad to meet as many people as I can."

Jake rose from the swing. "Care for a stroll, Ruth?"

"I'd be delighted," Ruth agreed.

"See you later, Sid."

The two of them headed towards the woods.

Tom arrived on the front porch and Rachel jumped up to introduce the boys. They shook hands and Tom sat on the porch swing. He was a few inches shorter than Sidney, and stocky, with dark, untamed hair.

"So, the Whites have told me you're a real scholar." Sid settled back into his chair.

Tom reddened. "Not really."

"He's at the top of his class," Caroline offered.

"Good for you!" Sid said. "I was always too busy playing around to do well in school. I enjoyed reading, but I never did well in other subjects. I didn't have time for homework between social events."

"What kind of social events?" Tom raised his eyebrows.

"Oh, nothing fancy," Sid explained. "My best friend Drew and I went fishing together a lot. We went riding, too. Sometimes Catherine came with us. Lots of the families in Roswell give barbecues and garden parties. And recently there have been some balls and bazaars intended to generate support for the Cause. Drew and Catherine and I went to all of those."

"Who's Catherine?" Tom asked.

Sidney flushed. "Well, she was my sweetheart."

"Was?" Tom persisted.

"I mean is."

"You needn't be so nosy," Rachel chided.

"Sorry," Tom said.

"No problem." Sid shrugged. "Do you like to fish?"

"I like the idea of fishing," Tom said. "I might like the reality better if I caught something once in a while."

"Maybe I could give you some pointers," Sid offered

"I'd be willing to try it," Tom agreed.

"Do you have a fly rod?" Sid asked.

"Yes, I do," Tom nodded. "My uncle left one to me, but I've never even tried it."

"Well, you have to change that!" Sid said. "You haven't lived until you've been fly-fishing!"

Sid was thrilled at any opportunity to fish. The boys made plans to meet at the River the next day as soon as Tom was out of school.

On Monday, Sid spent an uncomfortable morning working with Uncle Daniel. He tried to keep busy and avoided casual conversation with his uncle. At noon, they both went home for dinner, and then Sidney stayed home from the store to wait for Tom.

Bored with Shakespeare's sonnets, Sid wandered into the library to the rear of the parlor, looking for new reading material. Sarah's well-to-do family had passed down dozens of books to her. She and Daniel had bought a few over the years as well. He found a copy of The Canterbury Tales and settled on the sofa in the parlor. He had just begun reading "The Miller's Tale" when he felt a presence in the room. Rhoda was standing in the doorway with a bucket full of water.

"Am I in your way?" Sid asked.

"Mr. Sidney," she said. "I was just about to wash the floors, but if you're reading in here, well, I can work on some other rooms."

"It's all right, Rhoda." Sidney stood up. "I can take my book out on the porch while I wait for Tom."

"I don't want to trouble you, sir." She turned to go.

"It's no trouble," Sid said. "I'll enjoy being out in the sunshine."

She slowly turned back to the parlor. As he headed towards the front door, Sid wondered about her timidity. She seemed more cautious around him than she had. Then, with a sudden realization, Sid stopped and went back into the parlor. Rhoda was already down on her knees, washing the floor with a terrycloth rag. She looked up at him.

"Yes, sir?"

"Rhoda, you don't need to be shy around me. I know we started

43

off on the wrong foot, but I'm quite used to having colored people about and I'm very fond of the darkies on my own estate."

"Yes, sir." She lowered her eyes.

"Then, what is it?" Sid asked. He took a deep breath, then said, "You know what happened the other night, I suppose."

"Yes, sir. I know." She slowly rose to her feet.

"Well, it isn't what you think!" Sid went over to her. "I may find this place strange. I may not be used to living side-by-side with free darkies, but I wouldn't betray Uncle Daniel. I wouldn't—"

He stopped when he saw the wide, frightened expression in her deep brown eyes.

"Rhoda, you can trust me," Sid said. "I'm a Judson, just like Daniel and Sarah."

She nodded. "All right, Mr. Sidney."

"But you don't," he said.

"Well, sir, Mr. Daniel don't either." She wrung out the cloth, though she barely coaxed a drop from it.

"I'm going to prove you both wrong," Sid said. "You might not trust me now, but you will."

He turned away and took his book out to the porch. But he was too distracted to read any further. Instead he sat, slapping the book against his thigh until Tom came up the front walk.

"Something on your mind?" Tom asked.

"No," Sid said, laying the book aside. "Just didn't feel like reading." Sid pushed his thoughts away. There was no way he could reveal them to Tom.

The two boys went down to the river with their rods. It was a cool, breezy day, but the sun was shining. At first Tom just stayed on shore and watched as Sid stood in the River, knee-deep, casting his line. The fish jumped at his fly as soon as it hit the water. Tom waded into the chilly water and awkwardly cast a few times. He took some advice from Sidney and after a while he managed to catch a large rock bass.

"Wow! Caleb won't believe I caught something!" Tom struggled back to shore and tried to free the slippery fish from his hook.

"Who's Caleb?" Sid grasped the bass close to its gills and slipped it off the hook.

"My little brother. He's fifteen."

Sid handed the fish back to Tom. "Don't drop it or he really won't believe you." Tom kept his fingers clamped around the bass until Sidney offered him his creel and he dropped it in.

Sid checked his line. "Hey, is next year your last year of school?"

Tom nodded.

Sid's experienced cast made his fly dance above the surface of the water. He concentrated, giving life to the feather creation as it lighted on the river. He glanced at Tom and saw his awed expression. He hadn't meant to show off. He felt the blood rush to his face for a moment. He cleared his throat. "What are you going to do after you graduate?"

Sid yanked on his rod, pulled, yanked again and landed an American shad. It was a good five pounds, much bigger than Tom's bass.

"Well…" Tom dug his bare toes into the pebbles at the edge of the water. "What I really want to do is become a journalist—a reporter for a newspaper. Not just for The Luzerne Union, though. That's where I work now. I'd like to write for something bigger."

Sid added the fish to his string in the creel. "Would you go to New York or something?"

"That's the problem," Tom said. "I'd like to, but I can't leave Ma and Caleb. Not right away. I have to take care of them, especially Ma. My father died when I was twelve."

"I didn't know that." Sid sat on a boulder by the path that led up the bank. "I'm sorry."

"Aw, it's all right, now." Tom turned and looked at the river, the afternoon sun beyond it. "It was horrible at the time. My pa was the son of a coal miner, but he married well and he spent his whole life trying to prove himself worthy of my mother. He worked hard and stayed away from the rough crowd he grew up with. But when he lost his job I guess he just felt he'd lost everything. He went out drinking that night and was killed in a barroom brawl." Tom stopped and clenched his teeth.

"I'm sorry." Sid said again.

Tom heaved a sigh. "Most people in town already know. There's no sense in hiding it from you. If you're going to think less of me for the way my father died, well—I can't help that."

"No—no, I wouldn't." Sidney didn't know what else to say. He sat watching the water go by.

"Well, you've lost both your parents," Tom said. "And here I am going on about losing my father like I'm the only one it's ever happened to. I hope this doesn't come across wrong, but be thankful for the way they died. An accident is just an accident and there's nothing to be ashamed of in that."

Sidney nodded politely, wishing it were as simple as Tom thought. At least Tom felt free to talk about his father's death. Perhaps that was better than holding everything inside. Sid refused to let his mind go back to that day, to the events before his parents left for Atlanta. He couldn't—not in front of Tom. But Tom's back was turned anyway. He was kicking at the stones at the water's edge. As long as Sidney focused on Tom and how his father had died, he could ignore the panic rising in his chest. No shame, he had said? What did Tom know of shame? He carried his father's, but it was not a heavy, secret shame of his own doing, like Sid's. Sid forced himself to breathe slowly. He watched the water flowing by.

After a little while, Tom turned back towards Sid.

"I probably should be getting home."

"Yeah, me too," Sid rose.

They gathered their things and headed up the path.

"Thanks for helping me, Sid. I really appreciate it. You're an expert, so I'm sure it's no fun helping a novice like me."

"Don't be silly," Sid said. "Fishing is always a good time."

They crossed River Street, heading toward the Judson's house. They heard a shout from down the road and turned to see Jake

Samuels. He rushed towards them, a big smile on his ruddy face.

"Hey. I didn't see you at the store this morning," Sid said.

"I know, I know," Jake panted. "We had to get the last of the corn planted. And last night, everyone had gone home when Ruth and I finished our walk so we didn't get to share the news!"

"News?" Tom's lips turned up in a mischievous grin. A broad smile lit up Jake's face. "I proposed to Ruth last night and she accepted!"

"Congratulations!" The boys beamed as they shook Jake's hand.

"I had no idea," Sid said.

"How could you have no idea?" Tom asked. "The way those two moon over each other—it's pretty obvious!"

"Oh, I knew something was up," Sid said. "I just didn't know Jake was about to propose."

Jake stood on the front steps, beaming. "She's beautiful, isn't she?"

Sid did not remember thinking this and struggled to recall Ruth's face.

"Aw, she's all right," Tom said.

"Great Jerusalem, Tom!" Jake said.

"I'm joshing you!" Tom said. "Of course she's beautiful. You know I'm only jealous."

"Come in and tell my Aunt Sarah," Sid said. "If you want."

"He wants to tell everybody!" Tom smiled. "I have to head home, though. Thanks again, Sid."

Sid pulled Tom's fish from the creel. "Would you like to go again later in the week?"

"That would be great!" Tom started down the street. "Wednesday is my day off from work, since the paper comes out that morning. Let's plan on Wednesday after school."

"Sounds good." Sid and Jake went into the house and found Aunt Sarah in the kitchen. Jake practically exploded to Aunt Sarah with his news. Sidney pulled out his string of fish to examine them.

"I'm so happy for you, Jake," Aunt Sarah said. "You and Ruth will have a wonderful life together!"

Then she turned and saw Sidney standing there with his fish dripping on her clean kitchen floor. The look she gave him was enough to send him scurrying out the back door. He cleaned the fish in the backyard, thinking about Tom and Jake and how their gentle banter put him at ease. Tom's naive honesty was somehow both unnerving and comforting at the same time. Sid chose to hang onto the comfort in it, believing that Tom had recognized in Sidney a friend he could trust. If he clung to that, perhaps with him he could face the distrust of those living under the same roof. Perhaps he could even become worthy of Tom's trust—and theirs.

four

Sidney went to Tom's house for tea on Wednesday after they finished fishing. Mrs. Mahoney was a small woman, with ivory skin and jet black hair. Even if Tom hadn't told him she was well-bred, Sidney would have guessed it from the way she carried herself. She was poised, comfortable in the role of hostess, which put Sidney at ease as well. Caleb had Tom's dark hair and stocky build, but spoke much less. Unlike the Whites, the Mahoneys had servants—a maid and a butler. They served the family a leisurely meal of corn bread, cold ham and preserves, with sponge cake for dessert. Sidney had quickly become accustomed to being on guard against abolitionist views. He found himself a little bit surprised when they reached the end of the meal and the subject of slavery had not been broached. Instead, he'd enjoyed relaxing conversation with Mrs. Mahoney and her sons. After dinner, Tom and Sid sat on two hassocks with a low table between them and played checkers while Caleb read in a nearby chair. Tom was much more skilled at checkers than fishing.

After Tom's second victory, Sid said, "That's enough. I'd show you a thing or two if we played chess."

"Hear that, Caleb?" Tom interrupted his brother. "Sid wants

to play chess."

"We have a chess set." Caleb jumped up and went to the cupboard.

He brought it over and began setting up the pieces. "I'll let you beat Tom a couple times but then you have to play me."

"Thanks a lot." Tom grimaced at Sidney. "I'm awful at chess. Maybe you should just play Caleb."

Sid shook his head. "No way. I want to win something tonight."

Early in the game, Sid could tell he wouldn't have any trouble beating Tom. He leaned forward on his hassock, making the defeat lighter with conversation.

"Your family seems to be mysteriously silent on the subject of slavery."

Tom scowled at the board, brightened, and took one of Sid's pawns with his knight. Sidney had been expecting that move.

Then Tom looked at Sid. "Not everyone in Wilkes-Barre opposes slavery like your uncle."

"Guess I was just lucky, huh?" Sid used another pawn to take Tom's knight.

"Thunder!" Tom grimaced, then smiled, accepting the blow. "Actually, there are only a handful of abolitionists in this town. Most of the people here have Southern sympathies."

"Really?" Sidney was surprised. "The people I've met seem to look down on Southerners."

"It's no secret that your uncle is involved in the Underground Railroad." Tom leaned back on the hassock, propping himself up with his arms.

"Yeah," Sid said. "I figured that out."

"Naturally, some of his friends have views on slavery."

"Don't you?"

"Well, I support the Union. But as for slavery, my family's always been somewhat neutral. Most of the people in Wilkes-Barre aren't thrilled about the growth in the Negro population."

Sid moved his castle to corner Tom. "Checkmate."

"Land sakes!" Tom's mouth dropped. "Well, there you go. I told you I was terrible at chess." He started setting up the pieces for another game. "There are some radicals in town who hold very different views from your uncle's. They've even inflicted some persecution."

"Persecution?" Sid looked sharply at Tom.

"Of abolitionists. I haven't heard of anything happening recently, but there are some horror stories from when my mother was young."

"Really?"

"I really don't know the details," Tom continued. "Rachel's tried to tell me some of the stories she's heard, but being neutral, I don't pay much attention."

Sid looked from Tom to Caleb. "Has my uncle been persecuted?"

"I'm sure he's faced resistance," Tom said. "But things have settled down quite a bit in the past five or ten years. I think it's because the controversy between South and North is getting more intense. Northerners are fighting less among themselves so they can unite against the South. I guess war really is just around the corner."

Sid shook his head. "Why would my aunt and uncle put their reputation on the line for... what? A few darkies making it to Canada?"

Tom moved off the hassock to a large, leather chair. "Here's how I look at it. The Rebels talk about having a cause. They—well, you—want to preserve your way of life. The abolitionists have a cause too. And I'd be willing to wager they believe in it just as strongly as the Southerners believe in theirs."

"Tom!" Caleb gasped.

Tom flushed. "It's just a figure of speech. I didn't mean I'd really bet on it."

"Don't even joke about it." Caleb shook his head.

Tom turned back to Sid. "After what happened to Pa, Caleb and I vowed to each other we would never gamble—or drink alcohol. We want to stay away from the kind of life that led to our father's downfall."

Sid nodded politely, hoping they wouldn't look down on him should they discover he had been known to play poker and sneak whiskey on occasion.

"But about the abolitionists," Tom continued. "I respect your uncle. He's willing to take chances for what he believes. He helps people he doesn't even know. I'm not sure I'd do it. Some of the kids from school are forbidden by their parents to even talk to the abolitionist kids. The Whites have a hard time because of their views. But they won't forsake them, not for anything."

As he walked home that evening, Sidney pondered what Tom had told him. He had thought that his uncle was just a stubborn man, set in the ways of the North. But the more he learned about this town, the more questions he had about his family. Why did Uncle Daniel so fiercely oppose slavery? The risk was even greater than Sid had imagined, yet it didn't stop him from helping fugitives.

The house was dark when Sidney reached it, so he went to sleep with his questions. In the morning, Sid was alone in the dining room when Uncle Daniel came in.

"Morning, Sid," he said, taking his seat and lifting his coffee cup.

"Morning." Sid stole a glance at his uncle. He seemed different.

"Good visit with the Mahoneys last night?" Daniel asked.

"Yes, thanks." Sid nodded.

Somehow, going to work with the man did not strike Sid as distasteful as it had earlier in the week. Perhaps there was more to him than Sid had reckoned.

That following Sunday, Sidney walked to the Presbyterian Church with Uncle Daniel and Aunt Sarah. Sunlight flooded the sanctuary through tall windows in the side walls. The very tops of the windows were accented with colorful stained glass. As he sat down in the family pew, he noticed a small brass plate beneath the nearest window. *In Loving Memory of David and Laeticia Judson.* He looked up in surprise and met Sarah's eyes.

She smiled at him and whispered, "We thought it would be nice to have a reminder of your father here."

Sidney nodded. Uncle Daniel sat looking solemnly towards the front of the sanctuary. Sid wasn't sure he cherished the memory of his brother. The minister gave the call to worship and they stood to sing "Blest Be the Tie That Binds." Sidney tried to concentrate on the service, but his eyes kept wandering to the plaque beneath the window. He could see his mother's smile as she stood at the bottom of the staircase at Tall Pine before she left. He shook the memory away and turned his eyes back to the minister.

After church, as they left the sanctuary, Daniel introduced Sidney to Reverend Holloway. He was a large man with graying brown hair. His handshake was firm. Sidney was inclined to like him, but his probing brown eyes left Sid feeling exposed. He avoided the minister's gaze and quickly stepped outside. Tom was there, on the sidewalk in front of the church, with his mother and Caleb. He shook Sidney's hand.

Caleb asked, "Are you going to the church picnic?"

"There's a church picnic?"

"Next Sunday. Didn't you hear the Reverend announce it in church?"

"I must have missed that." Sid flushed.

Jake and Ruth came out of the church, accompanied by a thin young man with brown hair. He appeared to be in his early twenties, like Jake.

"Well, now, I just wanted to congratulate you is all," the man said.

Jake stopped where Sidney stood. "Have you two met? This is Joshua Smith."

"You must be that Judson boy from the South." Joshua smiled, showing gaps between his teeth. "A descendant of the Judson brother who actually had some sense!"

Sid shook his hand, wondering exactly what he meant.

Jake grimaced. "Good afternoon, Joshua."

As soon as he was out of earshot, Jake said, "What a weasel!"

"He only wanted to congratulate us," Ruth said with a smile.

Rachel joined them. "Who wanted to congratulate you?"

"Joshua Smith," Jake said.

Rachel shuddered. "He makes my skin crawl."

Eliza came out of the church then.

"Oh, Sidney," Rachel said. "You've met Eliza."

"Yes," Sid nodded to her. "How do you do?"

"Fine, thanks," she smiled.

"You must be Reverend Holloway's daughter," Sid guessed. "I didn't realize."

"Yes, I am." She said. "Just put two and two together, did you? I'm proud of my father, but being a minister's daughter does have its trials."

"Does it?" Sid asked.

"Well, everyone expects you to be so well-behaved," Eliza said. "And I'm just not naturally refined like Rachel."

Rachel laughed.

"Well, it's true, Rachel!" Eliza lowered her eyebrows and shot her a scornful look. "Everything's so easy for you, being a farmer's daughter, but I have to know how to make polite conversation with everybody all the time and then I'm not naturally inclined to be well-mannered."

"Making conversation is certainly not a weak point for you, dear," Rachel said.

Sid and Tom laughed.

"Well, I can't argue with that," Eliza said. She was finally silent for a moment.

"Are you coming to the church picnic next week?" Rachel asked Sid.

"I don't know. I'll have to see what my aunt and uncle are planning, I guess."

"I have to go now," Tom said. "Are you and I still fishing Wednesday after school?"

"Absolutely. And Caleb's welcome to come as well."

"Thanks!" Caleb grinned as the Mahoneys headed towards their buggy.

Aunt Sarah walked up beside Sidney and put her arm through his. "It seems you're getting to know some nice young folks," she said.

Sid nodded. "Tom and Caleb are great fellows."

"And Rachel?" Sarah said.

Sid looked at her sidewise and cleared his throat. "Oh, yes, she's a nice friend, too."

"Friend—hmm?"

"Well, Aunt Sarah, you know I have a sweetheart back in Roswell." Sid felt his face growing warm.

"I know." Aunt Sarah smiled.

"And, I'm just here for a visit. It's not long term—I mean, you don't think that—"

"Oh, I'm sorry dear. I didn't mean to embarrass you!"

"Well, why don't you just run down the list of eligible young ladies in town, then?" Sid suggested. "Why not Eliza?"

Aunt Sarah laughed out loud. "Now, that's just plain silly."

Sid heard Uncle Daniel chuckling behind him and looked over his shoulder at him. "Now I am thoroughly humiliated."

"Don't mind your aunt," Daniel said. "Now that Ruth and Jake are getting hitched, she has to turn her mind to a new endeavor."

"That is not so!" Aunt Sarah scolded him. "I have plenty of endeavors to occupy my mind. Rachel is just my special pet, that's all."

"I'm sure some fellow like Tom will do just fine for her."

Sarah shook her head. "That's almost as silly as the thought of you with Eliza."

"Well, here's a thought," Sidney changed the subject. "What about that church picnic? When is it? Saturday?"

"Yes," Sarah said. "Of course we'll go. We always do."

"Good," Sid said. "I'll look forward to that all week."

"And what did you think of the plaque?" Aunt Sarah asked.

"The plaque?" Sid's heart dropped as he remembered his parents. "Very nice. That was a lovely gesture. Both of you." He looked back at Uncle Daniel, who nodded to him.

"Sidney, if you ever need anything," Aunt Sarah said. "Even just to talk about it... I'm here."

Sid nodded. He was afraid to speak. They walked the rest of the way home in silence.

⚜

Travis Walker hosted the church picnic at his farm. Sidney arrived with his aunt and uncle, but soon went off with Tom and Caleb to fish on Mill Creek, separating the Walkers' property from the Whites'.

"This is the best part of the picnic," Tom said, attaching a new fly to his line.

"That's not what you said last year." Caleb chuckled. "You said the best part was watching the girls swimming in the pond."

Tom grimaced. "That's because I wasn't a very good fisherman last year. Anyway, it's not hot enough for bathing today."

"But they're boating on the pond." Caleb craned his neck to see. "We have a pretty good view from here."

Sid watched as Tom cast. His fly danced down and perched on the surface of the water. He was improving all the time.

"Sid can't look at the girls, though," Tom said with a wink at Caleb. "He already has a sweetheart back home."

Sid shrugged and moved upstream to cast. After Tom had caught a few rock bass, he came over to Sidney's spot.

"I'm taking a break." He found a dry rock and sat down.

Sid watched the clear water as it wove its way between boulders. Oak and maple trees surrounded the creek, the sunlight filtering through their leaves and plunging down into the water, lighting up the creek bed.

"It's harder to see the girls from up here," Sid said.

"I want to talk to you," Tom said. "I told you how my father died, but you haven't said anything about your parents."

Sid's chest tightened. He took a deep breath.

Tom went on, "All I heard was that they were killed in an accident. I guess I didn't ask too many questions at the time, but now I'm wondering how it happened."

Sid took another deep breath, cleared his throat. "Yes... it was an accident. Their carriage went off the road and rolled down an embankment."

"Oh."

"My mother was thrown from the carriage and she landed on her head. It broke her neck. The doctor said she died instantly. My father was crushed beneath the carriage. His death was slow and painful. He bled to death. They were both dead when we found them."

"God, that's awful."

Sid shuddered. He reeled in his line to still the trembling of his hands. Holding his rod upright and leaning on it for strength, he closed his eyes to block out the memory of that day.

"Sid, I didn't mean to..." Tom faltered. "I was just curious... I forget that it's so recent for you. I ask too many questions."

"Sometimes." Sid turned and smiled weakly at Tom.

"I'm really sorry."

The flush was still there, in Sid's hands, in his face. But the cold knot deep in his stomach felt heavier than ever. He couldn't tell Tom the rest.

"Listen." Sid ran his fingers through his hair to steady their trembling. "I have my own questions. I don't know how much you can tell me, but it sure would make me feel better to have some answers."

"About what?" Tom sat up straighter.

The flush ebbed slowly from Sid's face.

"My father," Sid said. "Why did he leave Wilkes-Barre?"

"You mean he never told you?"

Sid picked up his rod and cast again before he answered. "He told me he was born to be a Southerner."

"I don't know very much," Tom said.

"Tell me what you do know." Sid stared out over the uneven surface of the water.

"I've heard he had different views. He wasn't an abolitionist."

"Obviously," Sid snorted. "We are slaveholders, you know." Then he glanced at Tom, who was biting his lip. He'd forgotten how sensitive he was. "I'm sorry. I'm just a little irked that you know more about my father than I do."

"All I know is gossip," Tom said. "I never met your father."

"Go on."

"Your father's family was always involved in the Railroad. The story goes that David Judson had Southern sympathies, that he bungled on Railroad business, quarreled with his father and then went South. I guess he just always felt that's where he belonged."

"He bungled?"

"I don't know all the details, but people say he was trying to get his family turned in. If that's true… I mean, even though I'm not an abolitionist, I think that sounds pretty awful. I just hope you wouldn't do that to your uncle."

"I wouldn't!" Sid thought of his single encounter with the Railroad. "I can't imagine my father turning in his own family either."

"Well, I don't know if it's true," Tom said. "People say your father hindered the Railroad and that didn't sit well with his family or the other abolitionists in town, so he went south."

"Hmmm…" Sid said.

"Doesn't fit with your impression of your father?" Tom asked.

"Not really. And I don't think Uncle Daniel would let us visit if my father was going to turn him in—oh, a bite!" Sid yanked on his line and reeled in a huge black redhorse. "Look at that! She's a beauty!"

Tom grinned. "Over twenty inches, I bet! Caleb!" he called. "Come look at this!"

Caleb ran up, rod in tow. "Great Jerusalem! That's a dandy!"

Sid added the redhorse to his creel. "That's enough for me. Let's see if we can find Jake and the girls."

"I think Jake's mooning over Ruth out in a rowboat," Caleb said. "But we can look for the others."

The boys set off towards the pond together.

❧

Later that week, while Aunt Sarah sewed and Uncle Daniel studied The Luzerne Union in the evening, Sidney tired of The Canterbury Tales and went in search of something lighter to read.

As he returned the volume to its shelf, it struck a smaller book that had fallen across the opening. Sid reached in and pulled the slim book from behind the others. It was a blank book. He flipped it open to the center. In curved, feminine handwriting, it read:

3 May, 1839

I'm not going to write any more on the previous subject. I have to set down exactly what happened last week. I often keep these events to myself, for fear of discovery. Yet, I know the newspapers won't report what really happened and I must remember.

Daniel and I went to the courthouse in the forenoon to hear a lecture. I might as well say it was an anti-slavery lecture by Charles Burleigh. I don't think our involvement can be much of a secret anymore, if it ever was. This was all Bill Gildersleeve's doing. He arranged for Mr. Burleigh to come. It had hardly begun when we were interrupted by a loud mob. They were so disruptive that Mr. Burleigh asked Bill if there wasn't a more private place we could carry on. Bill suggested going back to his house. Daniel asked me to go on home with Mary, but I wanted to stay with him. Most of the audience did go home, but we went to Bill's house and that mob followed us! I get chills when I think of it. As we walked along, some of them took handfuls of mud and dung and threw them at us! Daniel shielded me from most of it, but his duster was badly soiled. They were taunting, too. They took up a chant, "What black nigger are the Gildersleeve girls going to marry?" I felt so sorry for Bill. He took it in stride, though. They finally left us alone and we were able to finish our meeting. Burleigh had some good things to say, though I'm not sure it was worth the trouble. As we were getting our things to leave, there was a huge cry outside. Suddenly the same rioting people were all over Bill's porch, banging on the doors and windows and yelling all sorts of awful things. I was so frightened. Thank God, one of our group had a pistol with him. He held off the mob until we could get beyond them and we rushed home to safety. Such a terrifying day.

Sidney stopped reading. He was invading privacy. Quickly he shut the book and squeezed it back into its spot in the bookcase. He dug his hands deep into his pockets and bit his lip. This was exactly what Tom had referred to. Aunt Sarah and Uncle Daniel had been subjected to persecution. How much had they suffered? He'd just have to be content to wonder. He'd already read more than he should.

He turned from the bookcase to the library desk, where he found stationery and set his mind to writing a response to Catherine's latest letter. He'd received it that afternoon and found it disturbing. Every day she was faithfully taking flowers to his parents' graves. She wished he were there to go with her. She begged him to come home. He struggled over his reply. His first sheet of stationery ended up a mangled mess of ink, with whole sentences crossed out. He began on a new sheet, hoping that written words might soothe Catherine's feelings as a caress would have.

7 June, 1860

My dear Catherine,

I received your letter and I thank you for it. How I wish I could be there to visit the cemetery with you. I long to be by your side at this time. Nevertheless, I must remain here for the time being. As I see it, I am honoring the memory of my parents in my own way. I have already discovered much about my father's family and their history. How could I better remember my father than to learn who he truly was and why he traveled to Roswell so many years ago? Do not lose heart, my Love, and do not lose faith in me. I will return to you. I only wish it could be today. But though we are far apart, my heart is with you always. Remember me, your ever loving

Sidney

Sidney read the letter through once again and, satisfied, he sealed and addressed it. But he let it sit for a week before he finally took it to the post office. And even then, he could not help but wonder if his words to her held any truth.

The next afternoon, Sidney took a break from work at the store to get some air. It was a hot day and he was in a sour mood. He felt guilty for his lack of feeling for Catherine and he suspected his uncle had been about some Underground Railroad business the night before. He had gone out right after tea and Sid had watched from his window when he came home late. Someone else had been with Daniel, but in the darkness he couldn't tell who. Sidney brooded over this as he crossed Franklin Street and headed east on Market Street, away from the River. How could his uncle just ignore the law? Sidney couldn't do it. But he couldn't betray his family either.

A shop door opened in front of him and Rachel came out. When she saw him, she smiled. "Hello, Sid!"

"Hello," he forced a smile.

"Where are you going?"

"Just for a walk," he said, purposefully accentuating his Southern drawl.

"Mind if I walk with you? I'm going up Main Street."

"Not at all." They strode along in silence and Sid hated himself for not having anything to say.

The Square opened in front of them, inviting sunshine down into the street. The Market House was ahead, with the boys' academy and the courthouse beyond. As they started towards Main Street, Rachel suddenly turned and looked past Sid. She gasped.

Sid followed her gaze across the square.

Several officials were dragging two black men from the other end of the Square towards the courthouse. A small crowd followed, shouting. Atticus White brought up the rear.

"It's..." Rachel paused. "Never mind." She started towards the crowd.

Sid followed close beside her. "Runaway slaves?" he asked. "Are they fugitives?"

She did not answer, but quickened her step to catch up with her father.

Atticus looked up. "Rachel, go home."

"No, Pa. I won't!" She lowered her voice. "Those men... are they marshals?"

Atticus nodded. "Marshal Yost and two deputies. There's nothing you can do. Go on home now."

"Please, Pa. Let me come." Rachel followed the crowd with him.

Sidney did the same.

"Don't draw attention to yourself," Atticus told her. Then he added quietly, "I'm going to slip away through the crowd if I can."

"Like Jesus," Rachel whispered.

Sidney elbowed his way towards the courthouse where the marshals led the fugitives. As they reached the courthouse steps, one of the Negroes broke away from the deputy that held him. He took off running straight towards the crowd, as though he expected the people to part and make a pathway for his escape.

Shouts came from the group of people behind Sid.

Some cheered. "He's escaping! Run! Run for your life!"

Others clamored, "Stop him! Don't let him get away!"

As the fugitive bolted by the front of the crowd, Sidney burst towards him and knocked him to the ground. The man was strong. He fought hard. But someone was helping Sid and together the two of them wrestled the darky until he lay face down on the ground. His taut muscles relaxed. Sid kneeled on his legs while the marshal tied his hands behind his back. Panting, Sid looked up to see who had come to his aid. Joshua Smith was holding the runaway's shoulders to the ground. He winked at Sid.

"We stopped this nigger in his tracks, eh partner?"

Sid's stomach turned. He stood up and the marshal helped the fugitive to his feet.

"Wilson!" he said to one of the deputies. "You hold this one."

The deputy complied and the marshal turned to Sid. "I'm Marshal Jacob Yost."

Sid shook his hand. "Sidney Judson."

"On behalf of the United States Government, I'd like to thank you for your assistance."

Sid nodded. "My pleasure, sir."

Marshal Yost went to Joshua then. Sid turned his back on the runaways and stole a cautious glance towards the crowd. He'd seen them around town, but most he hadn't met. Then he saw Bill Gildersleeve, towards the rear. Their eyes met and Mr. Gildersleeve shook his head with a frown. Sid looked away, searching the other faces. Some turned to leave. Mr. White was nowhere in sight. Rachel stood in the center of the square, her hat hanging behind her windblown head.

A hand clapped him on the shoulder. It was Joshua.

"I knew having a southerner in town would come in handy," he said.

Sid swallowed. "Uh… thanks. Thanks for your help."

The marshals led the bound fugitives into the courthouse. Joshua left with the remnants of the crowd. But Sid stood by the courthouse, his hat in his hand, wondering what he had just done.

He wandered next door and sat on a wooden bench by the public office. He stared down at his hat. Dark spots appeared in the dust on the street below as sweat dripped from his forehead. What had possessed him? Loyalty to the law? He ran his fingers through the thickness of his hair.

In time, the officials came out of the courthouse with the fugitives and led them towards the marshal's rig, waiting by the office. Just before the darkies were put into the carriage, the one Sid had wrestled broke free again and began running desperately toward Main Street, his hands still tethered behind his back.

"Stop!" One of the deputies yelled, drawing his handgun. "Stop! Or I'll shoot!"

He kept running. He did not see Sid as he ran by him. The deputy fired. The black man fell, writhing in pain, holding his leg with both hands. Sid rose from the bench. The deputy ran over to the black man. Sidney began to follow. The Negro groaned, blood covered his hands as he held his leg.

"I'll teach you to run away from a U.S. Marshal!" the deputy pointed his gun at the pitiful figure.

Sidney felt as though he were watching something from a dream. He saw the deputy's hand as his index finger squeezed the trigger. A shot rang out, echoing on the buildings around the Square. The Negro's body jerked as the bullet hit his chest. He fell back, his eyes meeting Sid's for a split-second before they glazed over. A cold fist seemed to hit Sid in the stomach. He gasped.

"There was no call for that," he said.

Sidney turned and looked at Marshal Yost, standing by the rig.

"Damn you, Wilson!" he called. "You're going to catch some flack for that."

He put the remaining Negro in the rig with the other deputy. Then he strode over to Wilson, who stood silent by the body.

"I ought to take away your badge—at least for a while." He shook his head. "Go into the courthouse and get the Sheriff."

Wilson nodded and started toward the courthouse.

Sidney turned his back on them. He walked fast towards Market Street, taking big gulps of fresh air. But as soon as he thought his stomach was settling, guilt washed over him again. He was responsible for another death.

five

WHEN Sidney went into the house, voices were coming from upstairs. He stood in the foyer until he felt steady enough to face them. Then he went upstairs to find Rachel in the sewing room with Aunt Sarah. She must have forgotten whatever she needed on Main Street and come here to tell Aunt Sarah what he had done. A colorful quilt was stretched out on a frame in front of them. They sat together, working steadily. When Sidney entered the room, Sarah looked up at him but Rachel did not. Her cheeks were flushed.

Aunt Sarah's delicate eyebrows were drawn together. "Hello, Sidney. If you're hungry, there's a plate for you in the warming oven."

"Thank you." His voice was strained and unnatural.

Rachel looked up at last. Sidney met her eyes but he did not smile. She looked down again. He turned around and left the room, only wanting to escape their condemning eyes. He went to the kitchen and found his warm plate of roast pork and beans. What right had Rachel to tell Aunt Sarah what he had done? They didn't even know the worst of it yet and still he had hurt both of them. He didn't know the Negro would be killed. But he could not erase the image of the black man's eyes as they met Sid's, pleading for life. If only he had stayed out of it. He could have just stood in the crowd and watched. Someone else might have apprehended the fugitive. He might even have escaped.

Sid went back to the store. He did not know if anyone had told Daniel yet, but he did not bring it up. He didn't even ask why Sidney had been gone so long.

That evening, Sidney sat on the porch with Daniel and Sarah. The days were long now. Light and warmth invited them outside after tea. He held a book in front of his nose without seeing the words. Daniel read a newspaper on the porch swing. Aunt Sarah sat quietly next to him, her hands idle for once. Sidney looked at her. He longed to put his head down on her shoulder, to pour out the whole story and tell her how awful he felt. But he just sat, staring at the letters on the page in front of him. Daniel interrupted his turbulent thoughts.

"Sidney!" His sudden voice made Sidney jump.

"Yes?" He closed the book.

"You haven't turned a page for ten minutes."

"Oh." Sidney was stiff, bracing himself.

"Why don't you go on up to bed? You seem to be tired." Daniel looked at his newspaper again.

Sid relaxed. But as he walked up the stairs, his steps were heavy. He was weary with keeping things inside. Daniel must know what had happened.

Somehow Sidney survived the next few days. Neither Daniel nor Sarah mentioned the dead slave. Sid began to wonder if they had forgotten about it, or perhaps never even known. But that was impossible. The incident had even been in the newspaper, though it hadn't mentioned his name. He had a few strained conversations with Rachel when he ran into her. On Wednesday he went fishing with Tom. They did not talk at all at first, but just stood in the River, concentrating on their technique. Then Tom, in his abrupt manner, broke the silence.

"Rachel told me what you did."

"Oh." Sidney bent down to scratch his ankle. "Now you can be mad at me, too, I guess."

"Don't be stupid. I'm not mad at you. You know I don't have views on slavery."

"But the deputy killed one of the Negroes."

"Yes," Tom said. "I know the reporter who wrote the article."

Sid took a deep breath and forced the words out. "That man is dead because of me."

"He's dead because the deputy made a rash decision," Tom said.

"If I had just minded my own business..." Sid trailed off.

"Sounds like you're pretty mad at yourself." Tom reeled in his line.

Sid grunted.

"You didn't know that would happen, Sid. You're a good person."

Sid cleared his throat. "I don't know about that." Now that it was out in the open, he felt terribly vulnerable. He grasped for some way to steer the conversation away from his feelings. "Rachel knows you don't have views on slavery. Why did she tell you what I did?"

"I don't know. I guess she's pretty upset about it." He stood watching Sid, who could talk and fish at the same time. "I tried to explain why you'd do something like that but it's beyond her comprehension. She just got angry with me and said I must be a Rebel, too."

"I'm sorry. I mean... well, thanks for trying to explain, but I'm sorry she's mad at you too, now."

Tom shrugged. "She'll get over it. We don't agree on everything. But I consider her a good friend, just the same."

Sid heard himself asking, "You're just good friends? That's all?"

He turned and winked at Tom, hoping it would seem like friendly curiosity. That's all it was, anyway.

"Just friends." Tom smiled. "I don't think it will ever be more than that."

The next Friday afternoon, Sidney went home from the store early. Business was slow. Uncle Daniel didn't think he'd need him.

His aunt had gone to a quilting bee at the Holloways' home. Rhoda was working in the kitchen, so Sidney took that week's Luzerne Union and went to sit on the porch to read it. The day was muggy. He was just getting up to pump himself a glass of cool water when he saw someone running down the road in his direction. He shielded his eyes from the sun and waited. The figure ran up and stopped in front of the porch. It was a black girl, not much younger than Sid. She stood still, gasping for breath.

"They's afta' me..." she panted. "A lady told me Ah cou' fine help here."

"Who's after you?" Sid asked.

The girl froze at the sound of Sidney's voice. "Ah mus' have de wrong house." She turned to go.

"No!" Sidney shouted. "Wait! You have the right house. I'll help you."

She looked at him distrustfully.

"Come inside!"

The girl bit her lip and shook her head.

Sid turned and called through the open door, "Rhoda! Come quick!"

The girl wrapped her arms around herself and looked down the road. "They be here any second, now!"

Rhoda came out onto the porch, wiping her hands on her apron.

"Land sakes!" she cried, when she saw the girl hugging herself, almost in tears. "Come on up here, girl."

"They's gonna catch me and send me back," the girl moaned as Rhoda led her into the house.

"No they ain't. Not if they got me to deal with." Rhoda turned back to Sidney before she went into the house. "You just set yourself down there and act as if nothing ever happen', you hear me?"

Her dark eyes flashed at him as she disappeared into the house with the girl. Sidney found himself surprised at how stern Rhoda could look. Her face was normally smooth and peaceful. He sat down and picked up the paper. He was on edge—waiting. It was only a moment before he heard horses coming down the road at a good pace. He looked up and saw some officers approaching on horseback. They slowed their horses to a trot and stopped in front of the house. Marshal Yost dismounted and came up the steps to the porch. Sid stood up to greet him.

"Can I help you, Marshal?" Sid asked.

"Maybe you can. Is your uncle at home?"

"No, sir. He'll be at the Mercantile 'til six."

"Is your aunt here?"

"No, sir. She's over at the Holloway's place."

"All right," he grunted. "We're chasing a runaway slave. You seen her?"

"Hmmm..." Sid thought a moment. "Well, now that you mention it, I did see someone run by. They were going awfully fast, though. I didn't look up till she was almost gone. Can't be sure it was a darky, but she ran right on down the street, like the devil was chasing her."

"Must be her." Yost turned to his deputies. "Wilson, you go see if Mrs. Judson is at the Holloway's place. Harvey and I'll chase this rascal down."

They dispersed. Sidney sat down again and wiped the sweat from his brow. When the marshals had ridden out of sight in either direction, Rhoda came out on the porch and stood looking at him.

He glanced up at her and whispered, "Is she all right?"

"Yes. She's fine." She cleared her throat, crossing her arms under her full breasts. "Mr. Sidney, I didn't know what to do when I saw that girl. I didn't trust you as far as I could throw you. I just knew I couldn't leave the girl out here. But now... I heard what you said to those men."

"Oh." Sid looked down at the newspaper.

"You sure like to keep people guessing, don't you?"

Sid paused. "Maybe I just learn some things the hard way."

He stole another glance at her. She smiled.

"Your uncle's gonna get wind of this real quick."

"Oh, don't tell Uncle Daniel. Rhoda, please. I don't want him to hear about this."

"Nonsense, Mr. Sidney. Why would I keep it from him? Now, I'll go in and get you one of those bottles of soda water we're saving for Independence Day. You deserve it, if anyone does."

Just as Rhoda brought his soda out, Sarah arrived home.

"Rhoda," Sarah quickly mounted the steps to the porch. "Did something happen while I was gone?"

Rhoda tried to hide her smile. "Wait till you hear it, Missus!"

Sidney squirmed in his chair.

"What, then?" Sarah asked. "A federal officer came to the Holloway's just as I was leaving. He interrogated me. I thought something awful must have happened."

"Come on in and I'll tell you all about it."

Sidney stayed on the porch. Rhoda spoke more loudly than usual. Perhaps she wanted him to hear her. He rubbed his sweaty palms on his pants. He didn't know how to explain what he had done and he wasn't ready to try. Rhoda's voice was still going, more excited than he'd ever heard it.

"And then I heard Mr. Sidney through the window plain as day! I heard him saying 'that runaway run right on down the street, like the devil was chasing her!'"

Sid laid the newspaper on the floor. He sauntered off the porch and hurried to the riverbank.

Sidney emerged at dusk. He entered the house and let the door close slowly behind him. The house was quiet and dark save a small light in the kitchen. Rhoda sat silent, a Bible open on the table in front of her, the lamplight shining on her face. Her lips moved as she read, haltingly. Sid watched her for several moments before she looked up.

"Mr. Sidney," she breathed. "I wondered what happened to you."

"I had to get some fresh air, Rhoda." Sid shifted awkwardly.

"People been in and out of the house ever since you took off."

"Why? Where is everyone now?"

"Well," Rhoda began. "After I finished telling your aunt what happened, she figured that if the officers rode after the girl in the direction you told them, after a while they'd realize they weren't going to find her and then they'd come back looking for her. So, she sent for Mr. Atticus White. He came and took the girl with him. He didn't tell anyone where he took her. So's to protect the rest of us—and the girl as well."

"Yes," Sid nodded. "That was smart."

"So, about thirty minutes later, the marshals came back." Rhoda smiled. "It was the hand of Providence you were gone, Mr. Sidney! None of us knew where you were and so they couldn't interrogate you. They were mean, too. I know it would have been hard for you to keep your story straight if they talked to you. None of us knew anything about that girl, of course. But they didn't believe us, so they searched the house—and the carriage house and the root cellar! I just thank the Lord that girl wasn't here, because we would have been caught for sure! And that poor soul sent back to slavery. I'm sorry, Mr. Sidney. I know you're from the South..."

Sid smiled. "Where is everyone now, Rhoda?"

"I'm getting to that! After searching the house, they finally left and then they went to the store to interrogate Mr. Daniel. The Missus and I put the house in order and started making tea but just when we got started, your uncle burst in and he told us all about the interrogating and said there's an emergency meeting for the Railroad. I don't even know where the meeting is. They left and I just had some of the fish and cold bread we were making for tea. I made some for you too so you can have it if you want to. I don't know when they're coming back."

As Rhoda took out a plate for him and loaded it with fish and bread, he realized how hungry he was.

"Thank you, Rhoda." He took the plate from her and started towards the dining room. Then he stopped. His heart racing, he turned back to the kitchen table and set his plate down across from Rhoda. She looked up at him, her dark eyes wide with surprise.

"Oh, Mr. Sidney, you don't have to—"

"I'd rather eat in here," he grinned sheepishly, taking his seat. "That's the most I've ever heard you talk."

Rhoda pursed her lips and looked down at the Bible. "There's a lot you're going to learn about me once I know you've got a good heart."

six

SIDNEY dreaded the return of his Aunt and Uncle. After eating his tea, he went into the library and tried to write to Catherine but found himself so distracted he couldn't concentrate. He read the letter over.

My Sweet Catherine,

It is with pleasure that I write to you to let you know that I am well. I hope this will find you the same. I trust your studies are progressing. You will be pleased to know that I am reading Shakespeare's Hamlet. I am enjoying it immensely.

I am grateful that you have been giving attention to my parents' graves in my absence. Have you visited Tall Pine? I hope the slaves are cooperating with the overseer I left in charge.

Sid sighed in disgust. What difference did it all make? He crumpled the paper into a ball, went into the parlor and tossed the letter toward the fireplace. It bounced off the mantelpiece and landed on the lid of Sarah's sewing basket. He looked up at the clock—quarter past nine. The second hand slowly ticked its way around the face. He could not tell Catherine the things that were pressing on his heart. He couldn't tell her about helping a fugitive slave, or about the runaway shot in the chest two weeks ago.

Sidney went back into the library. There were things he had to know. He found the slim volume where he had left it, behind MacBeth. He took it and a lamp to the desk and opened to the first page.

Wilkes-Barre, Penn.
30 September, 1838

I don't know how I shall ever help Daniel through this. David has gone. He left everything. When I saw Melinda downstairs yesterday, her eyes were red-rimmed. She told me David didn't even say good-bye to her. She looked awful. I just don't know what to do. Daniel won't talk about it. I feel David will come back. He's always been wild, but not cruel. He wouldn't just leave Melinda forever, without explaining. But when I suggest this to Daniel, he says quietly, "He's not coming back." Then he speaks of something else. If he doesn't come back, he's not the man I thought he was. I don't know how I shall forgive him for hurting my husband—and Melinda.

Sidney paused. Who was Melinda? Surely it couldn't be Mrs. White. There must be another Melinda. He turned the page.

10 October, 1838

Will I never cease to be amazed? Not only has David not come back, but now Melinda is leaving as well. She came upstairs to our apartment a little while ago to tell me. I put on some tea for her and we had a good chat. I was so looking forward to having her for a sister. Now that is all ruined, thanks to David. She says she must get away, to heal. She's as sure as Daniel that David isn't coming back. Next week she's going to stay with relatives in the country. She says she doesn't know how long she'll be gone. I told her to come back and see me again before she goes, to say good bye. It seems that we're losing everything. This summer I really thought things were coming together for David. He was settling down and he'd managed to catch such a respectable girl. I don't blame him for leaving. But I don't think he handled it properly at all.

Sidney sighed, flipping the book shut. There were only more questions here, not answers. It sounded like his father had planned to marry this Melinda, whoever she was. Why would he start to settle down here if he always felt he belonged in the South?

He went for his box of fly-tying supplies and brought it downstairs. Rhoda had retired for the night, so he had the kitchen table to himself. Questions continued to run through his brain as he worked. He still didn't know why his father had gone South—or why he himself had helped that girl today.

Uncle Daniel and Aunt Sarah came home at ten o'clock. Sarah ruffled Sid's hair with her fingers and smiled.

"You're a good boy."

Sid smiled uneasily.

She kissed his cheek and went upstairs to bed.

Daniel looked at Sid. "Do you have a few minutes?"

Sid set down the fly he was working on. "Of course."

Daniel settled himself in a chair across from Sid. "Your aunt's opinion of you is obvious. I'm not sure why you helped that slave girl but in light of recent events, I have a hard time believing your motives were pure." Daniel paused.

Sid looked away. "Which recent events?"

"You talked back to Rhoda the first day you were here. You eavesdropped till you discovered I was involved in the Railroad. You tried to get me arrested—"

"I didn't!" Sid protested, but his uncle went on.

"You wrestled and apprehended an escaped slave, an action which resulted in that slave's death—"

"That wasn't my fault!" Sid burst out. "I didn't know that would happen!"

"If you had minded your own business," Daniel said quietly. "Perhaps it wouldn't have happened.

"Perhaps," Sid repeated.

"Do you want to explain why you helped that runaway today?"

Sid raked his fingers through his hair, letting out a heavy sigh. "I wish I knew."

Daniel waited quietly.

Sid got up and went to the cook stove. He leaned on the cold, black top and took a deep breath.

"I felt horrible when that man was shot." He turned back to Uncle Daniel, but couldn't quite meet his gaze. "Really, sir. I guess I just saw someone in need today and… knew I could help instead of hurting. And there's no way I was telling the marshal where she was after what happened in the square."

Uncle Daniel took a deep breath. "I see."

"And one more thing, Uncle Daniel," Sid stepped forward, looking into Uncle Daniel's face. "I was not going to turn you in!"

Uncle Daniel's eyes softened. "I'm sorry I mistrusted you."

"Listen, sir," Sidney said. "If it's just too much of an imposition—having me here. If it interferes with your work, then… I'll go."

Daniel shook his head. "Don't be ridiculous. I would never turn you away. You need a home."

"I don't need a home," Sid said quickly. "I have an estate in Roswell."

Daniel smiled. "A house isn't a home, son. Besides, I've gotten used to having you around."

"But I've been nothing but trouble," Sid said quietly.

"I've had trouble before," Daniel said. "You're no trouble… well, not much anyway." He chuckled.

Daniel rose and touched Sid's shoulder. "I don't think it's time for you to go yet."

Sid was silent as his uncle left the room. He stared at his flies, laid out on the table in front of him. He picked up their wooden box and swept them into it in one big tangle of feathers and hooks.

He went upstairs to bed. He was not going to find answers tonight. Maybe never. Nothing fit together neatly anymore, the way it had before the accident. Sidney fell into a troubled sleep and dreamt of his mother and father.

They were in their carriage, pulling out of the drive at Tall Pine. Sidney sprang onto his horse and spurred him on, desperately trying to catch up with them. He must stop them. He rode harder but the carriage was always in front of him, the dust from its wheels choking him. And then, at that too-familiar bend in the road, he watched it plummet down the bank. And he was with them, tumbling over and over, hearing his mother scream. Then all was quiet, and he stood looking at the Negro in the Wilkes-Barre Square. Rachel was there, pulling on his arm. And the air was full of her screams, just like his mother's. But he couldn't stop looking at the man's accusing eyes. They seemed to be pulling him closer. And Joshua Smith's cackling laugh was behind him. Pushing him into the guilt and pain.

⚜

The following evening, Sidney attended an ice-cream social at church. As he approached the church with Tom and Caleb, he grew uneasy. He hadn't spoken to Rachel since the day the fugitive was shot. She had avoided him at church and in town. Maude had brought the eggs to the store today, and had been so shy that Sid dared not ask after Rachel.

Why do you care what she thinks of you? he asked himself. *She's just a Yankee.*

They met Eliza Jane on the way into the vestibule.

"Hi, boys!" she said. "How are you? Surviving this heat wave, I hope?"

They nodded, murmuring their assent.

"Well," she continued. "I guess we can't complain when all we have to deal with is the heat. It's better than smallpox."

"Smallpox?" Sid replied. "Who has smallpox?"

"You haven't heard about the outbreak?" Eliza asked.

"No," Sid answered.

"Where have you been, Sid?" Caleb asked.

Sid shook his head and waited. He knew Eliza would be happy to explain it to him.

"It started in Philadelphia a few weeks ago," she said. "But there have been several confirmed cases in Allentown. And I just heard from Mary Beth Conyngham that a man in Hazleton came down with it. That's a little too close for my liking."

"Hazleton?" Tom said. "That's too close for me as well. How did Mary Beth find this out?"

"Her father's brother lives in Hazleton. He was up to buy some cattle from them this morning and he told them about this case. It's downright frightening, Tom!"

Sid stood nearby, listening. He didn't remember where Hazleton was and he couldn't conjure up the concern Tom seemed to feel. Caleb went off in search of ice cream. Sid found himself scanning the groups of young people for Rachel's familiar smile. A flash of chestnut-colored hair caught Sid's eye and he turned. Ruth and Jake made their way into the church. Sidney let out the breath he had momentarily held. He nodded to the couple.

Then he heard a familiar voice behind him. "There you are! I've been looking everywhere for you."

Sid turned back to Tom and Eliza. Rachel stood between them. She'd been addressing Eliza. Then she saw Sid.

"Hi!" Rachel smiled. "I heard you disappeared yesterday. But I see you're back, safe and sound!"

"I only went down to the River," Sid replied.

"He missed the fish!" Tom winked at Sid.

Eliza had moved on to less concerning topics. She said to Tom, "You have to lend me one of your books. I really want to read a Charles Dickinson novel."

Tom drew his eyebrows together and cocked his head at her. "You mean Dickens?"

"Yes, Dickens!" Eliza laughed. "That's it! We were supposed to read one for school last year, but I couldn't get past the first chapter."

"Which one?"

"Umm..." Eliza paused.

Rachel answered for her. "*The Old Curiosity Shop.*"

"Oh, that's a tough one." Tom stepped closer to Eliza, leaving Rachel standing alone. "But why do you want to read Dickens if you didn't enjoy the book?"

"I don't know," Eliza said. "I don't think I gave it a fair chance. If you could lend me one, maybe one that you've made notes in, I think it would make it a lot more interesting."

Rachel said, "You should start with *Oliver Twist.* You might like it better."

Eliza went on, as though she hadn't heard Rachel. "Do you think you could lend me a book? One you think I'd like."

"Sure," Tom said.

Neither of them made any move to let Rachel join their conversation. If he had not been preoccupied with what she must think of him, Sidney might have been amused by the situation. Someone handed him a bowl of strawberry ice cream and he took it out to the front steps of the church, where he found Caleb. They sat together, eating their ice cream, and enjoying the breeze, the sounds of the crowd inside drifting out to them in little fragments. Presently, Rachel came out the front door.

"Good night, gentlemen," she said.

Sid rose. "Going home already?"

"Yes," she nodded. "I'm tired. Eliza and Tom are engaged in scintillating conversation and I'd rather go than stay."

"May I walk you home then?" Sid asked.

"Oh." Rachel looked away. "I suppose."

The uncertainty in her voice was discouraging, but Sid accompanied her down the steps, leaving his bowl with Caleb. As soon as they were out of the gate, Rachel spoke up.

"I didn't mean to be rude. I'm more than happy to have you walk me home... it's just—"

"You'd rather it were Tom," Sid finished for her.

"No!" Rachel protested. "I did feel a little excluded, so I finally left them alone."

"People seem to be pairing up these days," Sid said.

"I know," Rachel said. "Sometimes I wish we didn't have to grow up."

"And other times?" Sid asked.

"Other times I can't wait to get away from my mother." She chuckled, then closed her mouth. "I shouldn't say things like that."

"I can't believe my sister's getting married," she continued. "Things will never be the same again."

"I guess not," Sid remarked. "Everything changes when you grow up."

Rachel looked at him out of the corner of her eye. "And you've had to grow up a lot faster than I have."

"Yeah." Sid cleared his throat. "Want to know something funny? I couldn't wait to get away from my parents, either. But now that they're gone, I'm not so sure of myself."

Rachel sighed. "Forget what I said about my mother. Losing my parents would kill me!"

She stopped walking and turned to him. He cleared his throat again, afraid to meet her eyes.

"I wanted to ask you something," she said. "My father told me what you did yesterday." She paused, but Sid just stared up over the treetops to the clear sky above the river. "Why did you do it, Sid?"

Sid looked at the ground. He rolled a stone around with the toe of his boot.

He sighed. "The girl yesterday... she was in need of help. She was scared. That's the only thing I can figure out. I didn't really think—I just acted. I guess that's why. But it doesn't mean I'm joining the Railroad."

"Well, I didn't think so." Rachel frowned. "It just confused me. I thought maybe you were trying to win our approval."

Sid laughed out loud. "I wouldn't even attempt that!"

Rachel smiled. "My father likes you."

"I don't know why," Sid said. "Except that your father likes everyone."

"That's true," Rachel agreed. She began walking again. "Thanks for walking me home."

They were at the Whites' gate. She opened it and stepped inside. Then she looked over her shoulder at him.

"I think I'm beginning to hold my father's opinion of you, too. Good night!"

She was in the house before Sidney could respond.

seven

On a Wednesday afternoon in mid-July, Tom met Sidney at the river for their weekly fishing foray.

"I've been here two months today." Sid fastened a brand new fly to his line.

"You don't say!" Tom said. "It seems like it was yesterday I was meeting you over on Rachel's front porch."

Sid nodded. He began casting, skillfully floating his fly down to land on the water.

Tom prepared his line, looking almost the expert. "So, you're still planning to go back?"

"Sure," Sid said. "I'm not sure when, but... eventually."

"Huh," Tom grunted. "I thought maybe once you got used to us you'd change your mind."

"Well," Sid said. "I'm not sure I'm used to you, yet. This town is full of surprises. As soon as I think I have it figured out, I'm completely caught off guard by something."

"Such as?"

"Oh, you know... helping that slave girl for instance."

Tom chuckled. "You must know that has nothing to do with this town and everything to do with you, Sid."

Sid shrugged. "Well, I have to admit I do enjoy being here much more than I expected, but I never intended to stay forever."

"Let's always be friends, Sid," Tom said. "Even after you go back. Even if war breaks out and we fight on opposite sides." Tom was suddenly solemn, gripping his rod in his fist. "If I see your face at the other end of my musket, I won't pull the trigger."

Tom's dramatic oath embarrassed Sid. He swallowed hard, tapping his fly rod on the top of his bare foot. He looked at Tom and grimaced. "I think maybe you'll see my face in every man at the other end of your musket. And you'll have to pull the trigger."

He watched the water of the Susquehanna flow past, hoping he hadn't hurt Tom's feelings.

"You're probably right," Tom admitted. "I wish it didn't have to come to that. I don't want to shoot a man! I just can't imagine it feeling right."

"Well," Sidney said. "What are the odds that we'll end up in the same battle, anyway?"

"I wouldn't bet on it—if I were a gambling man!" Tom laughed.

"I didn't mean it literally," Sid said. "But I just don't see the harm in a bit of gambling."

Tom shook his head. "That's one of those things we're not going to agree on, Sid. You'll have to play your Poker and drink your whiskey without me. But I'm more than happy to fish with you."

"So let us fish," Sid said. "War seems inevitable, but there's no sense in worrying about the future just yet."

"No, there isn't." Tom began casting.

Sid watched his clumsy efforts. They were adequate. Tom's skills were improving every week. He made his fly dance, and it often fooled the fish. Perhaps they thought it was a fly with a broken wing, but they still thought it was a fly.

"So," Tom said. "You say you'll go back eventually... are you going to wait for the war to start?"

"Well, I'm not sure," Sid drawled. "I reckon if war breaks out and I'm still here, I'll head back right away. But I'm not in a hurry if it doesn't."

Tom frowned, reeling in his line. "But you've got a sweetheart to get home to, don't you?"

"Yeah." Sid's smile faded. He cast, expertly dancing his fly over the rippling surface of the water. "Catherine isn't too keen on me being up here at all. I tried to explain to her that after my parents' deaths I just needed to be with my own flesh and blood for a while. I don't have any family in Roswell."

"Did she understand?" Tom asked.

"No. But she was part of my reason for leaving, anyway..." Sidney had not meant to tell anyone that. It had just slipped out.

"How so?" Tom queried.

"Oh!" Sid jerked his line. "Is that a bite?"

But it was not a bite. He turned to Tom's probing eyes.

"Tom, I can't... I don't know how to explain," he stammered. "My parents thought we were too young to get married. So, after they died, I don't know. I guess I just don't want to rush into anything. It's easier being away from her."

"Is it?"

"Sometimes."

"You don't want to do the wrong thing?"

"Exactly."

"Have you cried?"

"Excuse me?" Tom's abrupt questions always caught Sid off guard.

"About your parents, Sid. You'll go crazy if you don't."

"I don't cry."

"Never?" Tom asked.

"Men aren't supposed to cry." Sid pulled his line in and waded out of the water.

"There is 'a time to weep, and a time to laugh,'" Tom quoted.

"Well, I'm not laughing, but I haven't wept either." Sid was stubborn.

"You feel better if you do. That's all I'm saying."

Tom's tone was gentle, but Sid set his jaw. He hoped Tom didn't know that he was holding back tears.

✣

That evening Daniel left after tea. Sarah began sewing in the parlor. Sidney took Hamlet and sat on the sofa near her. But he couldn't read. He sat slapping the book against his thigh. Sarah stopped her sewing and looked at him.

"What's troubling you?"

"Nothing," Sidney answered automatically.

"That's not true," Sarah said. "You're more like your uncle than you realize. I can always tell when something troubles him and I know something's bothering you, too."

"Why do you say that?" Sid burst out. "I'm not like Uncle Daniel!"

"Now, Sidney." Sarah put her hand on Sid's arm. "Daniel's a good man."

"But I don't want to be like him! I wanted to be like my father! But I was never good enough and now it's too late."

"Sidney," Sarah said firmly. "David loved you. You were his only child. You meant the world to him! I'm sure he was very proud of you."

"No, Aunt Sarah." Sid's voice was choked. "He wasn't proud of me. I didn't give him any reason to be."

Sarah set down her mending. "What makes you say that?"

It was Catherine. She was the biggest bane between Sidney and his parents. They had their worst argument on that horrible afternoon at the end of April. Sidney came in the front door to find his mother floating down the mahogany staircase, peach-colored organdy wafting about her, giving her glowing skin an angelic hue.

"Sidney!" she said. "I'm glad you're home. I can't get anyone to hitch the horses. Lem is busy at the moment, and your father is wearing his fine suit."

Sid took his mother's hands in his own. "Anything you want, Mother!"

She chuckled softly as she put on her gloves. "Where have you been this morning?"

"I went over to the Cartlands' to call on Catherine," Sid said.

David Judson appeared at the top of the steps, fastening his stock around his neck. "I think you ought to tell us when you're going courting from now on."

"Father, must we discuss this?" Sid turned away from his parents.

"It seems that we must!" David came down the stairs. "I don't know how many times I have to tell you before you get it through your head. You are far too young to have serious intentions towards any girl. In fact it would be best if you restrain yourself from calling until you've finished your education!"

"I will go calling whenever I please!"

"Sidney, don't speak to your father that way!" his mother scolded.

"I'll speak the way I want to speak!" Sid faced his father. "Why do you think you can tell me how to live my life?"

"I'm your father," David said. "Your actions affect this family."

"I don't have to do what you say!" Sidney shouted.

"We're only thinking of what's best—" Laeticia began.

"I know what's best for me!" Sid cut his mother off. "I'm going to marry Catherine! I'm not going to wait."

"Sidney!" his mother said.

"You don't say?" his father replied. "And where do you think the two you will live? How will you earn a living?"

"You've said yourself I can have a position at the Mills."

"Yes," David said. "After you've finished your education."

"Well, you'd better let me have it sooner." Sid felt the heat in his face as conviction and anger surged through him. "We've already made our plans. I spoke to her father this morning. There's nothing the two of you can do about it!"

His mother looked as though he'd struck her. She turned away.

His father went to her. Her shoulders shook as he embraced her. He turned to Sidney, his lips tight and colorless.

"You went against us intentionally." His eyes were steel. "You knew we did not approve."

"You can't keep us apart!" Sid retorted.

"Sidney, we have nothing against Catherine," his mother said through her tears. "You're just very young. And we made it clear you were not to speak to Mr. Cartland."

Sid opened his mouth to reply, but David held up his hand.

"Stop! We will discuss this at another time, when you can be respectful. We are going to town now. Go hitch the horses to the carriage."

"Fine!" Sid's voice was still sharp.

He turned from his parents and fled the house. It felt good to run, to get some of his anger out. He hadn't mentioned to his parents that Catherine's father had not exactly promised him her hand. Still, they were both determined to marry before the summer was over. Sid was rough with the harness, but he tried not to take out his frustration on the horses.

"Sorry, chaps!" he said as he buckled the straps. "I know it's not your fault."

He patted the bay on its neck and led the team out to the hitching post. He tightened the girth and looked over the harness to make sure it was adjusted properly. Then he stopped. There was a worn spot on the trace, right where it attached to the hames. Sid fingered it thoughtfully. He checked the other trace and it was weak at the same point.

"Oh, drat!" he exclaimed. "I don't have time to get new traces now. It'll be fine till tonight."

Sid turned away from the horses, kicking the gravel in the drive. He needed to get away. He began running again, this time in the direction of Peachtree Creek.

"Sidney, what are you saying?" Sarah's voice broke into his story.

"It was my fault." Sid choked over his words.

"No! Oh, no!" Sarah's hand went to her mouth.

Sid searched her eyes for some sign of forgiveness, of compassion.

✤

When Daniel came in from the Railroad meeting that night, he found Sidney asleep on the sofa, his head on a cushion in Sarah's lap. Sarah looked up and smiled sadly at her husband.

"He's finally grieving," she whispered.

✤

Sidney told no one of his talk with Sarah. The next morning at the store as he counted the eggs Maud brought in, he could hardly concentrate. Suppose Aunt Sarah thought less of him now. He couldn't bear the thought of that. When he went home for dinner, he asked her.

"Sidney," she said sternly, her hands on her hips. "I don't even think it's your fault that your parents are dead. Why would I think less of you?"

"But it is my fault!" Sid said.

"First of all, you don't know that the weak harness caused the accident."

"Yes, I do," Sid said. "Lem brought the harness back to the carriage house. I had to know, so I looked at it the day before I left to come here. Both traces were broken. If I'd just taken the time to change them-"

"Stop," Sarah said. "Nobody knows what happened. They were already worn, so the traces would likely have broken in the fall, even if something spooked the horses and caused them to go off the road."

For the first time in months, a glimmer of hope shone into

Sidney's heart.

"And," Aunt Sarah said. "Even if that was the only reason the carriage went off the road, I still don't see it as your fault."

"Why not?" Sid asked.

"You didn't intend to kill your parents." Sarah shook her head as she wrapped up some ham for him to take to Daniel. "You made a mistake. The same decision could easily have had no repercussions. It could have resulted in the safe return of your parents that evening. And you all might have forgiven each other for the harsh words you'd spoken."

She looked up at Sidney as he brushed a hand over his eyes.

"Oh, dear," she said. "You see—it was their time. But it's important for you to know that even if you had done something horrible, it wouldn't change our love for you."

Sidney didn't believe that was possible, but Sarah's perspective had eased the burden of guilt he'd been carrying. He went back to the store with a lighter step than he had used in some time.

Nighttime was an entirely different matter, however. Sharing his pain with Aunt Sarah had uncovered the grief he'd kept inside. He had not realized the depth of his sorrow over his loss as well as the unresolved argument. At night, he lay awake, often in tears, until he finally fell into a shallow and troubled slumber, plagued by nightmares.

A week had passed before Sid's grief was spent. He stretched out on the mattress with a peaceful feeling for a change. Perhaps tonight he could sleep more easily. Maybe he would not wake in a cold sweat to find Sarah standing by his bed saying, "You called for them again."

Aunt Sarah was not home tonight. Smallpox had finally spread to Wilkes-Barre, striking a few families in town. Sarah and Rhoda had gone to tend the sick.

Sid had just closed his eyes when a sharp knock at his door roused him. He sat up, blinking the sleep away.

"Come in," he called.

It was Daniel. He stood for a moment with his hand on the doorknob, the light from the hallway behind him making a sharp silhouette of his broad figure.

His voice came through the darkness. "Are you up?"

"Yes." Sid swung his feet to the ground and, striking a match, lit the small lamp on the table. "Is something wrong?"

Daniel came in and stood, surveying him. Sid rubbed the sleep from his eyes, trying to hide his annoyance.

Daniel cleared his throat and spoke. "I hate to put you to any trouble of this kind. I only come to you out of dire need. Atticus is all the way in Scranton. Bill Gildersleeve is tied up with other Railroad business and won't be free till morning. I just got word of these passengers tonight and I can't reach anyone else. I'd do it myself but I have a matter just as pressing to tend to. All I need is for you to help me and keep your mouth shut about it. This is a matter of life and death. Can I trust you?"

Sidney rubbed his eyes, trying to wake himself up. "You... you want me to help you with... runaway darkies, sir?"

"It's you or nobody. And I sincerely hope you are better than nobody in this instance."

Sidney gulped. "Aunt Sarah's not back yet?"

"She and Rhoda might be gone all night..."

Sid stood and reached for his pants. "Okay. I'll do what I can."

Daniel relaxed a little. As Sidney buttoned his shirt, Daniel explained the situation. Five slaves were traveling together from Virginia. They had gotten as far as the village of Nanticoke, south of Wilkes-Barre. Tonight a conductor was bringing them up the Susquehanna by rowboat.

"This conductor, Ned Faux, has brought slaves to Wilkes-Barre before," Daniel said. "He knows the general area where he should land. But in the dark, it's hard to find. And he's never been to my house before. He needs someone to guide him. When he gets close to Wilkes-Barre, he'll light a lantern."

Sidney was to watch from the shore until he saw a light on the water. He would then light his lantern and signal—two flashes. If the light on the water signaled three flashes in return, he was to guide them to shore and bring them to the carriage house until Daniel returned. He would not tell Sidney where he was going.

"You know too much already." He sighed.

They left the house by the back door and Daniel picked up an unlighted lantern on the way. Sidney followed him silently through the side yard, to the front of the house and across the street. Once they reached the riverbank, Daniel showed Sid how to signal with the lantern.

Then he said, "I need to go. Remember, if the boat doesn't land here it might go further up river and get into trouble. Don't take this lightly."

Sid only nodded, faintly aware of his incompetence. Daniel was gone. The night was cool for the end of July. In Georgia it would still be stifling. He settled himself on the ground. It was damp, but not wet. Enough dry grass surrounded him to make it comfortable. The river was silent and dark. It must be nearly midnight. He'd spent so many nights unable to sleep in his own bed across the street. Now, when his mind was finally at rest, he was not in bed but on a cold, damp riverbank staring into the pitch-black night, listening to the sound of the river flowing towards his homeland.

eight

Rays of light played over the rippling waves and danced across Sidney's hair as the sun emerged from the mountains behind him. The boy felt rough hands on his shoulders, shaking him awake.

"Get up!" Daniel was angry.

Sidney struggled to sit up, to push the weight of sleep from his head. No sooner had he sat up than he was pinned to the ground again by Daniel. His eyes were inches away from Sid's. A crashing in the bushes warned that they had company. Atticus White sprang into the clearing at the water's edge.

"Stop!" He grabbed Daniel's arms and pulled him away from Sidney. "Get a hold of yourself!"

Sidney lay on the ground, catching his breath. A sick feeling crept up from his stomach—he had fallen asleep. He sat up again and shook his head to clear it. Mr. White still held Daniel's arms but Daniel angrily threw him off and stormed up the path. Breathing hard, Atticus turned to Sid.

"I was never any match for him." Atticus panted. "He'll be all right. What about you?"

"I'm okay." Sid gasped for air, but could not meet Mr. White's steady gaze.

The queasy feeling in his stomach was growing stronger.

"I think I'm going to be sick," he managed to say. Then he turned around and dry-heaved into the bushes.

Atticus offered his canteen and Sid took it gratefully.

When he gained his composure, he said, "Thank you for stepping in there, sir."

"Don't mention it." Mr. White shook his head. "We were on your porch and when Daniel came after you, I thought I'd better intervene."

"I appreciate it." Sid rose wearily. "What... happened to the darkies?"

Atticus' face clouded. "Bill Gildersleeve found a rowboat upriver a bit. My guess is they're hiding in the brush somewhere. We just don't know why Ned didn't come to my house when he couldn't find you. He knows I'm in the Railroad."

Atticus paused. The silence was unbearable. Sid wished Daniel hadn't dragged him into this in the first place. He felt he must say something to this man who, for some reason, found no fault with him.

"Mr. White, I... I didn't mean for this to happen." His voice sounded more like a sob or a whine than a dignified apology. The whole situation was too much for him. But he had to explain.

"I didn't do it on purpose!" His voice caught in his throat.

"I know you didn't." Atticus' tone was calm. "Daniel does, too. He's mad at himself, really. If it's any comfort, the situation is no worse than if you had not been here at all. But it will be if the marshals discover us in this conspicuous spot on the riverbank. Come on."

Atticus slapped Sid's shoulder and they went up the path together. The world seemed to reel around Sid. When they got to the house, Sarah met him in the kitchen. Two lines were already deeply embedded between her eyebrows. She put her hand on his arm.

"Oh, Sidney! If only I had been here," she whispered. "I would never have let him send you."

Atticus spoke to Daniel. "Bill and I will scour the woods for Ned. I can't imagine what's become of him."

"Let me help!" Sid said.

"Haven't you done enough already?" Daniel asked.

"It might be good for him, Daniel," Atticus said.

"No." Daniel's voice was steel.

"All right, then," Atticus replied. "It's your decision."

When Atticus had gone, Daniel put on his hat.

"Where are you going?" Sid asked.

"I have a store to run," answered Daniel.

He strode off without another word. Sid turned to Aunt Sarah. "What have I done?"

"Sidney, don't you worry about a thing. I need to get dinner started and then I'll fix you some breakfast. You just sit here at the table for now."

Sid obeyed meekly, but in a moment he suggested, "I'll pack my bags right after I eat."

Sarah turned and stared. "Sidney Judson you'll do no such thing! You are a part of this family and we are not turning you out."

"But, ma'am," Sid protested. "You saw Uncle Daniel's face. I'll be lucky if he ever speaks to me again!"

"You are not going anywhere, young man." Sarah set the large stockpot on the woodstove with a bang. Sid jumped. "The idea," she muttered.

She opened the stove and stoked the fire, then slammed the door. Sidney watched from the table, afraid to speak. He had never seen her so upset. She began chopping onions in quick, jerky motions, pounding the knife through them into the cutting board.

She turned to him. "Let me explain something to you. Your uncle may have his quirks." She shook her knife with each point. "You two may not see eye to eye. But he is not the kind of man who sends away his own nephew!"

She turned back to her chopping. When the onion lay in a mangled mess, she spooned some lard into the stockpot and dumped the onion in after it. The mixture began to sizzle and pop.

"He's only angry because he loves people so much." Her voice softened. She took a wooden spoon to the pot and stirred up the beginnings of soup. "He's upset about the slaves. But he loves you, too."

Sid shrank into his chair, trying to make himself as small as he felt inside. But it was no use. He could not disappear. Aunt Sarah boiled some eggs for him.

As she set them in front of him, Sid finally gained the courage to speak again.

"I need to help," he said. "I'll go try to find Mr. White and Mr. Gildersleeve after I eat. Maybe I can help them find the slaves."

Aunt Sarah shook her head. "Sidney, I know you mean well, but you haven't had any experience. If you go traipsing around on the shore, you might draw attention to yourself. We never know when the marshals are coming to town. You could make the situation worse."

Sid ate silently for a moment as Sarah began slicing carrots to add to her soup.

Then he said, "I have to do something. It won't hurt anything if I just go to the Whites' farm and ask if they have any news."

Sarah stopped slicing and wiped her hands on her apron.

"I suppose that couldn't hurt," she said. "But you need to be very careful if you meet anyone else. When you're in the Railroad as long as we have been, you learn how to get out of sticky situations."

Sid grinned at her. "Aunt Sarah, didn't Rhoda tell you how suave I was with those officers last month?"

Aunt Sarah smiled. "All right. I suppose you can handle interacting with marshals just fine."

"Yes," Sidney said. "It's just staying awake all night that poses a problem."

Sarah laid her hand on his shoulder. "Don't be too hard on yourself."

Sid grimaced as he rose. "Well, sitting around here will only make it worse."

"Be careful," she said.

Sid put on his hat as he headed out the front door. He felt better as soon as he was on his way. Perhaps there would be good news from the Whites. Maybe they had found Ned Faux and the fugitives were safely hidden now.

He knocked on their door, trying to look nonchalant. There was no answer. It seemed that nobody was home. Disappointed, he turned and started off the porch.

Then he heard the door open behind him. Ruth stood in the doorway.

"Come in, Sidney," she said.

She led him through the dining room into the kitchen at the back of the house.

"It's just Sidney," she announced.

Atticus and Jake sat at the kitchen table.

"Well, look who it is." Jake smiled grimly.

"Good morning," Sid said.

Atticus stood up and knocked twice on an interior door. The door opened and William Gildersleeve came into the kitchen from an enclosed stairwell. He was followed by a slight, middle-aged man wearing brown trousers and a linen shirt. The man was shaking. He held a jacket over his arm. His sleeve was torn close to the elbow and the hem of his trousers was muddy. Sid knew it was Ned Faux without any introduction.

He took a deep breath. "Where are the darkies?"

Atticus spoke to Ned. "This is Judson's nephew. He was watching for you from shore."

"Or rather, I wasn't. I can't tell you how sorry I am." Sidney offered his hand, surprised at the strength in his own voice. "Please, say the slaves are hidden somewhere."

Ned shook his head. "I narrowly escaped capture myself." His handshake was firm, but Sid could feel him trembling underneath. "It's my fault, really. I should have kept them hidden till I had planned our route better. But as it was, I lead the runaways across a road and we were spotted."

Sidney sat down hard on one of the chairs and buried his face in his hands.

"Sit down, Ned," Bill directed. The two of them joined the others at the table.

"I'll make some coffee," Ruth said. She went to the cook stove.

Sidney picked his head up and looked at Ned. "How did you get away?"

Ned sighed. "I hate to think of it. I was ahead of the others. Once I realized the officer was after them, I ran for my life. I was still in the woods, so I don't think he ever saw me clearly enough to add me to the count. Then I came out below Atticus's barn and I knew I was close to safety."

"I'm glad you made it," Sid said.

Mr. Gildersleeve spoke again. "Five fugitives are going to be returned to slavery."

"Bill," Atticus said. "The boy feels bad enough. Why do you think he's here?"

"I'm not sure," Bill said.

"I hoped I could help somehow." Sid met his eyes.

"Ned isn't really safe until he gets back home," Atticus said. "If the wrong people discover he's here, they will certainly arrest him."

"Can I help?" Sid asked. "Can I take him home?"

"I think that's too risky, Sid," Atticus said.

"I'll go home the way I came," Ned said. "In the rowboat, under cover of darkness. There's no need to involve anyone else."

Atticus nodded. "We can hide you here till tonight. But if your boat is discovered, that might be a problem."

"Then they'll know the fugitives came up the River," Jake said.

"They might figure it out, yes."

"I'll go row the boat to your landing," Jake said. "If anyone asks about it, I can say I borrowed the boat from Rev. Holloway."

"For what purpose?" Bill asked.

"Put it at Daniel's landing," Sid said. "Say I went fishing."

Jake's blue eyes turned to Sid. He blinked. "Good idea."

"What will keep you from turning us in?" Bill asked. "How do we know you won't tell the officers where that boat really came from?"

"What will keep me from turning you in?" Sid asked. "My conscience. My love for my aunt and uncle. My respect for Mr. White. How do you know I won't tell them? I'll be working at the Mercantile the rest of the day. I'll be with Daniel until Ned is on his way. I can't talk you into trusting me, Mr. Gildersleeve."

"That is true," he said. "I'll walk with you to the Mercantile after we finish here."

"Fair enough," Sid said.

Ruth set a cup of coffee in front of each of the men.

"Thank you," Sid said. Ruth met his eyes and smiled.

Please put in a good word for me with Rachel, he silently pleaded. He could not imagine what she must think of him now.

After he finished his coffee, Mr. Gildersleeve walked him to the store. Sidney did not know what to say to Daniel, so he didn't try to make any more excuses. Daniel walked out to the front stoop with Bill and they stood in front of the open door talking for a few minutes. Sidney couldn't hear much of what they said, but he figured Bill was explaining all that had transpired. Soon after he left, customers came in, so there was no more opportunity for discussing what had happened the night before.

Around three o'clock, Jake came into the store for a new ax head. Daniel helped him find what he needed and Sid rang up his order.

"How's your day going, Sid?" Jake asked.

"All right," Sid answered. "Considering I'm a prisoner, I'd say I have it pretty good."

Jake shook his head as he gave Sid the money.

Daniel walked over and put his hand on Jake's shoulder. "Would you mind walking Sid home?"

"Uncle Daniel!" Sid said.

"I don't want to keep you here on such a slow day," Daniel said. "There's no need."

"And you can't trust me to walk home?" Sid's clenched his teeth.

"I think I can," Daniel said. "But Bill would have my head. I promised him I wouldn't let you out of my sight."

Sid slammed the cash drawer shut and stalked out the front door.

"Sidney, I don't mistrust you," Daniel called after him.

Jake had to jog to catch him. "I don't think he meant it the way it sounded."

Sid slowed down so they could walk together. "I can't believe this!"

"It's just for a day," Jake said. "It's just to appease Mr. Gildersleeve."

"Why does everyone cater to him?"

"I don't think they do, but he's been around at least as long as anyone else," Jake said. "If it were Atticus or your uncle asking for this, everyone would comply in the same way."

"I feel like a child," Sid said.

"Keep your voice down," Jake said. "You must understand that he means well."

"Just tell me, Jake," Sid spoke softly. "You don't think I'd turn you in, do you?"

"No, of course not," Jake said. "But Bill doesn't know you as well as I do."

As they approached the house, Sid noticed Aunt Sarah and Rachel talking on the porch. When Jake and Sid arrived, Rachel swept down the front steps right past them.

"Good day, Jake," she said briskly and continued down the street.

Sid stared after her in disbelief. He went up the steps to Aunt Sarah.

"That was a deliberate snub."

"Oh, I don't know about that," Sarah said.

"I'm not saying I don't deserve it," Sidney went on.

"We all know you didn't do this on purpose," she said.

"But Rachel? I thought she was my friend!"

"Oh, Sidney." Sarah sighed. "I had to beg Rachel to come for her sewing lesson!"

Sid sat down heavily on the porch swing.

Sarah went on, "Atticus ordered her to come. I think you can depend on him. And Jake, of course. But I can't guarantee anything for the rest of the Railroaders. All we can do is wait and see."

Jake went back to work and Sidney told Sarah his version of what had happened at the Whites' that morning. He hoped that sometime that night Daniel would be able to find out that Ned Faux was safely on his way. But Daniel only came home to fetch Sarah for an emergency meeting, leaving Rhoda and Sid alone. It was the first he had seen her since the occurrence of that morning and she was strangely silent as they ate together at the kitchen table. Finally, he could stand it no longer.

He took a deep breath. "Rhoda, I don't know what you've heard or what you think, but I want you to hear it from me that I didn't intend to get those slaves caught."

Rhoda's voice was quiet. "I didn't think you did, Mr. Sidney."

"It was an accident," Sid said. "I swear it to you on the Bible."

Rhoda nodded, her russet lips solemn. "I'm just sad it all turned out this way."

Sid heaved a sigh. "So am I."

The next day, Daniel and Sidney left for the store together. Ned Faux had gone quietly during the night. As far as anyone knew, he was safely home by now. Daniel was quiet, as though nothing had happened. Sid wasn't going to ask about the emergency meeting, even though he desperately wanted to know what had transpired. He was certain it had something to do with him.

He busied himself taking inventory and swept out the back room while Daniel waited on the first customers of the day. When he finished, he went out to see if Daniel could use some help. Jake stood at the counter, scanning the walls behind it.

He smiled when he saw Sid. "It's a new day, brother."

"Thank God," Sid answered. "Atticus sent you on some errands again?"

"Yes. We were repairing the thresher this morning and it came apart." He held out his hand, a rusty bolt in his palm. "I need a bolt just like this one."

Sid took it from him. "All right. I'll take a look in the back."

As Sid rang up Jake's order, the lever on the cash register jammed. "Damn it!" he muttered. "This thing is so old."

"Maybe it needs a new bolt, too," Jake said.

Daniel came over and worked the lever free. "There you go, son." He patted Sid's shoulder and walked back to his customers.

Sid stared after him. "What is going on?"

After Jake left, he looked at Uncle Daniel, talking and laughing with Reverend and Mrs. Holloway. There was no sign of the animosity he'd shown Sidney yesterday. That evening at tea, as soon as grace was said, Sid mustered his courage.

"So," he began, as he buttered his bread. "Does anyone have anything to tell me?"

Sarah, Daniel and Rhoda all looked at him, eyebrows raised.

"You know," he went on. "Something that has to do with me, that you've perhaps forgotten to share?"

Daniel shook his head. "I'm afraid I haven't the slightest idea what you mean."

"I mean what happened at the meeting last night." Sid bit into his bread.

Rhoda sat up straighter and smiled. "Yes! What did happen at the meetin' last night? I've been meaning to ask you that myself!"

"That meeting was private," Daniel said.

Sid put his butter knife down with a clang. "I know it was about me! You can't keep something private that was all about me!"

Sarah put her hand over Daniel's. "I think we should tell him."

Sidney steadily gazed at Uncle Daniel until he looked up. "What are you afraid I'll find out? That you don't hate me?"

Daniel shook his head. "I don't hate you."

"Then why don't you tell me what happened?" He chewed a bite of stewed apple, looking back and forth from Daniel to Sarah.

"It's my story. I'll tell him." Daniel looked at Rhoda, then Sidney. "This stays in this household. No one else can know. Understand?"

Sid nodded mutely. And Daniel began....

The meeting had started as most do. Daniel and Sarah had sat with the others in William Gildersleeve's parlor. Every healthy railroader in the county had turned up.

Travis Walker had been the first to speak about the situation. "Last night five of our Negro brothers and sisters were sent back to the institution of slavery that wreaks havoc in the lives of so many men, women, and children. And why were they not allowed to live peaceable, honest lives like the rest of us? Because a young man, a rebel straight from the South, wheedled his way into the affections of the good-hearted men and women of this organization. We trusted Southern blood. And this was a grave mistake!"

"Send him home!" someone shouted.

Melinda White rose and cleared her throat. "I think sending him home is a fine idea. However, that is a decision that will have to be made by Mr. and Mrs. Judson." She cast her eyes at them for a moment. "I think it's my duty to do what I can—to protect our youth from the influence of such Southern vermin! I should have done it long ago, but I have now forbidden my daughters to have anything to do with that boy. They are not even to speak to him!"

Sarah gasped. Daniel decided it was time to have his say. In two strides he was in the center of the room, looking into the circle of faces.

"I've known you my whole life. Most of us have grown up in this town. We went to school together. And we've worked towards a common goal: the abolition of slavery. When someone gets in the way of our cause, we are enraged. My nephew has gotten in the way, hasn't he?

"You all know I couldn't find anyone to cover the River. I

knocked at each of your doors. I went to Sidney out of desperation. But I should never have left him with that responsibility. I thought he would do in a pinch, but I was wrong. And you can blame me if you want. Blame me, not him. Being a boy, being exhausted, he fell asleep. Being a Southerner, he took his responsibility too lightly. Being his father's son, he did not quite measure up."

Daniel paused. "Most of you remember my brother David. You know what a rebellious lad he was. He always ran with the wild crowd."

A few members chuckled.

"But what you don't know is that he was not against the abolition of slavery. He was quite in favor of it—until a certain night. On this night David was sent south on the Indian Path to meet a conductor traveling with fugitive slaves. The conductor was new, so he needed someone to guide him into Wilkes-Barre. Unfortunately, David lost his way that night.

"I know all the stories. People said David went off to the saloon with his friends. That he went out to the bootlegger's hut instead of to meet the conductor. And I know why you believed them. I might have, too. But my brother came to my home that next morning—sober, but a mess of tears. He'd taken a wrong turn. He'd been unable to find the runaways.

"He was terrified of my father, and even more so of the Railroad. And with good reason, it seems. When the conductor was caught and sent to jail, you all claimed David intended to get him in trouble. You accused him of going to the authorities before he went to the saloon to get drunk. Most of you stopped talking to him. Rejected by his friends, having shamed his father, David left. He ran away and found a home in Georgia. He became what you said he was."

The room was silent.

"Now, I've gotten over all this long ago. I've been able to let it go. But I will not see my nephew run out of town in the same way my brother was."

Daniel strode to his seat and took it, still trembling with emotion. Sarah squeezed his hand.

Atticus rose and spoke from where he stood. "I think we can all agree with Daniel that the treatment of his brother was unfair and should not be repeated with his nephew. If Sidney leaves Wilkes-Barre, it should be of his own free will. Let's all go on as we have, realizing that what occurred last night was unfortunate. Let us show God's love to our white brethren, as well as black."

Sidney stared at Daniel, his heart pounding. "And that was the end of the meeting?"

"Well, aside from some people shouting rather loudly, 'hear, hear.'" Daniel nodded. "That was it."

"So my father didn't have Southern sympathies? Everyone up here says he did."

"Gossips seldom get the facts straight," Daniel said.

"The only reason he left was because of his public image?"

"Don't get me wrong," Daniel said. "He was no angel."

"I thought you hated him."

Daniel shook his head. "David and I never saw eye to eye. But he was my brother. I always cared about him." He began eating again.

"Then why don't you act like it?" Sid asked.

Daniel finished chewing before he answered. "I guess I never forgave him for leaving—until yesterday."

"Why yesterday?"

Daniel sighed. "When I found you asleep by the river, it was David all over again. I couldn't stop thinking about him leaving. He didn't say good-bye. Not to anyone. And I never let that go."

"Until yesterday."

"I realized it wasn't doing me any good. I remembered the way his friends had treated him. I remembered why he left. You know, we reconciled for a while, when you were young. But it was never the same. There was always something in the way."

"And then you quarreled." Sid took another bite of bread.

"Yes. I was wrong to hold a grudge. Maybe we couldn't be close, but I wish I had forgiven him long ago. Anyway, I didn't want the same thing to happen to you."

Sid looked at Daniel again. He was chewing, loading his fork with stewed fruit.

Sid cleared his throat. "Thank you."

Daniel met his eyes. He nodded. "It was the least I could do."

nine

I N the middle of August, Ruth and Jake were married. Jake had bought a farm of his own, just over the hill from the Whites. He planned to continue working for Atticus until the following spring, when he would plant his own fields. Unless war broke out, of course. Everything was dependent on the state of the Union.

August turned to September. Sidney, Tom and Eliza spent an autumn evening at the Whites's to welcome Jake and Ruth home from their wedding trip. The weather had turned chilly even though August had just slipped behind the bend. The young friends gathered around the fireplace to pop corn and talk.

These days, conversations always seemed to lead to the inevitability of war. And talk of war made Ruth leave the room. She couldn't bear the thought of Jake going off to fight. Jake didn't avoid the subject, though. He was excited about the prospect. Rachel stayed, sitting on the ottoman next to Eliza, but she kept silent, staring into the fire. Sidney, too, was quiet and moody. Tom argued with Jake.

"We could die, you know."

"We could stay here and die from smallpox," Jake said.

"Not nearly as likely." Tom shook his head.

"Come on, Tom," Jake argued. "You know it won't take long to put the Rebs in their place! A few battles should do it!"

He seemed to have forgotten Sid's presence.

"I hate this talk!" Eliza said.

Sid gave her what he meant to be a reassuring smile, but she just scowled and crossed her arms.

"No matter how brief the war is, someone is going to die." Tom was serious. "Besides, we're supposed to be one nation! Something changes about a nation when it turns against itself. 'If a kingdom be divided against itself, that kingdom cannot stand.'"

"Where'd you get that? One of your books?" Jake asked.

"The Bible, actually." Tom smiled.

"Oh, yeah. Thought it sounded familiar. What's it referring to, though?"

"I'm not sure." Tom shook his head. "I'll have to look it up. Rachel, your father would know. Where is he?"

Rachel turned slowly, pulling her eyes from the fire. "I'm sorry. What did you say?"

"Where were you? In another world?" Tom teased her.

Rachel smiled. "A far better one, actually."

"Your pa," Tom said. "Is he at home?"

"Yes," Rachel said. "I think he's in the kitchen with Mother."

Jake and Tom left the room in pursuit of Atticus.

Eliza got up. "I'm going with them."

Sidney looked at her with a smirk. "You care about a literary reference?"

"It's the Bible, Sid," she retorted. "I'm a preacher's daughter, after all!"

Eliza tossed her strawberry blonde curls as she left the room.

Rachel chuckled. "That's not why she's going with them."

"I know," Sid said.

"Wherever Tom is, Eliza wants to be," she said.

"Does that bother you?" Sid asked.

"What? No! I already told you I'm not interested in Tom."

"That was a while ago," Sid said. "You haven't exactly been talking to me for the past... oh, six weeks or so?"

"What do you mean?" Rachel said. "Yes, I have."

"No, not since I got those runaways caught," Sid went on. "I tried to explain to everyone who would listen, that it was an accident. But you seem to be avoiding me so I never got a chance to tell you."

"I know it was an accident." She gently slid from the ottoman onto the floor a few feet from Sidney. "I'm sorry about that day I wouldn't talk to you. I was so angry with you. I actually agreed with my mother when she told me I shouldn't associate with you anymore."

"And now?"

"Now I don't blame you," she said. "I think even Mother sees it. It's just one of those things. No use blaming anyone."

"Then why have you been avoiding me?" he asked.

Rachel shrugged. "I guess I've been a little afraid to trust you."

"Why?"

"I don't know." Rachel straightened her skirt. "There's a possibility you might turn us in," she said quietly.

Sid leaned towards her. "I would never do that."

"Why not? It would be for your 'Cause'."

Sid wished he knew what to say. Rachel looked at him, her brows drawn together, deep furrows between them.

"Things are just frightening right now," she went on. "With war coming, it seems like anything could happen."

"It does," Sid nodded. "But I'm not going to turn you in. So you don't have to worry about that. They can capture me, torture me and I'll still swear I never heard the name Atticus White."

Rachel smiled. "I hope it doesn't come to that."

"So do I," Sid said. "But in case it does, you have my word. And even if I go home and fight for the Confederacy, I'll carry your secret to my grave."

"If—" Rachel repeated. "You just said 'if'. You're not set on fighting for the Rebs?"

"If there's a war, I'll fight for them," Sid said.

"But why?" Rachel asked. "After all your time here, how could you fight against us?"

Sid swallowed hard and looked into the fire. "It's my home. I don't want to fight against you, but I'm a Southerner."

"You're only half Southerner, Sid."

"No—my father was—"

"I know all about your father," Rachel said. "He wasn't a Southerner twenty-five years ago."

"But my whole life, I—"

"Didn't know what the North was really like?" Rachel asked.

"Fine thing for you to say." Sid looked at her. "You haven't spent a day in the South."

Rachel was silent. She gazed into the fire again.

"You're right," she said. "I'm in no place to judge."

"I'm sorry," Sid said.

"Don't be," Rachel said. "I always want everybody to be on my side. I hate differing points of view. But it's part of life."

"Well, I don't like it either."

"It doesn't seem to bother you as much as it bothers me," she continued. "You haven't stopped talking to us yet."

"I wouldn't have anyone to talk to if I didn't talk to you. And—" Sid cleared his throat. "My judgment might be skewed by appearances."

"Are you hinting that I'm pretty?" Rachel looked at him.

Sid shook his head with a smirk. "I was talking about Tom, obviously."

Rachel laughed. "Don't start flirting with me, Sid. I know you're already spoken for."

Sid looked down. Her small, white hand lay on the carpet beside her. His strong, tan one covered hers. He did not remember putting it there. But he made no attempt to remove it.

The leaves turned color and the weather stayed cold. Sid grew aware of an underlying sense of unease. He was too accustomed to life in the North. He cared deeply for the family and friends he'd made here—too deeply, perhaps. One evening in October, he brought home a letter from Catherine. It alarmed him and brought Roswell back to the front of his thoughts.

"I feel I don't even know you," she wrote. "You're a stranger to me. It seems as though I had a dream once in which you and I were the most envied of couples. We would dance and ride and take walks together. It's hard for me to believe that these things were true. How often do you write? Once a month, perhaps? Jimmy Richardson asked me last week when my Yankee beau was coming home for me. It was difficult to hide my emotion because I've been wondering the same thing. Should I give up hope?"

After he read the letter, Sid dropped his face into his palms. How could he treat Catherine this way? She was back home waiting for him and he was here, practically forgetting her—and flirting with other girls. A knock on the door startled him out of his shame. Tom was standing on the front porch. Sid let him in and they went into the parlor together.

"I wanted to tell you I fished on Mill Creek the other day," Tom said.

"Without me?" Sid looked at him, wide-eyed in mock injury.

"You were working and I had a couple hours," Tom said.

"I figured you'd rather read a book."

"Anyway," Tom rolled his eyes. "The trout were really biting. We should go there on Wednesday."

"Okay—I guess," Sid said.

"You seem bothered. What's eating you?" Tom asked.

Sid ran his fingers through his hair. "It's Catherine."

"Your girl?" Tom said, taking a seat on the sofa. "You haven't been talking about her much."

"Haven't I?" Sid looked at Tom sharply.

"Not really," Tom shrugged. "I wondered if things were still going between you two. You did say it was easier to be away from her. I'm glad you're sticking around. It's just... I wondered, that's all."

"Why didn't you ask?" Sid settled into the chair across from Tom.

"I don't usually ask about those things," Tom said.

"You ask about everything else."

Tom reddened. "I guess that's true. I don't have much experience with girls. I wouldn't have any advice—"

"Well, I need your advice now. I've neglected Catherine horribly." He produced the letter. "Here."

Tom took a few minutes to read the letter written in Catherine's elegant slanted hand.

"Wow!" Tom grinned at him. "You were 'the most envied of couples'?"

"I guess." Sid shifted uncomfortably. "I don't know what to do."

"Tell me about her."

"Okay," Sid paused. "Catherine is... beautiful. Wait, I'll show you her photograph."

He rushed upstairs for the sepia photograph in its pewter frame. When he returned with it, Tom raised his eyebrows and snatched it from him. "Wow! What are you doing up here?"

Sid smiled. "She's even better in person. I was so lucky."

"Hmmm..." Tom nodded, with a smirk.

"She always had the most interesting things to talk about," Sid went on. "At least, they seemed interesting. Even if I didn't want to listen, just watching her talk was enough. The way the light would catch the gold in her hair. Everything about her is good to look at. The other boys were so jealous of me. It seemed like we were on top of the world..."

"And then that world came apart," Tom put in.

Sid nodded. "I realized it wasn't just the two of us after all. There are more important things in the world than Catherine and me and our balls and barbeques. I took everything else for granted."

"Yeah," Tom said.

"Reading this letter makes me feel like I should leave for home right now."

"You can't," Tom said.

"Why not?" Sid asked.

"You'll miss the bonfire and hay ride this weekend."

"Be serious," Sid said. "I'm about to lose my true love."

"Maybe," Tom said. "If she's your true love she'll wait for you."

"I can't lose her." Sid sighed. "I'm so ashamed. If I had written more often—even if I'd thought about her more often, maybe I wouldn't be facing this."

"I'm not very good at this, Sid," Tom said. "If you have to go home, you have to go. But maybe you could talk it over with Mrs. Judson before you decide."

"Okay," Sid agreed. "I'll talk to Aunt Sarah."

"Good," Tom said. "I don't want you to leave yet!"

🌱

Sidney found Aunt Sarah in her sewing room and told her about the letter.

"We've loved having you here, Sidney," Sarah said. "And you're welcome as long as you want to stay. But I can't make the decision for you."

"I know that," he said. "I just wish I didn't have to choose between two good things."

"Well… maybe you don't." Sarah drew her needle through a square of fabric in tiny, even stitches. "Your friends are welcome to visit here. If you're thinking of marrying this girl, it would be nice to meet her."

"Oh," Sid wrinkled his forehead. "I hadn't thought of that."

"I know you want to go back eventually," Sarah said. "But if you'd like, I could invite Catherine to come for a visit."

"I don't know how that would work." Sid leaned back in his chair. "I can't picture her in the North."

"Sometimes it's good to become acquainted with a young lady in different settings," Sarah said. "You might learn things about her you didn't know before."

Sidney decided his aunt was right. Even if it was a little awkward, having Catherine visit might be good for the two of them. He penned a letter explaining that an invitation from Aunt Sarah would follow. And with sudden certainty, he assured Catherine that, whatever transpired, he would come home in the springtime even if war had not begun. He hoped he would see her sooner than that—in the North.

Saturday evening, Sidney went to the hayride and bonfire at Jake's new farm. As he reached the fire pit with Tom and Caleb, Sid told them he'd made a decision to wait until spring to go South, unless war broke out sooner.

"You'll be around for Christmas!" Tom said. "You haven't had a real Christmas till you've spent one in Wilkes-Barre."

"Why's that?" Sid asked.

"You know, the snow and all," Tom said. "I bet you never even had snow for Christmas in Georgia."

"Actually, I have a couple times," Sid said.

"Well, you're practically guaranteed snow at Christmas in Wilkes-Barre."

Rachel and Eliza joined their circle.

"What's this about Christmas already?" Eliza asked.

"I'm just happy that Sid will still be here then. He was thinking about going back down South, you know."

"No, I didn't know." Rachel said. She sat down on one of the logs surrounding the fire pit. The light from the bonfire brought out traces of auburn in her hair.

"I guess that sweetheart of his pulled on his heartstrings a little bit, but she couldn't lure him away from us," Tom joked.

"Tom, don't—" Sid began.

"You should see this girl." Tom hooked his thumbs under his suspenders. "If I was the one courting her, I wouldn't stay up here with you folks more than a week."

Sid reddened. "Okay. That's enough."

"Did you lose her photograph or something?" Tom chuckled.

"I said that's enough!" Sid's voice was sharp. He stalked into the night, away from the fire. He walked to the gate at the edge of Jake's pasture. His heart was pounding and his face burning. Why was he so upset by Tom's words? Was it his guilt over not being there for Catherine? Or was it the look in Rachel's eyes. He felt a hand on his shoulder.

"I'm sorry, brother." Tom's voice was kind. "Don't be sore at me."

"I'm not." Sidney sighed. "I feel guilty, that's all."

Tom nodded.

Sid went on, "Aunt Sarah is inviting her to come up for a visit."

"Really?" Tom's raised his eyebrows with a smile. "We're going to meet her?"

"If she comes," Sid said.

"Sure she'll come," Tom said. "I bet she can't wait to see you."

"I don't know, Tom. Things change."

"If she's the girl for you, then things will be the same. Wait till you see her again! Then you'll know."

Sid looked at Tom's trusting eyes. "I hope you're right."

They went back to the fire. Eliza Jane and Caleb had joined other conversations. Rachel sat alone where they had left her, staring into the fire. She looked up and smiled. Sid hadn't expected a smile. How silly of him to think the talk about Catherine would upset her! He determined to stop his vain thoughts.

"Are you all right, Sid?" Rachel asked, smirking. "Tom was only teasing you."

"I know," Sid said, digging his hands deep into his pockets to steady himself.

Another boy called to Tom from the other side of the fire, some question about St. Augustine. Tom went over to share his knowledge. Sid sat on the log next to Rachel.

"I'm glad you decided to stay a little longer," Rachel admitted. "But I suppose you will be leaving us one of these days."

"Will you miss me?" Sid blurted out before he could stop himself.

Rachel's eyes opened wide. "Of course I will. I've become quite used to having you around." She smoothed her hair back from her face.

"I'll miss you, too," Sid whispered. He couldn't take his eyes away from hers.

Rachel looked back at him and her green eyes grew soft. "But you have friends back home, too—and your sweetheart."

"Yes," Sid said.

At that moment, he wished he'd never promised anything to Catherine. The air was heavy next to the bonfire.

Eliza danced over to them. "Come on another hayride, you two! Jake has the wagon all ready."

Sid shook his head. "You go ahead, Rachel."

Eliza led Rachel to the young people boarding the hay wagon.

Sid sighed with relief. He resolved to keep his mouth shut from now on. He was glad that Rachel had gone before he had a chance to say anything more foolish. He joined the group of young men on the other side of the fire. Tom and Caleb were among them and the conversation was rowdy. It was late when he went home. Most of the girls had gone already, so he walked with Tom and Caleb until they passed Union Street where the other boys turned to head home. Then he continued down River Street by himself.

When he reached his uncle's house, the windows were dark. He wondered if Uncle Daniel and Aunt Sarah were out on some Railroad business. Sid jaunted up the steps and then he stopped short. The front door stood ajar. Caught between the door and its jamb, was a pair of ladies boots.

ten

S IDNEY rushed to the door and pushed it open.

"Aunt Sarah!" he cried.

She lay curled on her side. It looked as though she had fallen across the threshold, her hat and shawl strewn next to her on the floor.

Sidney knelt by her, shaking her shoulders gently. "Aunt Sarah, what happened?" His fingers came away from her dress wet with perspiration. "You're burning up."

Sarah shivered. "Cold... So cold."

Sidney ran to the hall table for a lamp. He struck a match with shaky fingers and turned back to Aunt Sarah as the lamp began glowing. He had to calm the pounding fear in his heart and do something. He put his hands beneath her arms and pulled her into the house until her feet were inside the door. It closed with a dull thud. Aunt Sarah moaned again.

She shuddered. And then she vomited.

Sid nearly dropped her in shock, but he managed to keep hold of her shoulders as she spewed the vile substance onto her dress and all over the floor. He stood there gaping at the mess for a moment. Slowly he realized he was the only one who was going to do anything about it. He supported her shoulders with one arm. Reaching for a corner of Aunt Sarah's mantle, he wiped her mouth with it.

"All right," he grunted. "You're going to be all right. I need to get you to bed."

But how? He could carry her up the stairs easily enough, but he would soil the sheets if he put her in bed this way. He chewed his tongue to distract his senses from the stench of vomit filling the foyer.

Where's Rhoda when she's needed? Sid wondered.

"I'll wrap you in a blanket for now," he said

He ran upstairs and returned with two blankets and a pillow. He lifted Sarah and set her on the blankets, wrapping them tightly around her. Her body was hotter than a coal stove, but she shook with tremors as though she were chilled.

"First thing I'll do is go for the doctor." Sid wedged the pillow beneath her head. "You're going to be all right. Don't you worry."

"Daniel," Sarah's voice was weak. "I'm sorry, Darling. David will come home again."

Sid swallowed hard. She didn't know what she was saying. He didn't have time to be afraid right now. There was too much to do.

"Shhhh…" he said. "I wish I didn't have to leave you alone. I'll be back as soon as I can."

As he went out the door, Rhoda came up the front steps onto the porch.

"Where have you been?" Sid said crossly. "Aunt Sarah is burning up with fever!"

"Oh Good Lord!" Rhoda rushed to the door.

"I'm going for the doctor." Sid started down the street.

When Sidney returned with Dr. Jenkins, Rhoda had cleaned up the mess and dressed Sarah in her nightclothes. She was kneeling by her mistress, holding her hand. The doctor felt Sarah's forehead.

"Get her upstairs." His mouth closed tightly in a grim line.

Sidney lifted her in his arms and carried her up to the bedroom. Rhoda pulled back the bedclothes so he could lay Sarah down. He stepped out of the room while the doctor examined her. He gripped the banister and realized he was trembling again. Then the front door opened, and Uncle Daniel stepped inside.

He came to the foot of the stairs and peered up at Sid. "Is that Doc Jenkins' buggy outside?"

Sid went downstairs and put his hand on Uncle Daniel's arm.

"What happened?" Daniel started up the stairs, but Sid held him back. "Is she hurt?"

"She's sick," Sidney said. "I think—" Sid stopped. He did not want to say what he feared. He knew smallpox began with fever and chills, but it had been over two weeks since the last case. Maybe it was something else.

Uncle Daniel pulled away from Sid's grip and ran up the stairs. Sidney stood staring into the glow of the single lamp on the table. *Please, please, please don't let it be... please.* Sid wished he could cry, but all he felt was a sick kind of dread. He went through the parlor to the library. It had been some time since he'd looked at the little blank book, but he found it right where it always was. He flipped it open.

15 October, 1838

Melinda is gone now and the rumors are flying. I can't even bear to write them down. I know they aren't true. Everyone who asks me gets the same answer.

Melinda went away because she was heartbroken. There's no other reason. People in this town are such gossips. It gives me half a mind to go away myself. After what they did to David—and now Melinda. Daniel throws himself into his work. I'm afraid he believes the rumors. Last night I told him it wasn't possible. God wouldn't withhold something from us and give it to someone who didn't even want it. Melinda has always been a respectable girl.

Sidney turned a big chunk of pages.

16 June, 1839

I have so much joy inside me right now, I don't know what to do with it!

Doctor Jenkins confirmed it today—we are finally going to have a baby! I haven't seen Daniel so happy since before his brother left town. It is so good to see him smile again.

Footsteps descended the stairs. Sidney hurriedly shut the book and squeezed it back into its spot, his heart pounding. He tore out to the foyer. Daniel was just closing the door behind the doctor. He turned to Sid.

"The doctor thinks it's smallpox."

"But it's been so long since the last case."

"Not long enough." The glow from the lamp revealed the tautness of his face.

He moved wordlessly into the parlor and dropped into a chair. Sidney followed him, not daring to break the silence. His uncle's fear must be keener than any he had known. He leaned on the back of another chair and watched Uncle Daniel's face. The worry lines ran deep. His eyebrows drawn together, his lips turned down. Sidney suddenly realized that the feelings he'd had for Catherine couldn't compare to what years of love and devotion had nurtured in the hearts of his aunt and uncle. His eyes rested on the large family Bible on the table in front of Daniel. He moved to it, took it up in his hands and opened to the spot held by a silk ribbon.

"Remembering mine affliction and my misery, the wormwood and the gall. My soul hath them still in remembrance, and is humbled in me. This I recall to mind, therefore have I hope. It is of the Lord's mercies that we are not consumed, because his compassions fail not. They are new every morning: great is thy faithfulness. The Lord is my portion," he paused.

His uncle was crying. Sidney looked away.

"That's Sarah's favorite scripture," Daniel whispered.

"I'm sorry," Sid swallowed.

"No need. It's right that you read it." Daniel tried to gain control of his voice. "She read those verses all the time when we couldn't have children."

Sidney was quiet, surprised at Daniel's openness.

"She clung to them, believing they were true even when I didn't. I wanted children, too. But I couldn't make her understand that I was happy with her either way. Now that the time for children is past, she looks at those verses and tells me they are still true. She says the misery is just a memory and His mercies are new every morning." Daniel shook his head. "There was a time when I was so angry with God for holding back joy from us. But now I know she is right. It's nothing you can explain. The emptiness is gone. The Lord is our portion."

Daniel looked at Sidney for a moment.

"You and I both have pain over my brother's death. You'll find in time, the wound will heal."

"I know you're right," Sid whispered.

The next morning, Sarah's condition was the same. Doctor Jenkins was back to examine her. Sidney showed him to his buggy when he left.

"I don't want to frighten your uncle any more than necessary," he said. "Your aunt has a tough fight ahead of her. It's one of the worst cases I've seen, and the rash hasn't even started yet. We can only pray and hope for the best."

Uncle Daniel talked Sidney into going to church, while he nursed Sarah. Word about Sarah's illness had traveled quickly. After the service, a small crowd gathered around Sid, inquiring about her. Finally, Sidney managed to make his way out the door and he started for home. When he got to Market Street, he met Rhoda, walking home from her service at the African Methodist Episcopal church. He fell into step with her.

"I can't wait to get home to the missus," Rhoda said as they headed towards River Street.

"Neither can I," Sid replied. "I thought people would never stop asking me questions!"

Sid heard footsteps behind them. Rachel was running down the street.

Sid stopped to wait for her.

Rhoda said, "I thought you wanted to get home, sir."

"It's Rachel," Sid said.

"Ah!" Rhoda raised her eyebrows and muttered. "You're a man all right."

"I'll be along soon," Sid said.

Rhoda continued on her way, shaking her head.

"Sidney," Rachel said as she caught up to him. "I want to know how she really is. I know you were mobbed back there, but please, I have to know."

Sidney was silent for a moment, his hands in his pockets. He sighed.

Rachel went on. "You must know something. The doctor must have said—Oh, Sid! Why won't you tell me? Is it bad?" Her eyes grew large.

Sid's voice was quiet. "The doctor told me it's one of the worst he's seen. He said we have to hope for the best."

"Oh, no!" Rachel sat down on the curb, staring into the dusty street.

Sid dropped down next to her.

"How could this happen?" she cried. "It's been weeks since the epidemic." She turned to him. "You must be so worried." She took his hand. "Can I come see her? If Mr. Judson says it's all right?"

Sid nodded, hoping his uncle wouldn't mind. It was easier to face whatever news waited at home with Rachel by his side.

Daniel sat alone in the parlor. He looked up and half-smiled at them as they stood in the doorway together. There was no change.

Sidney swallowed. "Can I go up and see her?"

Uncle Daniel shook his head. "I think you should leave the

nursing to Rhoda and me. There's no reason for you to be exposed."

Sid's mouth dropped open. "But I'm the one who found her! I've already been exposed!"

Daniel paused. "I'll have to talk to the doctor about it."

"I want to help," Sid said. "I can't just sit around and do nothing."

"I'll need you to take more responsibility at the store. That will be a big help."

"No! I want to help Aunt Sarah get better."

Daniel stood up. "I will talk to the doctor about it. But until then, the answer is no."

Sid took a deep breath, ready to fight back. Then he felt Rachel's hand in his, tugging. He looked at her. She pulled his arm, opening the front door with her other hand. He followed her out onto the front porch.

"What is it?" he asked.

"Don't you think Mr. Judson has enough to worry about without you getting huffy with him?"

"Now you're against me too?" Sidney took a deep breath. "Rachel, I'm the one who found her. I went for the doctor."

"Right," Rachel said. "You've already done more than your uncle. Now he needs to take care of her. Don't make it harder for him."

"You wanted to see her, too."

"Yes, but I understand why he wouldn't want me to. Leave the nursing to him and Rhoda, if that's what he wants."

Sid hated admitting she was right. Angry tears stung his eyes. He turned away from her and looked out across the street towards the river.

"Sid, I'm not saying—"

"I know what you're saying," Sid snapped. "I just don't like it."

"I'm sorry." Rachel took his hand and squeezed it again.

He held onto it. He was suddenly terrified, and he couldn't bear to let go.

"Sid..." she began, trying to pull her hand away.

He dared not look at her. "I just want to do something."

"Come inside and help me get dinner for your family."

He shook his head. "Rachel, you don't have to—"

"I want to do something, too," she pulled her hand away gently and touched his arm. "Come on."

❧

Rachel came to help often, as did Mrs. White and Mrs. Mahoney. Someone was at the house every day, cleaning and cooking. Mrs. Holloway had recovered from smallpox herself, so she frequented the sick room to relieve Rhoda and Daniel. Daniel rarely came to the store, so Sidney practically ran it himself. The customers buzzed with debates over the upcoming election, though everyone inquired about Sarah's health. Tom came in on Wednesday afternoon.

"I went to your house to look for you, but my mother said you haven't been around much."

"The store's too busy." Sid shook his head. "I wish I could be home more. How does my aunt fare today?"

"Mrs. Holloway said the rash has started," Tom said.

Sid nodded. "The doctor told me last night that it would start soon. They won't let me see her."

"Rachel told me," Tom said. "How are you holding up?"

Sid shrugged. "I don't have much time to worry."

"But you worry anyway, right?" Tom said.

Jake came in then. "How's Mrs. Judson?"

Tom answered Jake while Sid directed a customer asking for dress patterns. He turned back to Jake. "What can I do for you today?"

"I'm making some repairs around the house. I know where the nails are, but I need glue as well."

"I'll get you a jar of Spaldings," Sid said.

When he brought it back to the counter, Jake had collected a sack of nails. He was still talking to Tom.

"I know John Bell is the safe choice," he said. "But the more I consider it, I have to vote for Lincoln."

"That's absurd!" Tom said. "If Lincoln's elected, there will be war."

"Most likely." Jake nodded. "But I still think he's the better man."

Sid interrupted. "That'll be seventy-five cents."

Jake dug in his pocket for the change. "What about you, Sid? Voting for Breckinridge?"

"Tom and I are too young to vote. Remember?"

"That's exact change." Jake handed Sid some coins. "I've debated voting for Stephen Douglas, but since he's no less controversial, I'll vote for Lincoln."

"Vote for Bell," Tom said. "A Constitutional Unionist will satisfy everybody."

"Sorry, Tom!" Jake laughed. "Even if I didn't think Lincoln was the best choice, I'd have to vote for him. I'm married to a White!"

"Do what you have to." Tom sighed. "Sid, you'd vote for Breckinridge?"

"I don't want to talk about it," Sid said. "I have no influence in the matter."

At the moment, Sidney did not care who won the election. The fever in the nation seemed as high as Aunt Sarah's, but all he wanted was for her to pull through. Tom stayed the rest of the afternoon and helped Sid close up.

"I'll walk home with you," he said.

Since Mrs. Mahoney was still at the Judson's, Tom stayed for tea. Sid couldn't help thinking that only one week ago, a meal with Rachel and Tom would have been a lighthearted, talkative one. But tonight silence overtook the table.

When Tom and Mrs. Mahoney started into the night together, the doctor arrived to examine Sarah. Sid went into the kitchen where Rachel was washing the dishes.

He slumped into a chair with a sigh. "You don't have to do so much, Rachel."

"Nonsense," Rachel said. "It's nothing. You know I want to help."

"Well, thank you," he said. "You make the best apple pie I ever tasted."

Rachel grinned. "What about your mother?"

Sid shook his head. "My mama didn't do much baking. We had darkies for that."

"I forgot," Rachel said. "You're probably working more now than you ever have in your life."

"Is your father voting for Lincoln?" Sid asked.

Rachel turned to him, drying her hands on her apron. "Yes."

"I'm so sick of hearing people talk about it at the Mercantile," Sid said. "They're so worked up. I don't even care who wins."

"I don't have much heart for debate right now, either." Rachel leaned against the sink, crossing her arms.

"I know you're probably closer to my aunt than I am," Sid said.

"Oh, I don't know," Rachel said. "My parents have always been friends with Mr. and Mrs. Judson. I've come to visit since I was a little girl."

"So you probably know her better than I do."

"She's not my aunt, Sid," Rachel said. "And I still have my mother."

"Not a very good one, though."

Rachel turned back to the basin and plunged her hands into the water.

"I'm sorry." Sid got up and put his hands on her shoulders for a moment. "I shouldn't have said that."

Rachel sighed. "No, you shouldn't have. But perhaps I have some idea how you feel about Mrs. Judson's illness. She has always been here for me. And she's so much more motherly than my own mother."

"She's the only mother I have now." Sid swallowed hard, leaning against the counter next to the sink. "I can't—I can't lose her, too."

Rachel was silent. Sid looked at her face and saw that she was biting her lip. She drew a shaky breath. "You won't lose her. I've been praying too hard."

Footsteps descended the stairs and Sid went out to meet the doctor. They stepped out onto the porch together.

"I have to know how she is, Dr. Jenkins. Be honest with me."

"Well, son, it's hard to say." The doctor shook his head. "She's still so weak with fever. And the rash is spreading now. The lesions start in the mouth and spread to the face, forearms and hands, then the rest of the body. It's already to her hands, and it's pretty bad. She'll have some serious scarring. These next few days are crucial. By Sunday or Monday we should know."

Sidney slept little that night. He kept waking to hear Sarah calling out. Once he got up and went to her door, listening with his heart pounding.

"Daniel!" she cried. "I'm sorry!..." Her breathing was heavy, labored. "You'll have to tell him, Doctor. I can't!... He won't understand." Then came a loud wail, "My baby's dead!"

Sid had to go in. No sooner had he reached out for the door handle, than Rhoda's hand came from nowhere and slapped it away. He hadn't even heard her come up the steps. Now she stood in her chemise with her hands on her hips. Her voice came in a loud whisper.

"Mr. Sidney, there's nothing you can do by going in that room. Mr. Daniel's in there and he's the only one can help."

"What's going on?" Sid backed away from the door.

"She's delirious. Reliving the past." Rhoda shook her head, sniffing. "Might have known this is what would come out."

"The baby died?"

"Lived less than a week."

"I didn't know."

"Course not. It was before you were born," Rhoda said.

Sid heard Daniel's voice, low and soothing. "No one blames you, darling. It's not your fault."

Rhoda's voice softened. "Go get some sleep, Mr. Sidney. There's nothing you can do for her."

Sidney crept back to bed and tried to go to sleep.

Every day at the store seemed unending. Sid longed to get home to see how Sarah was. Yet when the time came, he dreaded it. And his heart pounded with fear all the way there. Her condition stayed the same, though. Since he had no school Saturday, Tom helped Sid at the store all day and then walked home with him. It was a little easier, having him along. On Sunday, Sid couldn't drag himself to church. After dinner he tried to take a nap so he could face another week at the store.

It seemed he had barely dozed off when he woke to a knock on his bedroom door. He turned over and looked out the window. It was dusk. The knock came again.

"Come in!" Sid sat up.

Uncle Daniel burst into the room. "She's going to make it!"

"What?" Sidney sprang from the bed.

"The doctor was here. He said she's going to pull through!"

Sidney threw his arms around his uncle. And suddenly Daniel was sobbing. The weight in Sid's heart had disappeared. The night's coming didn't seem so dark. Daniel pulled away and wiped the tears from his face with his handkerchief.

"I'm sorry." He chuckled at himself. "It's no use trying to be stoic."

Sidney went to his window and threw it open. He bellowed across the street to the river common, "She's going to be all right!"

Daniel and Sidney laughed together.

eleven

SARAH was still very ill. She had come through the most dangerous days, but she stayed weak and delirious with fever while bumpy pustules took over her extremities. Life in the Judson household continued in its altered state, with Sidney taking on most of the responsibility at the store, and ladies helping out in any way they could. It was easier now, though. Hearts were lighter.

As October turned to November, Sarah's fever subsided. On Election Day, she was sitting up, eating broth by herself. She was thin and very weak, but good health was in sight at last.

Daniel came into the store and resumed his usual duties that day. By the next morning, everyone had the news. Abraham Lincoln had been elected. The store was filled with customers voicing their opinions.

At the counter in front of Sidney, Joshua Smith growled at him. "I bet you're about as happy with the results as I am!"

"Maybe less," Sid said. Secretly, though, he was almost glad he was too young to vote. He wasn't sure he would have made the right choice.

"This country's going to the dogs," Joshua said.

Jake appeared next to Joshua. "Lincoln's going to do wonders!"

"Shut your trap," Joshua said. "A few months ago, you were voting for Douglas, like me. You and your father-in-law are probably the only reason Pennsylvania came in Republican."

"Well, I'd be proud of that," Jake beamed. "But the margin was greater than two."

Daniel was smiling, too. As were his abolitionist friends. But Sid thought there had to be uneasiness behind the smiles. Everyone knew South Carolina had vowed to secede from the Union.

By Thanksgiving, Sarah was herself again. Although thin, she was up and about, busying herself with her old housekeeping duties. She continuously apologized for all the trouble she had caused by being ill. Daniel insisted she not host Thanksgiving dinner and she grudgingly gave in. They joined the Whites, who had invited relatives as well as the Mahoneys.

As they gathered at the Whites' dinner table, their joy was evident. Sarah's beautiful face was now scarred with pockmarks, but that made no difference in Daniel's love for her. Sidney knew that whomever he ended up marrying, he wanted to be sure that he loved her as much as his aunt and uncle loved each other. Rachel met his eyes across the table and smiled at him. Sidney felt a twinge of longing as he suddenly thought of last year's holidays in Roswell, but this was a day of giving thanks to God. And they had much to be thankful for.

After dinner, the young people played cribbage in the sitting room by the fire, while their elders continued visiting in the dining room. Laughter drifted through the house, despite the shadow of war clouding the future.

When the games had ended, Rachel went to see her cousins off. Tom turned to Sid.

"Caleb won't help me out, but maybe you will. I want to give Rachel a Christmas present. I know she wants a copy of Dickens's Oliver Twist, and there's an autographed copy at home in our library. My mother's cousin brought it over with her from England. But I'm afraid Rachel might think it's inappropriate."

Sid raised his eyebrows, suddenly a little queasy. "You're giving Rachel a Christmas present? What happened to Eliza?"

Tom blushed. "It's not like that!" he said. "Not with either of them!"

Caleb laughed, sprawling out next to the fire. "I'm with you, Sid! Tom's stringing both of them along!"

Sid laughed too loudly. "It's not like that? I think you've paid quite a bit of attention to Eliza."

"Well, I don't know," Tom admitted. "I think very highly of Rachel and Eliza both. But I certainly don't have any serious intentions towards either of them... yet. It's just that Rachel and I both have a respect for literature. I know she would like it and I care about her getting it."

"You care about her?" Sid grinned.

"Stop it, Sid!" Tom frowned; his color had only deepened. "It's not that way between us. I don't want to send any messages I'm not ready to follow up on."

Sid swallowed, trying to calm the storm in his gut. His face was hot.

"Then don't give her a Christmas present," he said.

"But I want her to have that book."

"There will be plenty of time when you're ready to follow up on it."

Tom sighed.

"Rachel and I share a respect for literature." Caleb mimicked, winking at Sid. "One girl's not enough for you, is it Tom?"

"Shut up," Tom said.

Sid picked up a newspaper and rolled it up in his hands, needing to busy his sweaty fingers.

"Why so serious?" Caleb asked him. "You're not jealous of Tom's charm, are you?"

Sid made himself laugh. "At least my girl knows I'm her beau!"

Rachel came in as Sid playfully pounded Caleb with the rolled up newspaper.

"Hey, be careful," Tom said. "I know someone who writes for that rag."

"What's all the ruckus about?" she asked.

"We're talking about girls!" Caleb said.

"Really? Who were you talking about, Caleb?" Rachel asked. "It wouldn't happen to be one of my sisters, would it?"

Now it was Caleb's turn to blush. He suddenly became interested in Sidney's newspaper. Sid and Tom let Rachel's comment drop. Sidney felt warm. Somehow his face didn't want to return to its usual temperature. The four friends sat silently, Caleb reading the newspaper, the others just pondering.

"You boys are awfully quiet now that I'm here," Rachel said.

"Don't be silly," Sid replied.

Mrs. Mahoney appeared in the doorway, telling Tom and Caleb she was ready to go home. They went without protest. Sid was left alone with Rachel.

"Did I come in at a bad time?" Rachel asked him.

"I don't know. They were talking about girls, so I guess they didn't want to continue in front of you."

"They were? You weren't?" she smiled.

"Well, Tom wanted advice," Sid explained.

"And you're the one to come to for advice," Rachel went on.

"I don't want to talk about it," Sid said.

His heart was pounding. He wished he could just ignore the shine of Rachel's hair, the way his heart jumped when their eyes met across a room. He should have told Tom to give her the book. Sid would be leaving. Why make it harder than it would be?

"I was just teasing you," Rachel said. "You know, because you and your Catherine are pretty well set to get married, right?"

"Yes, we are," Sid lied. "We probably will when I go South in the spring."

"I didn't mean to pry. I guess I should know better since you got so sore at Tom that night at the bonfire." Her voice was so kind he could barely stand to hear it.

They must speak of something else.

"The bonfire," he repeated, thinking how long ago that seemed.

"That's the night you went home to find Mrs. Judson sick."

Sidney was relieved at the change of subject. "I'd never seen Uncle Daniel so worried. I didn't know till then how much he loves her."

"It seems like he's softened a lot," Rachel said. "I always knew he had a good heart, but he's not so stern since your aunt's illness."

"Yes." Sid nodded. "Although it's probably also that I understand him better. But he's so happy now that she's well again."

"I know." Rachel smiled. "So am I. Doesn't it seem strange with all the unrest in the country? We're all so joyful today, in spite of our differences. We're not even thinking of what lies ahead. Even Mother seems happy—and she rarely does anymore."

"She used to?" Sid asked without thinking.

Rachel paused. "My mother is a complicated woman. I've heard things about her younger years. It took a long time for her to get close to my father. For years after they were married, she still wasn't really his. Then, while I was growing up, she was mostly happy. Until recently."

Daniel was ready to go. Sidney reluctantly got up. He must not interfere in Rachel's life. As he went home that evening, he resolved to do what his mind told him was right and ignore his heart.

❧

On the 4th of December, President James Buchanan gave his State of the Union address to congress. His message upset everyone in Wilkes-Barre, abolitionists and Southern sympathizers alike. Customers came into the store irate. Their comments fumed around Sidney as he worked.

"What a weakling! He has no plan."

"At least he knows what he believes. He condemns secession!"

"But he won't do anything about it!"

Daniel let Sidney go home early. Business was slow. The townsfolk had only turned out to talk.

When he stepped inside the front door, he heard female voices in the kitchen. Sid planned to slip upstairs unnoticed, but he couldn't help hearing Rachel's voice as it rose with emotion. She still came to help quite often, even though Sarah was better.

"He didn't say anything against slavery!" Rachel was exclaiming. "Not one word! And not only that, he said the Free States should mind their own business and not try to control what the slave states were doing. Maybe not in those words but... oh, and he said fugitives should be returned to their owners!"

"Oh, Miss Rachel," Rhoda said. "Don't you go scaring me like that."

"Rhoda, you bought your freedom," Rachel said.

"That don't mean anything to some folks," Rhoda growled.

This confirmed Sidney's suspicion that Rhoda had been a slave herself. He headed through the dining room, towards the kitchen.

"Don't worry," Rachel went on. "When Mr. Lincoln gets into office, he'll set this country straight!"

"I wouldn't be so sure about that," Sid said, joining them.

"Mr. Sidney!" Rhoda exclaimed. "We didn't know you was here!"

"I just came in," he said.

Rachel turned to him. "I know you don't agree with us, but that's how I feel. Maybe the country won't be the way you want it, but Mr. Lincoln will certainly help with our cause. Another thing! Can you believe Buchanan proposed an amendment recognizing slaves as property!? Sickening!"

"The Slave States hold that view already," Sid put in.

"Sid, I really don't want to argue with you about it," Rachel said.

"I don't want to argue, either," he said. "But your views should hold up against opposition—if they're correct."

"I know, but... I just..." she paused.

Sarah saved her. "I'm no happier about the President's address than you are. We're certainly thrilled with Mr. Lincoln's abolitionist leanings. But Sidney's right about one thing. Don't be certain that Lincoln will set the country straight. We don't know that at all."

"He hasn't said anything about what he's going to do!" Sid exclaimed.

"He doesn't have to! Everybody knows where he stands!" Rachel said.

"But he ought to give some answers about what his plans are. Honestly, we can't know what to expect if he won't give us an agenda!"

"We can't know what to expect, no matter what," Sarah said softly as she took the bread from the oven. "That's the reality of life all the time. The current situation just makes us aware of it."

"Well, I have to get home," Rachel said. "Mother will be waiting for me. I'll see you tomorrow, ladies."

Rachel refused Sid's offer to walk her home, but he went out on the porch with her anyway as she buttoned up her coat and wrapped her scarf around her neck.

"You're not going to stop talking to me just because our opinions differ so slightly, are you?" he asked her.

"I haven't yet. Why would I now?"

"You won't let me walk you home." Sid wrinkled his forehead.

"I know you're tired from working all day." She laughed at him and shook her head. "Why do you think I didn't want to argue with you, Sidney?"

"I don't know."

"I want to go on being friends," Rachel said. "I don't want to get mad at you about differences in opinion."

"Well," Sid said. "Why don't you try changing my opinion?"

"Impossible!" She laughed again. "You know I've tried. If living here with us, watching your aunt and uncle, and knowing Rhoda hasn't done it, I don't know what will!"

"So you've given up on me? Like the president, I must not have a conscience?"

She shrugged. "I have to go home." She turned and walked to

the street. Then she looked back and saw him still gazing after her. She waved before she disappeared around the bend.

As December wore on, talk of secession continued. But Tom and Rachel became too caught up in their studies to debate politics with Sidney. They were preparing for the annual competition among the top students from the Wyoming Valley schools. The competition would take place across the River at Wyoming Seminary in the town of Kingston on December 21st. All subjects and grades were included. Rachel was competing in spelling and literature. Tom had worked his way to the finals in history, literature, and writing. Caleb, Caroline, and Maude were competing as well. Eliza had not qualified for the competition in any subject, but planned to go along as part of the audience. After a little coaxing from Tom and Caleb, Sidney agreed to do the same.

He rode with the Mahoneys. There was enough snow on the ground that Tom decided to take the sleigh instead of the buggy. As they crossed the bridge, Tom and Caleb recited their lessons to each other. Sidney became disinterested somewhere between the definitions of iambic pentameter and blank verse. He turned his thoughts from academics and wondered what he should give Daniel and Sarah for Christmas. Even though Uncle Daniel needed new boots, Sidney knew he would never buy the ones he wanted because they were too expensive. But Sid had written to the lawyer left in charge of his father's finances, asking him to send some money. Now he had enough to buy those boots for Uncle Daniel and to get something special for Aunt Sarah. He had already made arrangements for amethyst earrings to be given to Catherine. Before he left Roswell, he had planned to give her an heirloom pendant of his mother's for Christmas. But now he couldn't bring himself to do that. She had not yet responded to Aunt Sarah's invitation. He couldn't imagine why. Perhaps when he returned to Georgia, everything would be clear again.

The competition began at ten o'clock in the morning. Though it was a short trip, they arrived with just enough time to find seats in the classrooms. Tom and Caleb had to go to different classrooms to compete, so Sid followed Mrs. Mahoney to the literature competition for Tom's grade. Eliza was there, too, with Ruth, who had come to watch Rachel. The other Whites had gone to see Caroline's spelling competition.

"During the next session, I need to watch Caleb compete in mathematics," Mrs. Mahoney told Sidney. "That means I'll miss Tom's writing competition, but he says it's not very exciting to watch."

Eliza sat next to Sid and talked of school and how smart Tom was and why didn't Sidney come to school and what did he think of North Carolina's threat to secede. Sid was glad when the competition began and she was forced to be quiet. Each student recited a poem, paying particular attention to alliteration, rhythm, and rhyme scheme. Then each competitor read an explication they had written. Rachel had done an explication of Shakespeare's sonnet 18. "Shall I compare thee to a summer's day?" she read. "Thou art more lovely and more temperate." As she talked of the poem, Sid thought it sounded as though it described Rachel perfectly. Rachel was so eloquent, so poised in front of the audience. She looked at the people watching her more than the papers she read. The words rolled out from between her lips in soothing rhythm, varied and similar.

"Wow," Eliza whispered. "I don't know how she does it. You'd never know she was nervous!"

"Is she?" Sid whispered back.

"She's always tense before these things!" Eliza exclaimed in a loud whisper. "Even when it's just in front of our class, she practically gets sick. You should have seen her on the way here! She was absolutely trembling. And I'd say the color of her skin was closer to green than I'd ever seen it."

"I didn't realize," Sid murmured.

"She was more nervous than I'd ever seen her," Eliza commented. "Tom's never nervous, though. He just works hard and gets up there and does so well! He's amazing." She flushed.

Tom took second place and Rachel third. Sid thought Rachel had done better than the girl who took first, but he didn't get a chance to tell her because no sooner had the winners been announced, than the students had to rush to prepare for their next competition.

Rachel's spelling competition was last, and ended at four o'clock. Rachel was brilliant, but she missed a letter in the last word, taking second place. Frowning, she took her seat in the first row with the other students. The competitors received their awards, and then it was time for refreshments. Sidney stayed with Eliza and Ruth while Tom went off to speak to some boys from the other schools. Presently, Rachel appeared, trembling and pale. Sid thought she looked more nervous than she had during the competition. Eliza and Ruth showered her with praise. And when they rushed to the buffet to get her a plate of well-deserved nourishment, Sidney turned to her.

"You were amazing," he said.

The anxiety drained out of her face. "Really?"

"You were better than that girl who won in Literature. Much better. Your essay—and the recitation. I knew you were smart, but—"

"She was better. She wins every year. Fortunately for me, she's graduating this spring." Rachel smiled.

"You were better," Sid insisted.

Before he could say more, Ruth and Eliza returned with a full plate for Rachel. Then Mr. and Mrs. White gathered around her, exclaiming over her success. The upper-grade students were asked to stay for a special session concerning higher education. Mr. White asked Tom if he'd mind taking Rachel home after it had ended. They'd take Mrs. Mahoney with them, as the adults wanted to leave. Eliza stayed to ride home with Tom, Caleb, and Rachel. Sidney decided to stay as well, since it would be a good chance to go down the street to see if any of the stores had the boots Daniel was hoping for.

"I'm going to do some Christmas shopping," Sid told Eliza. "Make sure they don't leave without me."

"Can I come with you?" she asked. "I'll help you decide what to buy for your aunt. Boys can't pick good presents for women!"

Sid laughed. "Sure, come along. I'd like the company."

"Did you get something for your sweetheart yet?" Eliza asked as they walked along the street, all bundled up against the cold and snow.

"Yes. Amethyst earrings," he answered. "Now do you think boys can pick good presents for women?"

"I don't know," she said. "I'd have to see them. I was afraid maybe you got her an engagement ring!"

"Would that upset you?" Sid smirked at her.

"No, not me!" Eliza laughed.

A gust of wind blew the snow into their faces. They had reached the main avenue in town. They went into a mercantile much like Daniel's with a sign over the window, which read, "Edwards, Morgan, & Co." It didn't take Sidney long to find the boots. As Sid paid for them, Mr. Morgan told him about a fine jewelry store across the street. He tucked Eliza's hand under his arm as they headed towards it. It was snowing rather hard.

"I want something simple. Something she'll wear," Sid explained as they shook the snow from their boots. "You know my Aunt Sarah. She's beautiful, but understated. I wish I had thought earlier to have Chloe send up something of my mother's to give her."

The jeweler showed them a set of silver combs.

"These are beautiful, Sidney!" Eliza exclaimed. "You have to get her these! If you have enough money."

"Of course I have," Sid said. "Are you sure she would wear them?"

"Definitely on Sundays," Eliza assured him. "They aren't too showy."

As he paid for the combs, Eliza turned a sly look on him.

"You're not finished with your shopping, are you?" she queried.

"I think so."

"Are you out of money?"

Sid laughed. "Hardly! What are you getting at? Did you want something? I could give Tom a hint. He's a little dense about these things."

"No, not me!" Eliza tossed her reddish-blonde hair. "But Rachel did an awfully good job tonight. Don't you think it would be nice to give her a little present of congratulations?"

Sid's heart pounded and his face grew hot. He avoided Eliza's gaze as he put his change in his billfold. He cleared his throat.

"I couldn't do that. You know it."

"I don't know it! Why couldn't you?" she exclaimed.

"She might think I meant something by it."

"She's not a goose, Sid! She knows about Catherine! You ought to give her something."

Sid pulled at one last straw. "Why don't you pick something out to give her and I'll pay for it."

"I don't need your money! Besides, I already have something for her. I got her a fancy leather blank book to write in."

Sid looked at her. "Is it the custom to give gifts after these competitions?"

"Of course!" Eliza smiled. "Tom told me he's giving her some autographed Dickens book."

"Oh, really?" Sid raised his eyebrows. "And won't she think he means something by that?"

"I don't think so." Eliza scowled. "It's just the thing to do—I have something for Tom, too."

"All right then." Sid was convinced. "What should I get?"

"How about amethyst earrings?" Eliza grinned. "No, I'm only teasing. Come look, they have some beautiful brooches." She led him towards a display case.

"I think jewelry would be misconstrued," Sid said uncertainly.

"They have other things here," Eliza encouraged him.

Sidney looked around a little bit. Then he found it in a glass case in the corner—a tortoise shell pen.

"Eliza," Sid called her over. "What about this?"

Eliza's eyes grew wide. "Perfect," she said.

The jeweler had soon wrapped the pen in an attractive box. He looked up at the two of them as Sidney handed him a bill.

"Some news today, eh?" he said.

"What news, sir?" Sidney asked.

"You haven't heard about South Carolina?" The jeweler raised his bushy gray eyebrows. "They've seceded. They voted for it yesterday."

"They did?" Eliza's voice was high.

Sid glanced at her. She was paler than usual.

"How did you hear this?" Sid asked.

"Read it right here." The jeweler took a newspaper from the side of the cash register. "Philadelphia Inquirer. My brother gave it to me a little while ago. Can't stop thinking about it."

Sidney read the headline. "Secession of South Carolina! The Lost Star of the Republic!"

"Oh my goodness!" Eliza covered her face with her hands.

"Thank you for sharing the news, sir," Sidney said.

He put his hand on Eliza's elbow to guide her towards the door. Tears were running freely down her face. Sid offered his handkerchief.

"Your face will freeze," he said.

"Oh, I have my own!" She dug in her purse and dabbed at her cheeks as they left the store.

"I'm sorry, Eliza. We'd better get back, though." She took his arm again as they hurried back to the school with his packages.

Tom, Rachel, and Caleb were all waiting for them when they reached the entrance.

"We'd better hurry," Tom said. "It's snowing hard! It might be difficult to get home."

Eliza, still sniffling, grabbed a hold of Tom's arm with her mittened hands.

"What is it?" he asked.

"South Carolina," she said. "They've seceded!"

"No!" cried Rachel.

"The Union is dissolved," Sidney said. "We saw the headline ourselves."

Caleb shook his head.

"What will come next?" Tom asked quietly.

Sid looked down at the snow around his feet. He was as sad as they were, wondering what the future could hold in a country divided.

Rachel said, matter-of-factly, "Whatever this means for all of us, we still need to start for home. It's after six o'clock and this is a real blizzard. We can talk as we ride."

But they didn't talk much as they rode. The furious wind and snow kept them from discussing the news, and their spirits were no longer gay. Seeing the joy gone from Rachel's face, Sidney wished the jeweler hadn't told them the news. Then they all might have had a happy ride home together. Tom was using every ounce of energy to fight the driving snow and keep the horses going into the wind.

They had been traveling for some time and there was no sign of the bridge. The snow was almost blinding, but it seemed there were fewer houses on the street. Tom stopped the horses.

Sid tapped his shoulder.

"Do you want me to take the reins for a while?" he shouted.

Tom shook his head.

"This is bad, Sid," Tom shouted back. "I'm not where I thought I was."

"What?" Sid looked at Tom's face. His lips were set together and his eyes searched the sides of the street. "I meant to follow Market Street over the bridge, but somehow . . ."

Tom slapped the reins on the horses' backs and they began moving slowly. Soon he pulled them up again.

"Damn it, Sid! I'm on Plymouth Street!" Tom shouted.

"That doesn't mean anything to me, Tom," Sid said.

"It means we're going the wrong direction," Tom went on. "If I headed off another direction without realizing it, there's no telling what could happen in this storm. I can't see a thing. We might run into the river."

Caleb reached up from the rear seat and laid a hand on Tom's shoulder. "Where are we?"

"We're heading into Plymouth for God's sake!" Tom said.

"Aunt Rose lives in Plymouth," Caleb said.

"That's right, Caleb!" Tom smiled. "Why didn't I think of that! We could spend the night at her house."

"I think we'd better," Sid said. "If you can find it."

"I can find it," Tom said. "It's on a side street off of this one. As long as we go slowly and look at each street, I'll be able to tell which one it is."

"What's the matter?" Eliza called from the rear seat.

Sidney shouted to her, though she was only a few feet from him. "We're going to Tom's aunt's house for the night."

"But our parents will be worried sick!" Eliza said.

"It's snowing too hard," Caleb said. "We can't go on if we can't see."

Tom had to climb down from the sleigh and lead the horses through a few snowdrifts before they found his aunt's house. Rachel and Eliza struggled to the front door while the boys went to stable the horses. Aunt Rose was heating some mulled cider for them when the boys came in, stomping and brushing off the snow.

"I can't believe you young people were out traveling in this weather!" she said. "What were your parents thinking, leaving you at the Seminary in a blizzard?"

"Well, it was hardly snowing when they left," Tom said. "But by the time Sidney and Eliza came back from Christmas shopping, it was really coming down."

"I'll say it was!" she said. "Let me just dish up some cider for you folks and you can let your bones thaw out."

The young people sat in the kitchen, sipping hot cider around the stove. They popped corn and chatted about the competition for a while. Then Aunt Rose took them upstairs and helped them get settled for the night. Exhausted as they were from fighting the snowstorm, it didn't take them long to get to sleep.

Sidney woke in the middle of the night. His throat was parched, so he went downstairs for some water. He was surprised to see a fire still going in the parlor fireplace. Rachel sat by it, wrapped in a blanket. After getting a drink from the pump in the kitchen, he went into the parlor. Rachel's hair was down, but she was dressed, so he sat next to her.

"Couldn't sleep?" he asked.

"No," she replied.

"May I sit with you?"

"I suppose," she said.

"Is it the secession?"

"We needn't talk about it," Rachel said quietly.

"I'm sorry we heard that news tonight. You were so happy before." He paused. "I have something for you. It's not much. It's just a gift of congratulations, because you did so well. It's nothing more than that."

"You didn't have to get me anything."

"Well, Eliza kind of convinced me to," he said. "She got you something, too."

Rachel laughed. "That little weasel!"

He went to the foyer, where he had set his packages. He presented the long box to Rachel. She worked the ribbon off and opened the lid.

"Oh, Sidney," she breathed.

Her eyes filled with tears, and she half-turned away.

"Do you like it?" Sid asked, his voice quavering.

She turned back. "Why don't you let me stay mad at you?"

"You were mad at me?"

"I'm angry with you most of the time, just because you're a Southerner! And the secession just made it worse." She shook her head. "This must have cost you a fortune!"

"A small one," he said. "I had to sell my mother's jewelry to get it."

"Liar! You wouldn't dare!" Rachel laughed. "I will always treasure it."

They sat by the fire together, just watching the flames. Sidney wished this night would last forever—he and Rachel snug by the fire with the snow swirling outside. He didn't want to think about tomorrow or the next day. About what secession meant for him. He looked at Rachel, with firelight flickering over her troubled brow, highlighting the red hues in her chestnut hair. He wished he could comfort her. But even if nothing had held him back, he wouldn't know how. There was nothing to do but sit together and draw strength from one another.

twelve

B Y morning the storm had ended. The sun was shining and two feet of new snow covered the outside world. As soon as they had finished breakfast, the young people thanked Aunt Rose and went on their way.

"Let's hurry, Tom," Eliza said as they pulled away in the sleigh. "Our parents must be worried."

"It won't take long to get home now," Tom said. "We're only a few miles away."

"I think I'm going to be ill," Eliza moaned. "What if Father doesn't understand?"

"I know," Rachel said. "What if they think we stayed out all night on purpose?"

"We hardly had a choice," Sidney put in. "I think they'll be glad we're alive."

"Well, it's easy for you," Eliza said. "You're a boy."

"I'll explain," Tom called back to them. "I'm sure they'll understand."

Reverend Holloway was shoveling the front walk as they arrived. He met them at the manse gate. He was relieved to see Eliza safe. At the White's, they met quite a different scene. Mrs. White ran out of the house as soon as the sleigh came into view.

"Oh, no," Rachel muttered. "Where's Father?"

As they pulled up to the gate, Mrs. White gave Rachel no time to explain. She started into the sleigh, grabbed Rachel's arm and dragged her down from her seat, almost tumbling her headfirst into the snow. Sidney jumped up, trying to break Rachel's fall.

"Mrs. White!" he exclaimed, reaching for Rachel's free arm.

"You keep your hands off my daughter!" Mrs. White snarled at him. "I don't even want to hear what you've been doing all night."

"Mother!" Rachel turned scarlet.

"Quiet!" Mrs. White snapped. "This is disgraceful! A daughter of mine, gone all night long with three boys. I would have expected it of this Judson, but certainly not of the Mahoney boys. I have been sick with worry while you've been out joyriding and who knows what else! I see you took the Reverend's daughter home, but perhaps you thought a layman's daughter was easier to take liberties with. Is that it?"

"Mother, we just dropped Eliza off this morning!" Rachel exclaimed, her face growing redder by the second.

"Mrs. White," Tom said calmly. "If you will please let me explain—"

"I don't think so—" Mrs. White began.

"Melinda! Let the boy speak!" Atticus strolled up the walk from the house.

Mrs. White's thin lips shut tightly.

Tom breathed a sigh. "I don't think you can honestly believe we were out joyriding in that weather last night. We tried to come home in the snow, but I lost my way and it was just too dangerous to go on. My aunt lives in Plymouth and she was more than happy to put us up for the night. We came home this morning as soon as we could. We were well supervised. I assure you my aunt is a respectable woman. You may ask my mother about her if you like."

"Well," Atticus said. "I think we can be glad that Rachel was with such responsible young men last night. Thank you, boys. Your foresight probably saved your lives—and Rachel's."

Sidney thought Rachel had probably not heard the last from her mother, yet he deemed it best to remain silent.

As they drove away from the White's, Caleb said, "What a witch!"

"I can understand why she's upset," Tom said. "But my God!"

Caleb looked back at Sid from the front seat. "It's a good thing she doesn't know you were up with Rachel half the night!"

"What?" Sid flushed.

"Oh, you think we didn't know where you were?" Caleb laughed. "I woke up and saw that you were missing. I bumped into Eliza in the hallway. She was looking for Rachel. So where did you hold your little tryst?"

"It wasn't a tryst!" Sid was angry. "We just sat by the fire and talked. Nothing happened."

Tom's voice was level as he glanced at Sid. "Could something have happened?"

"No!" Sid said. "Anyway, who are you to talk? You went ahead and gave Rachel that book against my advice."

Tom looked over his shoulder at him. "Everyone was talking about giving gifts at school. It didn't seem like a big deal."

"Still," Sid said. "Rachel and I were just talking."

"Well," Tom said. "It would probably be better if Mrs. White didn't know you were in the parlor alone with Rachel all night. She'd be convinced her daughter's a whore."

Sid shook his head in disgust. "How could she think that? Doesn't she know her own daughter?"

"That's just the way she is," Tom said. "She thinks the worst of everybody."

They rode in silence for a moment. Then Tom turned to Sid again. "Does Catherine know you sit all night by the fire with other girls?"

"Come on, Tom!" Sid said. "Don't start about Catherine."

"No, you come on! When is she coming up to visit?"

Sid shrugged. "She hasn't answered yet."

"You haven't heard from her? How long has it been?"

"Since before Aunt Sarah was ill. Two months, I guess."

"Jeez, Sid! I'm sorry, brother."

"It could be the mail," Sid said. He paused and bit his lip. "I doubt it, though. I don't know what's going on."

"You'll work it out," Tom said. "You love each other, right?"

"Yeah," Sid said. "Of course we do."

Tom pulled the sleigh up in front of the Judson's home.

"Thanks, Tom." Sid climbed down into the snow. "Later, Caleb."

Aunt Sarah met Sidney at the front door, relieved at the sight of him. He waved good-bye to Tom and Caleb as they headed home to calm their own mother's fears.

Sidney saw little of the Whites for the next few weeks. They were busy with relatives over the holidays, so he never had an opportunity to find out if Mrs. White had more to say to Rachel about her scandalous behavior. Christmas came and went without incident. One of Aunt Sarah's brothers came from New York, bringing his wife and their two young sons to celebrate with the Judsons and Rhoda. In spite of the modest joy shared in their household, the state of the nation cast its shadow over the holiday.

When Sidney arrived at the store the day after Christmas, Uncle Daniel handed him two letters he'd picked up at the post office. Sid stared at the envelopes for a long moment, finally tearing open the letter from Drew.

Dear Sid,

How are things in Yankee territory? It has become difficult to remember that you were ever part of our lives here. Catherine is depressed. She thinks you're never coming back. It's difficult to cheer her. I think the only thing that will do that is your coming home again.

Written before the secession, Drew's letter did not mention the recent news. But his tone sounded as though Sidney were a traitor. Sid set the letter aside. Then, his hands shaking, he opened the letter from Catherine.

Dearest Sidney,

I cannot imagine what's kept you in the North so long. When you wrote saying your aunt would invite me to visit, I didn't think you were serious. What I want is you back home, but it's becoming quite clear you do not care enough to return. Father absolutely forbids me to travel with the nation in its current condition. Otherwise, I might have come. I have written my regrets to your aunt. She seems like a fine lady, for a Yankee.

I've wrestled for some time wondering if I should share this with you, but I now feel that I ought to tell you. Father has urged me to give up on you altogether. When first he brought it up to me, I told him right away not to be silly, for I knew you'd come back to me soon. But now I am beginning to think he may be right. It's well into December and I haven't received a word from you about Christmas. What kind of beau forgets his sweetheart so utterly? Should I simply accept the harsh truth that all is lost?

Sid folded the letters together and crammed them into the pocket of his overcoat. Then he hung his coat on the peg in the stock room and returned to the front to see Uncle Daniel.

"I'll start tidying the stock room, all right, sir?" Sid asked him.

Daniel stood behind the counter rifling through the ledger from the week before. He looked at Sidney over the top of his reading glasses.

"I thought it was quite organized when I closed up on Christmas Eve," he said.

"I'm going to give it a good sweep, anyhow," Sid said.

"Anything bothering you, Sid?" Daniel looked back at the ledger.

"Why?" Sid shrugged.

"The letters I gave you," Daniel said.

"Just friends from home," Sid said. "They're getting anxious for my return."

"Well," Daniel said. "Don't go back until you're good and ready."

Sid nodded. He headed to the stockroom and took the broom to it with vigor.

That evening, Sid wrote in reply—first to Drew, hoping to revive some of the camaraderie he once shared with his friend. The letter dissatisfied him, but he decided to send it anyway, knowing it would take a long time to get there. With secession in progress, it was quite possible that war could call Sidney back to Georgia very soon.

Next he penned his response to Catherine. Of course she couldn't know that Chloe was to give her his gift on Christmas Day. He hoped she liked the earrings he had chosen especially for her. All was not lost. He would likely come home very soon, since war was certainly not far off. All of her fears would be put to rest when he held her in his arms once again. Reading the letter over, Sid was pleased with it. He was certain his words would allay her fears and all would be well.

On the way to work the next day, he stopped at the post office to mail the letters. As he walked to the store, though, he regretted sending them. Nothing he'd written to Catherine was true. He had no idea how he'd feel when he saw her again. Before his parents died he had known exactly what lay before him. Catherine as his wife, his father's estate as his home. That was his goal a year ago.

Since his arrival in the North, though, a vague memory had returned to him. It had become clearer as the months passed. As a young boy, he had visited Uncle Daniel's store and marveled over it. He'd told Drew about it when he returned home and they'd set up a store in Sid's back yard, playing shopkeeper. His father had scoffed at their little game when Sid came into the house that night.

"You want to be a shopkeeper?" he'd laughed. "You'd choose dry goods over the Roswell Mills?"

Sid hung his head, his cheeks burning. His mother hurried to

154

his rescue.

"David, it's just a game," she said. "Just a little fun the boys are having. Every child plays at all sorts of things. Why, I used to pretend with other little girls that we were darkies and we had to work from dawn till dusk. Can you imagine? We thought it was fun to play such things, but today I'm the mistress—there's no doubt of that."

"And you'll be the master," his father had said to him. "Of this estate, not of a no-name establishment. You're my only child—most boys would be thrilled to have an estate coming to them, free and clear."

So Sidney had put the shop-keeping dream, if it was a dream, aside and planned for a future that would become reality. Now that reality seemed to be dissolving in his mind.

Sidney went to the Whites for wassail on New Year's Eve. It was not much of a celebration, despite everyone's attempts at gaiety. The future looked bleak. General Anderson had moved his federal garrison from Fort Moultrie to Fort Sumter. The Southern states viewed it as a direct violation of President Buchanan's promise that no changes in position would be made. The Secretary of War had resigned. As talk of recent occurrences went on around them, Sidney found himself standing next to Rachel.

He drained his mug of wassail and realized he had nothing to say to her. Her mother's words hung in the air between them and there was no way to erase them. The only thing to do was to behave as though they were simply friends. If he could be nothing more than polite towards her, then eventually they would both believe they were only casual acquaintances.

"Good evening, my lady," he said.

She laughed, in that clear, lilting way that he wished he'd never grown to care so much for. "Good evening, sir."

"Did you have a fine Christmas?"

"We did, thank you," she answered. "Very fine. And you?"

"Very fine indeed," Sid nodded.

Eliza meandered over just in time to save them from more awkward conversation. And so the two of them survived the evening and the politeness between them continued for several weeks.

Sid worked hard at the Mercantile, hoping that it would keep his mind off Rachel. In early January, they received word of Mississippi's secession. At the store, Sidney heard every side of every debate in Wilkes-Barre. At times the discussions grew almost riotous. Some men argued for secession. Some believed strongly in the Union. Others thought the states should be given more rights. But it didn't matter what they thought. Buchanan was anti-secessionist and Lincoln was against any compromise. What control did any of Wilkes-Barre's residents have over the situation? Most were infuriated by Southern troops opening fire on the Star of the West as it tried to deliver supplies to Fort Sumter. War seemed imminent now, yet it had not officially been declared. So Sidney did not leave, even though he knew his presence was becoming more awkward every day. Florida and Alabama closely followed Mississippi in secession.

On a Saturday in mid-January, Rachel appeared at the Mercantile. She didn't even smile when Sid greeted her.

"Why so cheerful today?" he asked.

"No one's very cheerful, are they?"

"No," he agreed, looking around the store at the groups of men.

"Actually," Rachel said. "There is a reason I'm particularly not cheerful today."

Sid raised his eyebrows.

"The State Convention of Georgia met today," she said.

"Yes," Sid looked away. "I knew they were meeting. I didn't think you followed their actions, though."

"Only this one. I think I'm the first to know because I was in the telegraph office when Mrs. Goeringer received the news. So I hate to be the one to tell you, but I'd hate more for you to hear it from all these vultures in here."

"Yes?" Sid leaned on the counter, knowing what she was about to say.

The bell on the door jingled as someone stepped in. Joshua Smith.

"Georgia seceded from the Union!!!" he shouted.

Rachel's face fell.

Joshua continued, stalking towards Sidney, pointing with an outstretched arm. "I believe that's where this old boy comes from!" Joshua grinned his ugly grin. "You gonna go home where you belong now? I bet your niggers miss you, huh? Gonna go back and crack the whip a little? It looks like you'll be able to now, without any interference from Washington!"

Sid ignored him, tidying up the shelves behind the register. Rachel stood at the counter, her face pale, her forehead creased with lines of worry.

"Can I get you something?" Sid asked her.

"Yes, please."

"Candy?" he asked.

She nodded. While Sidney got her a peppermint stick from the jars by the cash register, he tried to steady his shaking hands. He had thought the secession of his home state wouldn't make much difference to him. At one time he had believed it might be the right thing. Now his stomach was in knots. Georgia was no longer part of the Union. It belonged to a separate nation. It made Catherine and Drew seem even further away. Rachel bit off the end of the peppermint stick, the color slowly coming back to her cheeks. Uncle Daniel came out of the stock room and patted him on the back.

"Go home if you want, son," he said. "I can handle the store for the rest of the day."

Sid nodded, swallowing. "Thanks, Uncle Daniel."

He got his coat and walked out with Rachel.

"Oh, wait! I need to pay for the peppermint." She turned back.

Sid took her arm. "No, it was a gift."

"Thank you. Do you mind walking me home?" she asked. "I have to ask you something. I hate to bring this up, but it's been bothering me."

"Go ahead."

"Please," she said. "I don't mean anything by this."

She took a deep breath and went on as they started down Franklin Street.

"Perhaps I'm imagining it. I just need to know."

Sid's stomach refused to untie itself. "Just ask whatever you want to ask."

"Okay," she said. "Have you been avoiding me? I mean, not exactly avoiding me, but avoiding talking to me. Before Christmas we were friends, weren't we?"

"We are friends," Sid said quickly.

"No," she said. "I mean, at Tom's Aunt's house and even before that. Lately it seems like you don't want to talk to me anymore. Are you afraid I thought more of the gift than you meant? Because I know it's just a gift from a friend. So you don't have to stop talking to me to make me see that."

She stopped and looked at Sid, biting off another bit of the peppermint. He stuck his hands in his pockets.

"I'm sorry," he said. "I don't really know how to explain it. I do want to be your friend, even if this war separates us."

"Don't talk about the war," Rachel said.

"Why?" he asked.

"I'll be sorry to see you go," she said.

"Thank you," Sid said. "I—" He almost said it, but the words stuck in his throat. He couldn't tell her he would hate to go. His hands were suddenly damp. He ran his fingers through his hair to busy them. "I think your mother will be glad to see me go."

"Oh good Lord!" Rachel put the second half of the peppermint stick in the pocket of her coat. "I'm so sorry about that day. The things she said."

"It's not your fault." Sid shook his head.

"Sometimes she says things she doesn't mean," Rachel continued. "Is that why you've been avoiding me?"

"Partly," Sid admitted.

"Please, just forget everything she said."

"I just hope she doesn't make it a habit to accuse you of such behavior," Sid said. "That would be absurd."

Rachel didn't answer. They had reached her gate. She said good bye and flitted up the walk and through her front door.

thirteen

S IDNEY waited for war to start. Farmers and businessmen argued about the latest news at the store every day. In the beginning of February, Texas departed from the Union, bringing the total number of seceded states to seven. On February eighth, the newly formed "Confederate States of America" adopted a provisional constitution and on the following day elected Jefferson Davis as its president. Sid was occasionally the brunt of jokes about the Rebels, was often asked why he was still in the North, and avoided political conversation whenever possible. Joshua Smith made that difficult at times, harassing him with questions about how he felt on specific issues. Sid wondered why someone with Southern sympathies wasn't more sympathetic towards an actual Southerner.

Tom was neutral. If he fought, he'd fight for the Union, but he'd avoid fighting as long as he could. Tom, Caleb, and Sidney hadn't been fishing since the river had frozen. Tom wanted to ice fish, but Sid was unused to the cold and to stand out on a frozen river did not appeal to him even if fish were involved. So they played checkers and tied flies indoors.

Sid left Tom's house one February evening and made his way home through the wind and light snow. When he stepped through the front door, he heard low voices in the kitchen. Leaving his dripping boots in the foyer, Sid went through the dining room to the kitchen door. He stopped and stared. Two darkies were sitting at the table. Rhoda, her chocolate skin glowing in the lamplight, brought them each a plate of corn bread and stewed fruit. The Negroes were slaves from Tall Pine.

The woman looked up and saw Sidney standing in the doorway. Her hand flew to her mouth and she stood up so suddenly she knocked her chair to the floor.

"Hattie," Sid said, moving into the room. "Lem."

The man turned and looked at him.

"Oh, ma Lawd! It's a trap! All dis way an' we fine ourselves in a trap!"

"No, no," Sidney said. "It's not a trap! These people will help you! I was just surprised to see you, that's all."

"Mr. Sidney," Rhoda said, putting her hands on her hips. "How do you know these poor souls?"

"They belonged to my father, Rhoda," Sid said.

"Well, you listen here." Her eyes flashed at him. "You better just stay out of this!"

"No," Sid said. "I want to know what happened. Were you mistreated at home?"

"Mr. Sidney." Lem's voice was thick and tremulous. "Please don't send us back there. That new overseer, that Mr. Pierson, he's just as mean as they come. He beat us and then he say he gonna sell me... an' not Hattie."

No one ever beat the slaves at Tall Pine. Sidney looked at the two of them. His property. But instead he saw a black man writhing in pain on the ground in Public Square. He couldn't bring that man back to life now, but he could keep Lem and Hattie from having to face an officer like Wilson.

"I'm not going to send you back," he said. "I'm going to give you your freedom."

Silence ensued. All three of them stared at Sid.

"You-you're going to what?" Lem gasped.

"You're free," Sid repeated.

"Mr. Sidney," Hattie breathed.

Lem covered the distance between them in two big strides and took his hand in the strongest handshake Sid had ever felt. "I knowed you was gonna turn into a good man—even back at Tall Pine when you was but a whippersnapper wit' a surly mug!"

Sid patted Lem's shoulder and breathed a sigh of relief when he released his hand.

"I'm not sure what this will involve, as far as papers and whatever else," he said. "I'll do it on one condition, though. No one can know that I've set you free. I've been the subject of enough ridicule in this town already. I don't need to add fuel to the fire."

"Oh, yes Mr. Sidney," Lemuel lowered his eyebrows. "We promise we won't tell no one. We just tell people our Massa give us freedom, but we won' tell no one who that Massa is! If you want us to keep moving on from here, that's fine too."

"You can stay in Wilkes-Barre if you want to." Sid ran his fingers through his hair. "I don't think I'll be here too much longer myself. Whenever war breaks out, I'm going back South. Rhoda!" Sid's voice was suddenly sharp. "This goes for you, too! I know how you like to tell my stories, but not this one. Do you understand?"

"Mr. Sidney!" Rhoda's hands went to her hips again. "If you want me to be quiet, all you gotta do is ask. Don't go bossing me around like you're in charge of my soul! Ain't nobody got a hold on my soul but the good Lord Jesus!"

Sid sighed. He felt like someone was struggling for a hold on his soul. But whoever it was had lost the battle and he was free for the moment.

✤

While Sidney signed the papers to free Lem and Hattie, Daniel began looking for a place for them to live and work. He couldn't pay anyone else to work in the store, but Atticus White needed a new hand, now that Jake had his own farm. Talk about the new Negro couple seemed to permeate the store, adding a new facet to the general political chatter.

"I don't understand why they're here!" Seamus MacIntire exclaimed. "If their master set them free, why'd they come up to the North to settle—and why Wilkes-Barre of all places?"

"Good question," Joshua Smith snarled. "I don't think their master really set them free. I think they're just runaways and they tell people they're free because they're tired of running."

"If that's the case, we should do something about it!" Joshua's brother, Bill, pounded the counter.

"No, no! You're wrong about that," said Terrence Williams. "My brother saw their papers and he told me it's a firm fact. They are free."

"He saw their papers?" Joshua asked. "Why'd he see their papers?"

"He's an attorney, you know. Perhaps they were investigated when they got here. I heard there was a little fuss at the court house when they first arrived."

Although the talk made Sid a little nervous, it also brought a quiet smile to his face. He tried to steer clear of Lem and Hattie. He nodded and smiled when he passed them in the street. They nodded back and smiled a little too broadly. When they came into the store, he simply took care of their orders, praying that nothing he said or did would give him away to the men who stood by, gaping at the newcomers. Not all white storeowners did business with colored people, but Daniel did. Sidney hoped the gossipers would chalk up his uneasiness to his Southern blood.

The first week of March, Tom came into the store after school, stomping the snow from his boots.

Sid shook his head at him. "How can we still have snow in March, Tom? When does it finally melt?"

Tom laughed. "That all depends on Old Man Winter. He has

a mind of his own."

"Guess that's true," Sid said.

Jake came through the door as well, letting in a burst of cold air and snowflakes.

"Brrrr!" Sid grumbled. "Shut the door!"

"All right," Jake chuckled. "What a welcome! Is that how you treat your customers?"

"My apologies," Sid smiled. "I'm ready for spring."

"Not me," Tom said. "I think I'll be losing a friend come spring."

"Well, I wasn't thinking of that," Sid nodded. "Just the weather."

"I know," Tom said.

"Aw, you think he's really going to leave?" Jake said to Tom. "That war's never going to start. He might as well just stay."

"What do you mean it's not going to start?" Sid asked. "Of course it's going to start—sooner or later."

"I don't know," Jake said. "Lincoln's been inaugurated and nothing's happened yet. I think we might be able to go on the way we are. The Confederate States can just peacefully leave the United States and we'll continue with business as usual."

"Impossible," Tom said, leaning on the counter. "The president will have to address the situation one way or another. He can't just ignore it!"

"I don't like to discuss it," Sid said.

"We all know that," Jake sat on the bench against the front wall, next to the wood stove.

"Aside from that," Tom spoke up again. "There are two Federal forts in Confederate territory now. How long do you think the Confederacy will put up with our troops?"

"You've got a point there," Sid said.

But not only did Sid not like to talk about it, he didn't like to think about it at all. He was secretly glad that neither spring nor war had forced him to think seriously about going home. But he knew the current state of things could not last much longer.

That evening, Aunt Sarah brought the mail in and handed a

letter to Sidney. It was from Catherine. He took it into the library to read it. She thanked Sidney for the Christmas present. She said she could not wait for his arrival and looked for him as soon as spring arrived. The letter was less than warm. He took out some stationery to answer her, but soon set his pen down in frustration. He went to the bookcase and felt for Aunt Sarah's journal.

23 March, 1840

We had a letter from David today. We haven't heard from him since that first letter last spring when he told us he was in North Carolina. Now he's in Savannah. For love of a woman, he says. He's running away from this life—as far South as he can get. It sounds like he's serious about this girl. I can't help but feel sad about it, thinking of what I had prayed for. Melinda has taken up with Atticus lately, so I suppose there wasn't any hope of them ever reconciling anyway.

It was Melinda White. His father had been involved with that woman. What could he have possibly seen in her? He flipped to the back of the book.

20 June, 1841

David and Laeticia arrived yesterday. She is a lovely woman in every way, except that she comes from a slave holding family. It seems that David has embraced his new life. Laeticia's uncle from Savannah has offered him part-ownership in the new Roswell Manufacturing Company in central Georgia. I imagine they will be just like other Southern families. Perhaps they will even buy a few slaves of their own. It's so hard for us to watch him turn his back on the way he was raised. But I suppose there's nothing we can do about it. We will love David and his bride, in spite of our differences.

Sidney shut the book. They always had. Until their quarrel when he was eight, Sid had never known there was a potential for animosity between the two brothers. Uncle Daniel and Aunt Sarah made them feel welcome every time they visited. And Aunt Sarah had written to invite them even after the quarrel. But his father would never go back.

Sid's letter to Catherine seemed futile now. He left it for another day, wishing she were more optimistic. He did not want to travel until the weather turned warmer anyway. He would have to write explaining this to Catherine.

That Saturday evening the young people gathered at the White home. Caleb and Caroline sat by the fire, discussing their history lesson. Tom beat Sidney several times at checkers. Then, refusing to play chess, he struck up a conversation with Eliza instead. Ruth and Jake had shared dinner with their family and now sat talking with Rachel. Sid sat alone, thinking about his inevitable departure for once. It made him gloomy. He heard voices outside the door and slipped out of the room. Atticus was talking with Hattie and Lem in the front hall. They were about to leave. Seeing Sidney, Atticus put a hand on his shoulder.

"Here's someone who wants to talk to you, I think," he said to the couple.

Atticus knew, but that was all right. Daniel had explained the situation to him when he had agreed to let Lem work for him. Atticus would not tell anyone. Not even his wife.

"Mr. Sidney, how do you do?" Hattie grinned.

Lem's voice was low. "Let me tell you, Mr. Sidney. We've been doing mighty fine! We can't thank you enough for what you've done for us!"

"Don't mention it." Sid smiled, embarrassed. "I haven't had a chance to ask you about home. Can you tell me what's going on in Roswell? How's Chloe?"

"Well, when we left in the beginning of October," Lem said. "Chloe was still in the big house, managing everything just fine. She's a good woman. We didn't tell no one we were leaving. We didn't want no one to have problems with the officers."

"That was wise," Sidney agreed. "Have you seen Drew?"

"Drew been to the house a few times. I seen him," Hattie answered. "When I was up to the house helping Chloe with some work. He came to check up on things and his daddy come with him."

Sid swallowed hard. "And Catherine?"

It seemed an eternity before Hattie answered, with a glance at Lem, "She come too."

"She's been to the house as well?"

"Yes," Hattie met his gaze at last. "She come to see how things is going. She just as beautiful as ever, Mr. Sidney. And she's doing well, as far as I can see."

Sid breathed a sigh. "Well, I don't want to keep you two. Thank you for taking a few minutes for me."

"Oh, anything for you, Mr. Sidney," Hattie whispered fervently. "We're real grateful to you, sir!"

They left and Sid went back into the parlor. The door had been closed between the parlor and the hall, so he felt sure no one had heard their quiet conversation. Caleb and Caroline were now discussing English. Tom and Eliza were deeply embroiled in conversation, though its caliber hardly seemed to live up to Tom's potential. Rachel, Jake and Ruth were gone. Presently Rachel came in, from the opposite end of the room. She looked slightly flushed. When she settled back into her seat, Sid sat nearby on the hassock.

"Where's Jake?" he asked.

"Jake and Ruth went home," Rachel answered shortly. "I just saw them out."

"Oh," Sid said. "Why are you so flushed?"

"Am I?" Rachel put her hands to her cheeks, and grew more flushed.

"I'm sorry," Sid said. "It's none of my business." He smirked. "I just thought maybe you had a beau out in the kitchen—"

"No, Sid," Rachel interrupted him. "It is your business. I can't tell you here. Come with me."

He followed her out to the hallway again. They put on their coats and she led him through the kitchen and out the back door of the house. They sat on the stoop in the chilly night air.

"They were your slaves, weren't they?" Rachel burst out. "I shouldn't have listened. But I couldn't help it. I heard you talking to them as though you knew them and then I had listened to your whole conversation!"

"But how?" Sid was annoyed.

"I'm sorry!" Rachel's voice shook. "I walked Ruth and Jake out this way. They left by the back door. Then I wanted to go upstairs to get a book Tom lent me, but when I reached the doorway to the hall, I heard you ask about Drew. And I couldn't stop listening. I didn't even think of not listening."

"Gosh, Rachel! Just don't tell anyone."

"I won't. I promise! I won't tell a soul!" She looked at him, her eyebrows drawing together. "You set them free?"

"What about it?"

"Why would you do that?" she exclaimed. "And you're going to fight for the Confederacy? Do you believe in slavery or not?"

"The war's not all about slavery, Rachel," Sid said.

"But this doesn't make sense," she said.

"I'll tell you why I set them free if you'll keep quiet," he said.

"I will." She drew her coat closer to her and looked at him.

He told her of the February evening when he'd come home to find Hattie and Lem in his uncle's kitchen. How he'd felt sorry for them and wanted to help them.

Rachel was quiet for a moment. Then she said, "It still doesn't make sense."

"Why?"

"Slaveholders don't set their slaves free."

"It just seemed like the right thing to do."

"I'm sorry, Sid. It's just that I've never been able to figure you out."

"You think Southerners are all the same and you see them as your enemies. Well, I'm not like every other Southerner. I'm me." Sid's words surprised him. "And you can't see me as an enemy."

"No, I suppose I can't." Rachel looked at him. "As hard as I try sometimes."

They both laughed.

"You really love her, don't you?"

"What?" Sid's heart pounded.

"I heard you asking about Catherine," Rachel said quietly.

Sid didn't answer.

"Is that why you have to go back?"

"Partly," Sid spoke. "I promised I'd go back. I have to keep my word."

"Don't you want to go back?"

Sid was silent. He pushed the snow around with his boot.

"It's all right," she said. "You don't have to answer."

fourteen

As March came to an end, Sidney knew he could not postpone his trip home much longer. One evening as they closed up the store, he drew a deep breath and spoke to Uncle Daniel.

"I think it's time I made plans to go home."

Daniel stood by the door and slowly turned the sign in the window to indicate the Mercantile was closed. Sid's heart raced as he waited.

Finally, Daniel turned around and looked at him. "Are you sure you want to go back, Sid?"

Sid swallowed and shook his head. "No, I'm not sure at all."

"You don't have to go," Uncle Daniel said.

"Yes, I do," Sid answered. "I promised."

"I see." Daniel looked at the floor. "Well, as far as your Aunt Sarah and I are concerned, you can stay permanently."

Sid cleared his throat. Still, he had trouble finding his voice. "Thank you. That means a lot to me." He continued in a hurry, "I don't want to leave you without someone to help in the store. I think I can stay until the end of April, so perhaps you can find an employee before I head out."

"That's thoughtful of you." Uncle Daniel nodded. "Well, the end of the month then."

Sid started sweeping the smoothly sanded floorboards. He felt unsettled. The look in Uncle Daniel's eyes opened an ache in his chest. But he couldn't go back on his word.

That night after tea, he went into the library and wrote to Catherine, telling her of his plans. When he came out, no one was in the parlor, but he heard voices coming from the kitchen. Sid went to the door between the dining room and kitchen. Hattie, Lem, and Rhoda were gathered around the kitchen table.

Rhoda was laughing. "That's what I did, too! I found a lawn jockey with a lighted lantern and that's how I finally got myself to Philadelphia."

"But then you bought your own freedom?" Hattie said. "How'd you find the money?"

"Well, it was on account of my husband," Rhoda said. "He was a free Negro and he earned the money to buy me."

"You had a husband?" Sid said.

Rhoda looked up. "Mr. Sidney, you just can't do that! You got to announce yourself when you come in the room. Specially when there's a private conversation going on."

"I'm sorry, Rhoda," Sid said. "I was just surprised."

"Why?" Rhoda gave him a wide-eyed look. "You think I can't catch a husband?"

"No!" Sid wasn't sure how to respond. Without a doubt, Rhoda's smooth, glowing skin and womanly figure made her desirable. "I never thought about it before."

"Well, my husband was a fine-looking man, let me tell you," Rhoda said. "Laws, we were happy, what little time we had together. But he crossed the border into the South, you see, went back to help more runaways."

She looked at Sid, still standing in the doorway. "Pull up a chair."

Sid sat down with them. "What happened to him?"

"They caught him with the fugitives and he got sold into slavery," she said. "He's still down there somewhere. I keep hoping one day he'll walk through that door. Then maybe we'll get to make the babies we always talked about."

They were all silent.

Then Rhoda spoke again. "But I interrupted Hattie. You were saying the two of you stopped at a house with a lantern, too."

"Well, now," Lem said. "Hattie's telling the story all jumbled up like. The lawn jockey came after the freezing cold nights of walking through the woods."

"That's right," Hattie said. "We was just following the drinking gourd at first."

"And the moss on the trees," Lem added.

"Wait, what?" Sid asked. "What's the drinking gourd?"

"You look up into the sky on a clear night and you'll see it," Rhoda told him. She rose. "Come on out in the backyard."

She led them out into the chilly night, letting the kitchen door swing shut behind them. The snow had melted, but it was still cold. Their frozen breath hung in the air as they gazed up at the sky.

"Do you see it, Mr. Sidney?" Lem asked. He stretched his hand up and pointed out the constellation. "See the stars that make the drinking gourd?"

Sid searched the stars and then he saw it—the outline of a dipper. "Yes! I see it!"

"The two stars on the end of the dipper," Lem said. "They point to the North Star. That's the way you need to travel to get to freedom."

They traipsed back into the warm kitchen.

"And on cloudy nights," Hattie said. "You just feel the tree trunks. Moss grows best on the north side of trees."

"And what's this about lawn jockeys?"

"You know the little statues some people have out on their lawn?" Rhoda said. "The little stable boys?"

"Yes," Sid said.

"Well, if it's holding a lighted lantern, you know it's a safe house."

"I see," Sidney said.

"Thank the Lord for that!" Lem said. "The lawn jockey set us on a path from house to house. We didn't have to sleep out in the snow. We didn't realize when we left Georgia it get's colder as you head north!"

The three of them laughed together. Sid smiled. He'd spent plenty of time with Rhoda, but he'd never seen her quite so jovial before.

The next day he mailed the letter to Catherine during the dinner hour. Rachel and Tom came into the store together after school. Tom was looking for paper and blank books. Sid showed them some stationery that had come in that week.

"All this winter we've been wrapped up in schoolwork." Tom flipped through a blank book, then slapped it against his left hand and cocked his head at Sid. "I'm ready to go fishing again! The river is almost thawed."

"I know." Sid averted his eyes and returned to the counter to tally up Tom's bill.

"Don't you want to go fishing?" Tom followed him and leaned on the counter, watching.

"You goose!" Rachel said, joining Tom at the counter. "The only place Sid's going to fish this spring is Georgia."

"Oh, I forgot!" Tom shook his head at his absentmindedness. "I don't know what I was thinking."

"Just the paper?" Sid asked.

"And envelopes." Tom added them to his selections on the counter.

"Two dollars," Sid told Tom. "I'm planning to leave at the end of the month."

"Why haven't you told us?" Tom demanded.

"Relax," Sid said. "I just talked to Uncle Daniel about it yesterday. And I sent word to Catherine today. You're the first to know."

"The end of the month?" Rachel laid one hand over the other

on the counter, her long, slender fingers curving gracefully.

"Yes." Sid looked from her hands to her face.

"Oh," she met his gaze.

Tom raked his fingers through his hair and shook his head. "I knew this was coming, but still..."

"I know," Sid said.

Tom dug in his pockets and plunked some coins down on the counter. "Can't believe you're really going."

Sid forced a smile. "I'll miss y'all. A lot."

That Sunday, as parishioners milled about after church, chatting and making their ways to their buggies through the mud, Joshua Smith rode up on his horse.

"There's a war on!" he shouted.

Silence swept through the crowd, as anxious faces turned towards him.

"Confederate troops fired on Fort Sumter on Friday and the Federal garrison replied!" Joshua went on. "Fort Sumter surrendered! War at last!"

He rode away to keep spreading the news. Sid took a deep breath, trying to calm the rush of blood in his ears.

Sarah took Sid's arm gently. He looked up and saw Rachel staring at him. She flushed and looked away for a moment. When she looked back, he tried to smile at her reassuringly. She did not smile in return.

At the dinner table that afternoon, Uncle Daniel talked about the gall of Confederate troops. He shook his head and sighed, putting a forkful of roast beef into his mouth.

Sid cleared his throat. "Now that war's on, I think I'd better leave sooner than planned."

Aunt Sarah looked at him, the lines between her eyebrows deepening. Daniel stopped chewing, but did not look up.

Sidney continued. "I always said I'd stay until spring, or when war started—whichever came first. Now they've both come."

Daniel breathed in deeply. "Did you ever consider that just because you always said something, doesn't mean you have to do it?"

"I'm a man of my word," Sid said. He took a bite of roast potatoes.

"I'm not talking about breaking promises," Daniel said. "I'm just saying that when you make a decision, you might want to have a better reason than always having said you'd do something."

Rhoda picked up her fork, loaded it with meat, then set it down again. "I don't know how a boy like you thinks he can go fight for the South."

"Rhoda, I'm a Southerner."

"No, you ain't!" Rhoda pointed her fork at him. "You're from the South, but you ain't a Southerner, and you know it!"

Aunt Sarah spoke up, her quiet voice steady. "Sidney must do what he thinks is best."

Looking at his aunt, Sid took a breath. He wished he knew what to say to her.

Daniel said, "Of course you'll make your own decision. I just want you to be sure to think it through."

"I have." Sid thought his own voice sounded strangely weak.

Aunt Sarah got up and took the platter of meat and potatoes into the kitchen. Rhoda rose and threw her napkin down next to her plate.

"Time come, you might want to think about someone other than yourself!" She picked up her plate and stalked into the kitchen.

"Rhoda!" Sid stood up and followed her. "You think I haven't? You think this is easy for me? It isn't—"

Sid stopped short when he reached the kitchen and saw his aunt at the sink, back to them, shaking with silent sobs.

"Aunt Sarah!" He went to her and put his arms around her.

"Oh, I'm sorry!" Sarah mopped at her cheeks with her apron. "I knew you'd have to go. I just… it's hard is all."

"I'm sorry," Sid offered feebly.

"You don't need to be sorry," she said. "All boys grow up and leave—I can't imagine what it would feel like if we'd had you for all your eighteen years, instead of just one."

"See what you done," Rhoda mumbled, shaking her cornrows.

"Oh, Rhoda! Stop!" Sarah said. "There's no need for all this fuss. Sidney, please don't worry about me. I didn't mean for you to see me cry. You must know I love you and I'm sorry to see you go."

"I didn't want to hurt you."

"You haven't." Sarah shook her head at him. "Some things just hurt."

Sid went for a walk to get some fresh air. He only made it as far as the carriage house. As he scratched the team between their ears, all he could think about was Rachel. When Aunt Sarah was sick and Rachel had pulled him out onto the porch, he had held her hand longer than she'd wanted him to. And he couldn't forget how it felt. He wanted to hold it for the rest of his life. He had known then that he loved her. He'd been alternately toying with it and running from it ever since.

The black Morgan horse nuzzled Sid's shirt looking for treats. Sid dug in his pocket for some sugar cubes he'd picked up at the store. The horse chomped on one in pleasure.

Sid sighed. "I wish I never promised Catherine I'd come back."

The Morgan cocked its ears.

"I don't even know if she still cares about me," Sid went on. "I could be heading back to Roswell for nothing."

Sid held out his hand, another sugar cube on his palm. The horse took it gently with its lips.

"If she doesn't care about me, maybe Rachel could." Sid shook his head. "I know she must feel something. She has to!"

He was trembling as he left the carriage house. Halfway to Rachel's house, he lost his nerve. He walked around the block and headed home on River Street.

Then Rachel came around the corner in front of him and stood in his path. "Where are you off to, Confederate soldier?"

"I... uh.... Don't call me that." Sid lowered his eyebrows.

"I thought that was your plan."

"I have to talk to you," Sid blurted out.

"What about?" Rachel asked.

Sid put his hand on her elbow and guided her across River Street to the Common. "I'm leaving sooner than I thought."

"I figured that," Rachel said. "Now that war's started."

They found a bench under an oak tree and sat down.

"I want you to be here when I come back." Sid was sure Rachel could hear his heart pounding.

"I'm not going anywhere," Rachel said.

"No, Rachel," Sid took her hand and cleared his throat. "I want you to wait for me."

Rachel stood up abruptly. "I cannot believe you just said that!" She pulled her hand away. "Is that what you did to Catherine? Are you traveling the country, trifling with girls' hearts?"

"No!" Sid stood up. "Listen to me. I don't care about Catherine—except that I feel bad for not caring. And I don't think Catherine cares for me anymore, either."

"You don't think?" Rachel said. "All this time you put on a big show about your beautiful sweetheart down South. Bragging to the boys and flirting with the girls. Do you expect me to fall at your feet now?"

"No." Sid dropped down on the bench again. "I know I'm not good enough for you."

"Then how dare you ask me that!" Rachel crossed her arms, her face flushed.

"I'm leaving tomorrow," Sid said. He could still feel Rachel's hand in his. "I can't stand the thought of never seeing you again."

"Why are you telling me this?" Rachel asked.

"If I knew you cared about me, I would come back," Sid said. "I could make myself worthy of you."

"No. You would go South and fall in love with Catherine all over again."

"I wouldn't!" Sid stood up and reached for Rachel's hand.

She pulled back to avoid his grasp. "Anyway, I don't want someone who has to make himself worthy of me. I want someone who makes choices for the right reasons—not to impress me."

Sid sat down again. "You must think I'm pretty arrogant right now."

"I've always thought you were arrogant."

He rubbed his damp palms on his pant legs, staring at the ground in front of him. He had been foolish to think Rachel could care for him. What would an abolitionist want with a Southern slaveholder?

Rachel sat next to him. "I know you're scared about going South and fighting in the war. And maybe you're afraid things won't be the same with Catherine—"

"I know they won't be the same," Sid said. "Because I'm in love with—"

"What you're doing isn't fair," Rachel interrupted. "You want to have me waiting for you, in case things don't work out with her."

"That's not it at all!" Sid said. "I'm going to end things with her."

"You're going to regret this later, Sid. And then you'll be glad I said no."

Sid looked at her, unbelieving. "Please, Rachel," he breathed. "Say you'll think about it."

"Look, I'm sorry you're leaving. I really am. But let's not make it harder than it is. Okay?" She got up. "I'd better go now. Are you going to be all right?"

Sid shook his head in disbelief.

"I'm sorry," Rachel said. "Please let's still be friends."

"Sure," he said.

She walked away from him, across the Common to the street. Sid was numb. Why had he been so sure she cared about him? He went down to the river and sat on the bank until dark. Then he went back to the house.

He tossed and turned all night. When he slept, it was only to dream of Rachel. He sat alone with her in front of the fire at Tom's aunt's house, the winter storm howling outside. But instead of just sitting in silence, Sidney leaned towards her and kissed her, tasting her lips, her tongue. She pulled away for a moment to say, "Don't go. Stay with me." Sid jolted awake. Angry with himself, he rolled over and tried to sleep again. When Rachel had turned him down, he'd felt numb. But that had worn off. Every time he shut his eyes, Rachel was in his arms, his body against hers. And his anger surged because it couldn't be.

In the morning, he packed up his belongings. Aunt Sarah came into his room with a parcel.

"Here's some lunch for the train ride. Just some ham and a piece of bread. Sidney!" She put her hand to his cheek, looking into his eyes. "Didn't you sleep at all?"

"Not much," he said. "Thanks for the food."

"There's also a book in there I want you to finish," she said.

"What book?" Sid put the parcel into his satchel and fastened it.

"Make sure you return it," Sarah smiled. "That way you'll have to come back and visit us."

Sid grabbed his aunt's hand. "Of course I'll come back to visit!"

"It won't be the same, though," she said. "You've been like a son to us."

It was eleven-thirty and time to leave for the train station. Uncle Daniel strapped Sidney's trunk to the back of the carriage. Aunt Sarah sat on the front seat, smiling. But her face was white. Rhoda stood by the wheel as Sidney approached with his satchel.

"Are you going to the station?" Sid asked her.

She shook her head and Sid saw that her dark brown eyes were full.

"Rhoda," he didn't know what to say.

"I never thought I'd care for you, Mr. Sidney," she said. "Not that first day when you come here! But now you like family—though you won't listen to me!" She gave him a stern look. "I know you'll be back when you come to your senses."

They reached the train station with a little extra time. Tom and Caleb were there, Ruth and Jake, and Atticus. And Rachel. She stood apart from the others and Sid went to her, giving in to his anger.

"Forget what I said yesterday," he said.

Rachel's chin came up. "I already have."

"Good," Sid looked into her eyes, steeling himself. "I didn't know what I was saying. You were right—I was scared things wouldn't be the same with Catherine. But, I think they will be. I think things will be fine."

Rachel's eyes clouded, but she stood straighter. "Good. I wish you all the best." She reached out and shook his hand.

And Sid held it too long. "Write to me."

Rachel withdrew her hand. "Write to me first."

The others crowded in then. It was time to board the train. Tom embraced Sid. Caleb shook his hand and so did Jake and Ruth, wishing him a safe journey and bidding him come back to visit. Atticus gave him a firm, warm handshake and one of his priceless smiles.

He turned to Aunt Sarah. She put her small arms around him.

"Oh, Sidney," she wept. "I wanted to send you off with a smile. But I'm afraid I'm not strong enough."

Sidney's eyes were full as he kissed his aunt. He quickly turned to Daniel, who took his hand in a hearty handshake and said, "Sidney, we'll miss you. I-I'll miss you! And not just your work at the store." He gave him a hug.

"Me too!" was all Sidney could manage.

The whistle blew. He pulled away and stepped onto the train. Turned around for one last wave to the family and friends he had grown to love. He found a seat and watched them as the train jerked into motion, taking him away, back to the South. He had said good-bye. It was final. There was no comfort in this pain. It would always be there. It would travel with him.

After changing trains in Philadelphia, Sid opened his pack and took out the lunch Aunt Sarah had given him. Next to the ham and cold bread was a thin package wrapped in brown paper. Sid opened it to find the journal from the bookcase. He stared. She knew? He turned it over in his hands, wondering. Then he opened it and read the first entry again, about his father leaving for the South. Armed with Aunt Sarah's approval, Sid kept reading. He lost himself in the world of a younger Sarah and Daniel. Their joy emphasized his grief and their pain intensified his own.

fifteen

30 July, 1839

It is wonderful to see Daniel happy in this work. He's never wavered in his devotion to the Railroad. Even when we were courting, he knew it would always be part of his life. He loved me, but he still had to do what was right. It drew me to him even more, to know that he would do the right thing out of the goodness of his heart. His integrity was genuine, not something he put on to impress me. Now I cannot imagine why I ever doubted the righteousness of this cause.

Aunt Sarah's words ran through Sidney's mind as he plodded up the drive to his estate. He reached the great front door of the main house and turned the handle. Then he stood in the doorway, quietly taking in the scene before him. The staircase curved up to the open upstairs hallway. Its mahogany railing was polished to perfection. The marble floor of the foyer shone even more brightly than he remembered. On the right side of the front hall stood the large paneled door to the dining room. On the left, French doors opened into the parlor. Everything looked the same.

Sid looked from the parlor into the drawing room. He saw his mother seated in her chair taking a glass of sweet tea. Her white dress glowed in the sunlight, her dark hair pulled back from her delicate face, her slim figure held in perfect, dignified posture. Her scent, lemons and roses, filled the room. She looked up and smiled when she saw Sidney. Her soft voice floated out to him lovingly.

"Mr. Sidney! I didn' know you was home!"

Sid jumped. A small mulatto woman stood in the parlor.

"Chloe!" Sid swept her into an embrace, lifting her tiny frame off the floor.

"Put me down, Mr. Sidney! I'm too old for you to swing around no more!"

Sidney obeyed her. He always had. "Tall Pine looks beautiful! Just as it did when I left."

"An' you—you's tall and broad like a man." She covered her mouth, her face wrinkling in a thousand familiar places as she held back her emotion. "You gone and growed up!"

Sid laughed. "I think I felt more grown up before I went North."

"It sure is good to see your face," Chloe said. "But how come you didn't tell anyone you were coming home so soon? Miss Catherine said the end of the month."

"I left in a bit of a hurry once I got news of the war," Sid said. "There wasn't time to send word."

"Miss Catherine will be over to check on things sometime soon, I reckon." Chloe drew her eyebrows together as she studied his face. "She always comes on Tuesday afternoons—and Fridays, too. She's sure gonna be surprised to find you here!"

"I'm a mess," Sid said, looking down at his dusty, wrinkled traveling clothes.

"You sure are!" Chloe smiled, shaking her head. "You hurry and get cleaned up before she gets here!"

Sidney rushed up the staircase. As he walked down the hallway towards his bedroom, he reminded himself that Catherine was his only hope now. Then he stopped suddenly and turned.

The door to his father's study was ajar. The record book was lying open on the great ebony desk. David Judson's pipe lay where it so often did when it was not in use. Sidney went to the desk and flipped through the book, full of the finances and inventory of the Roswell Manufacturing Company. Looking up towards the door that led from the study into his parents' bedroom, he saw his father standing, pipe in hand, the smoke curling around his head. His black hair and mustache contrasted starkly with his fair complexion. The gray suit vest and trousers were pressed and spotless. He ran his fingers through his hair in the familiar gesture. Sauntering into the room, one hand in his pocket, the other holding his pipe by his lips, he spoke.

"Sidney, you've got to be more responsible. All you care about is fishing and riding," he paused. "And that silly girl you're pining after. Do you ever have a thought for your mother and me?"

How many times had his father said that to him? Yet he hadn't listened until it was too late. Sidney walked out of the room, closing the door behind him.

❦

Alone in his bedroom, his heart beat furiously. A bath had washed away the dust of his travels. His trunk was still at the station, but he found some good trousers and a shirt and vest, which fit him quite well. He sat on the edge of his bed, rubbing his palms on his trouser legs. What was the use of holding onto Rachel? Perhaps when he saw Catherine the old feelings would come back. He would marry her and then he would go to war. The abolitionists didn't want him anyway, so he might as well fight for people who did. He glanced into the mirror, pleased with his reflection.

He went downstairs. Her voice was coming from the parlor.

"My dear Chloe, do you really need my opinion on your sponge cake? Perhaps I can taste it another time. It's going to make me late for the barbecue."

"I'll go see if it's cool, Miss. I think you'll be glad you waited!"

"Very well."

Chloe came out into the foyer and all but ran into Sid.

She whispered, pointing towards the door, "Go on! She's waiting!"

Sidney walked into the parlor.

"Sidney?" Catherine rose, the porcelain skin over her high cheekbones turning crimson. "Sidney! You're home!"

She went quickly to him and then his arms were around her, holding her tightly. "I'm home," he murmured into her hair.

It smelled like lavender. He kissed her—fiercely, deeply. She drew back a little and looked at him with tears in her eyes.

"How I missed you..." she said.

"Catherine," he whispered. "You're more beautiful than ever! How could I...?"

"What?" She dabbed at her eyes with her handkerchief.

"How could I have stayed away so long?" he finished.

"I don't know." Catherine's lips turned down in a little pout and she patted his shoulder sternly. "Do you still love me after all these months?"

Sidney was breathless. "Of course I do!"

She looked down at her handkerchief, twisting it around her fingers. "Do come to the barbecue! I'm on my way, now. Drew will be there and you haven't seen him yet, have you?"

"No, but I want to see you. Let's stay here, please." He tried to kiss her again, but the pout returned.

"I promised I'd be there. They'll be unhappy if I don't show. That would be most impolite."

Sid sighed. "Yes, I suppose it would."

"Come on! You look dashing." Catherine clapped her hands. "I can't wait till everyone sees you again!"

She led him out the front door. They climbed into her carriage. Her parents' slave, Elijah, cracked the whip and they sprang into motion. Sidney pulled Catherine into his arms, kissing her again.

"Sidney." She sat up and pushed away from him. "You will have to stop this once we get to the party, you know."

"Why do you think I don't want to go?"

She kept back a little. "We must gain our composure."

"If you insist," he slumped back against the carriage seat.

When he held Catherine and kissed her, he could forget his conversation with Rachel. Maybe he had thought something could be better than this, but he was mistaken. He had forgotten the mystery of Catherine's deep blue eyes, the way her lips turned up at the corners, begging to be kissed. Even though he'd spent many lonely evenings trying, he hadn't been able to conjure up the curves her bosom and hips made beneath her dress. Now he remembered why he'd wanted her.

They arrived at the Richardson's estate for the barbecue. When Sidney emerged from the carriage with Catherine, a shout rang out from the boys. Jimmy Richardson ran over to greet him, pumping his hand vigorously.

"You're actually home!" he said.

"I can't believe it!" Drew arrived next to him, pounding Sid on the back.

Jimmy's brother, Sam, joined the group. "We were placing bets on when we'd see you again!"

"Looks like you lost, Drew!" Jimmy said.

Sid forced a jovial-sounding laugh. More boys thronged around him, surprised and expectant. He glanced at them, recognizing most. The pause lengthened.

"Well, it's good to be back!" he said, finally.

Some of the boys murmured in response, nodding.

Then Sid lowered his eyebrows at Drew. "You lost? What was your bet?"

"He bet you'd never come back!" Sam said.

One of the boys yelled, "He hoped!"Others snickered.

"It was just a game." Drew shook his head. "It's good to see you, Sid."

"Are you hungry?" Jimmy asked.

"Starving!" Sid said.

"Come on. Let's get you some food!"

He led the way to a picnic table with an ample spread. While Sidney loaded his plate with fried chicken, baked beans, and corn bread, Jimmy and Drew stayed close to him, asking the details of his arrival. Catherine strolled over to a bench under a tree where several other young ladies sat. Sam took his place on the ground next to one of the girls.

On his way to join Catherine, Sid and his companions were stopped by Charlie McMichaels, a gangly fellow he'd never liked much.

"When'd you get in?" Charlie asked.

"Just this afternoon," Sid replied.

"So you haven't had much time to get reacquainted with everyone, I guess."

"Well, no... but we're old friends—"

"So you think things will be the same as they were."

"For the most part, I expect," Sid said.

"Maybe... maybe..." Charlie stood nodding his head at them.

Sid wondered if it would be impolite to excuse himself. He didn't feel like talking to Charlie. But Charlie just stood there, nodding, and looking from Drew to Sid.

"Well..." Charlie paused. "Don't let me keep you. Drew'll be wanting to get over to Catherine, I reckon." He stepped back.

"You mean—" Sid began.

Charlie guffawed loudly. "I mean 'Sid'! All this time you've been gone, I practically forgot your name and mixed you up with your best friend! Sid will be wanting to join Catherine!" He slapped Sid's back as Sid turned towards Catherine.

"That was strange," Sid mumbled.

Drew chuckled. "He's a strange fellow. That's why we never passed time with him, Sid."

Jimmy ambled along silently. When they reached Catherine, the boys sat on a few logs placed strategically around her bench. Sid ate quietly, making polite conversation when required. At the end of an hour, he felt strained and exhausted.

Drew and Sid left early and accompanied Catherine home. In the carriage, Drew leaned over and slapped Sid's leg.

"It's good to have you back!" he said.

"Good to be back."

It was his same old friend. Surely he could be himself with Drew.

Sidney paid his respects to Catherine's parents, who greeted him politely and said they were glad to see him back in town. Then he and Drew took some of the Rushton's horses for a ride between the Judson and Rushton estates. They galloped through the open fields near Drew's stables, but when they reached the woods around Peachtree Creek, they slowed to a walk to give the horses a break.

"You haven't told me much about your time up North," Drew said. "You make any friends up in Yankee territory?"

"Sure," Sid nodded. "Quite a few."

"I guess I figured that, since you were gone so long." Drew shook his head. "What could you have in common with Yankees?"

"More than you'd think," Sid said. "It's not like everyone goes around preaching against the South all the time. They have lives just like we do."

Drew chuckled. "You're awful high and mighty."

"I don't mean to be," Sid said.

"You've seen the world." Drew guided his horse across the creek, Sid close behind. "While I've been left in the dust."

He turned and looked at Sid with a smirk. The horses trotted out of the water and up the bank.

"I won't be left behind for long, though," Drew continued. "I've been thinking about going to college."

"Really?" Sid was amazed.

"I'd have to make something of myself eventually. I guess I realized that while you were gone."

"Good for you."

"The University of Georgia will have to wait till we drive those damn Yankees off our land, though."

Sid grunted.

"Shouldn't take long," Drew said.

They had reached the edge of the woods and Drew dug his heels into his horse's flanks.

When they finished their ride, Sidney went home to bed. It was the first time he had slept in his old room since that terrible time following the death of his parents. It was strange and awful to lie down in the bed again. And sleep took a long time to come.

On Thursday night Sidney went with Catherine and Drew to see Thomas R.R. Cobb speak at a patriotic meeting in Atlanta. As Cobb expounded on the righteousness of the Cause and the justness of slavery, the fervor in the room increased.

"We must not allow the North to destroy our way of life!" Cobb said. "We must unite against the powers that be!"

The young men cheered in response. Wanting to appear concerned about the Cause, Sid stood to applaud as the speech came to a close.

The excitement among Sid's friends lingered as the young people gathered at Catherine's home for a bon fire. There was shouting and laughter. When Drew got up on the back of a wagon to give his own speech, the boys got even more fired up.

"We will not let the Yankees destroy our way of life!" shouted Drew. "We will fight! We will die for the Cause!"

Cobb's speech had stirred memories in Sid's heart—old times living the beautiful life of the South. Yet he felt nothing near the enthusiasm of the other boys. He wandered away from the crowd and sat down by a tree at the edge of the backyard. Before long, Drew was beside him.

"What's the matter? All that time up North make your Southern blood run cold?"

"Never!" Sid laughed. "Guess I'm just tired from my trip."

Drew paused for a moment. "You always were the thoughtful type—but you seem even quieter now. You're not very excited about this war, are you?"

Sid ran his fingers through his hair and sighed. "I'm not thrilled about killing other humans."

"You didn't used to be bothered by the prospect," Drew countered.

"Maybe I was a better actor then," Sid suggested. "Or maybe since I didn't know any Northerners, killing them didn't seem like such a bad thing."

"I knew it!" Drew said. "You are a Yankee!"

"No I'm not!" Sid protested. "I'm still a Southerner. I'm just a little more sober about it. Maybe you should think about what war really means yourself. We might die. Both of us. All of us boys might die. What happens to our women if we can't hold off the Yankees."

"They won't set a toenail on our land!" Drew picked up a stone and pounded it against the dirt.

"You hope!" Sid said. "Anyway, I'm not a Yankee."

"We'll see," Drew said. Then looked sidewise at Sid. "I have to know something, though."

"What's that?" Sid asked.

"What are you planning on doing about Catherine?"

"Same thing I always was." Sid wrinkled his forehead. "Why?"

"Well, you just seem to be taking your time." Drew shrugged. "When you were gone, she had a rough patch there at first."

"I know I wasn't good to her while I was gone." Sid looked down. "I can do much better than that."

"I sure hope so," Drew mumbled.

"What are we doing tomorrow night?" Sid asked.

"Didn't Catherine tell you? The Confederate Ball is tomorrow."

"She probably told me. But everything she says tends to run together, especially when it concerns galas and barbecues and balls."

Drew laughed, nodding.

"That's perfect, though," Sid said. "Tomorrow at the Ball—I'll ask her then."

"You're planning to propose." Drew looked at him.

"Yes," Sid said, getting up to rejoin the crowd at the fire. "You said yourself I've been taking my time. I'd better get a move on."

The rest of the evening, Sid pushed away his uncertainties, giving in to excitement over the upcoming proposal. He shunned every thought of his life in the North and joined in the fun, even sharing a flask of whiskey with Jimmy Richardson.

The next morning, Chloe showed Drew into the dining room just as Sid was sitting down to breakfast.

"Would you like something to eat?" Sid asked him.

Drew shook his head. "I ate already. Hurry up and finish your breakfast."

"Hurry up?" Sid cut into a sausage link. "Why?"

"It's time to sign up. You and me, Sid—we're going to the recruitment office today."

Sid almost choked on the sausage. "Today? What's the rush?"

Drew stared at Sid. "Can you honestly tell me you're not fired up at all after seeing Cobb last night? We have to stop those Yanks now!"

"Oh, I… I see the need. Yes. I just—"

"Fine. I'll go without you." Drew stood up. He pointed a finger at Sid. "You are proving to me that you're one of them."

"Calm down," Sid said. "I'm going to sign up. Let me finish my breakfast."

Drew sat down again, scowling. Sid was not eager to sign up. He had known he wouldn't be, but it had always been a moment in the future. He tried to calm himself. He was not at the office yet. He would just go along with Drew and see what happened.

They walked into town together. Drew sullen. Sid silent. They reached the recruiting station and waited in line behind a few boys who looked to be about fifteen. The officer turned them away. Drew stepped up to the desk.

"Can you believe that?" the officer said. "They tried to tell me they were nineteen. They don't even have peach fuzz. You fellows, on the other hand, look like the kind of men we need. You ready to sign up?"

"I am," Drew said. "This one's yellow."

Sid froze. "I'm not yellow, Drew."

"Call it what you want—I call it yellow." Drew chuckled as he signed his name, explaining to the officer. "He spent almost a year up North. Now he's scared to shoot a Yankee."

"I'm not scared."

"Prove it!" Drew stepped back and motioned for Sid to go up to the desk.

Sid was furious. "I don't have to prove anything to you!" he muttered.

"Then you're proving me right," Drew said.

"Maybe I just want to think about it some more."

"And sign up next week?"

"Maybe"

"Then you'll be in a different regiment. All our friends are signing up now. You know that."

Sid suddenly felt alone. He had always planned to fight for the South. If he thought about it more, he would likely sign up eventually.

Drew put his hand on Sid's shoulder and guided him up to the desk. Sid took the pen. He drew in a sharp breath as he watched his black scrawl appear on the line.

The boys walked home in silence. Sid was afraid to think about what he had done.

When Sidney reached home, he went to his mother's room. Last year he had planned to give Catherine the emerald ring passed down from his mother's grandmother. He found it right where he had expected it to be in its small velvet pouch. He carefully hid it away in his pocket.

As he left the room, he heard a voice in his mind, "You'll go South and fall in love with Catherine all over again."

He stopped in the hallway and shook his head. Why should he care what Rachel had said? Anyway, if she had accepted him, he wouldn't be… but he didn't finish the thought. Instead he went to his father's study and took a swig from the flask of whiskey stashed in a drawer.

That evening, Sid settled into the back of Drew's family carriage. They headed to the Cartland estate to pick up Catherine and her cousin, Minnie.

"So how come you have to escort Catherine's cousin to the Ball?" Sid asked. "Still haven't managed to snag a decent girl?"

Drew laughed. "What do you know about it? I've had my share."

The boys got out to help the girls board the carriage. Sid took his seat next to Catherine. "You look beautiful!"

She wore a mint green chiffon gown, with a hooped skirt and a fitted bodice that plunged at the neckline to show off her bosom. Her golden tresses were swept off her neck and fell in a cascade of curls over the crown of her head.

He leaned over to kiss her, but she held him back, "Stop—you'll muss my skirts."

She smiled as he sulked. "You look quite dashing yourself."

Minnie and Catherine chatted all the way into Atlanta. Sid responded politely when necessary, but most of the time he just gazed at Catherine.

The Confederate Ball was held at City Hall. The proud stripes of the flag of the Confederacy covered the walls. Young and old alike milled about, greeting each other as they waited for the dancing to begin. Sid and Drew went to get some punch for the ladies.

A hand came out of nowhere and slapped Sid on the back. It was Jimmy Richardson. Sam was close behind him.

"How go things on the far side of Roswell?" Jimmy asked. "Any news?"

"No news," Drew responded.

They started back to the ladies with two glasses of punch each. Sam asked, "No movement of the troops?"

"Well," Sid said. "Drew and I did sign up today."

"That's the spirit!" Jimmy said. "So did we!"

"Frank and George did as well," Sam said. "Everyone we've talked to so far. No one could resist after that inspiring speech last night."

"Guess not," Sid agreed. He sipped his punch and started back across the room.

"Aren't you excited?" Sam quickened his step to walk alongside him.

Drew laughed. "Don't mind Sid. He's just a little preoccupied with Catherine."

"Oh." Sam fell back to walk with Drew and Jimmy.

Sid pushed through the crowd and caught sight of Catherine. She stood next to Minnie, perfectly poised, holding her pocket fan coyly over her bosom as she waved it ever so slightly. Minnie made a comment, inaudible to Sid. Catherine laughed, casting a scornful look towards another girl. Then she tossed her head and whispered something back to Minnie. Her gaze met Sidney's and her blue eyes were empty.

Suddenly he knew he couldn't do it.

The band struck up a waltz. Catherine floated towards him and took one of the glasses of punch.

"Is this for me?" she said, sipping it.

Sid nodded. "Why don't we get some fresh air?"

Her lips turned down. "I thought we were going to dance—just like old times."

"Not just yet." Sidney led her out into the garden. She sat in a wrought-iron chair. Sid leaned against a lamppost.

"Sidney, I really want to go in with the others," Catherine said.

"I need to talk to you about something."

He took her hand and she rose to stand in front of him.

"I've been so much less than you deserve..." he began.

"Sidney," Catherine said. "Before you go any further, I need to tell you something."

"Let me finish, please."

"No," her voice was insistent. "I know what you're going to say and I don't want you to go on!"

"What?" Sid drew back and looked at her in surprise. "I don't even know how I'm going to say this—"

"Just listen, please!" she fidgeted with his hands as she spoke haltingly, unable to meet his gaze. "You were gone so long and you didn't write—hardly at all. I thought you'd found someone else. I don't... Oh blast! I don't love you anymore! I've changed... We've both changed... And we shouldn't be together."

Sidney stared, surprised that it hurt to hear the words. "I was going to say the same thing."

"You were?" Catherine looked up at him. "But Drew said—" She stopped, frozen.

"Drew said what? That I was going to propose!?" Sid pulled his hands away from her.

"Well, yes," Catherine said.

"What right did he have to tell you that? Is he your spy?"

"He just wanted to warn me," she said.

"Well, he was wrong," Sid said. "I realized something tonight. I don't love you. At least we both feel the same way."

"Oh, Sid!" Catherine burst into tears.

Sid pulled her to him, gently rubbing her back.

"I'm sorry," he said. "I'm sorry I didn't write. I wasn't fair to you."

"I was so afraid I'd hurt you tonight."

"Well, it doesn't exactly feel good." He offered her his handkerchief. "But I wish you'd done it sooner."

She wiped her tears away and quieted her sobs. "I'm all right," she said.

Sid nodded. He felt horrible. But he knew seeing the emerald on Catherine's finger would feel worse.

"Would you still like to dance?" he asked. "For old times sake?"

"I think I would." She smiled through her tears and took his arm.

sixteen

WHEN Sid awoke on the day after the Confederate Ball, he had no desire to rise. Without Catherine as a distraction, he had nothing to contemplate but the bleak reality of life without Rachel.

He rummaged in his nightstand for some writing paper.

My dearest Rachel,

I don't presume to think I could ever be worthy of you, but I had to let you know how wrong you were about Catherine and me. I am not in love with her. Last night I ended our relationship, just as I told you I would. I wish I had done it long ago. Then perhaps you would have been willing to consider me. I never loved any woman the way I love you.

Sid paused, reading over the letter. Chloe knocked on his bedroom door.

"Mr. Drew's here, sir," she called from the other side.

"I'll be right down," he replied, as he pulled on some trousers. He folded the letter and put it into his pocket.

When Sid emerged into the drawing room, Drew stood at one of the tall windows, looking out into the pine trees sheltering the west side of the house.

"I can't believe you're out calling this early," Sid said.

Drew turned. "Actually, I never went to bed."

Sid poured some gin into two tumblers and offered one to Drew, who waved it away and took a seat on the sofa.

Chloe came in with a silver tray holding an envelope.

"A message came for you this morning, Mr. Sidney."

Sid paused, mid-sip. "Thank you, Chloe."

He took the envelope and read the cover:

"Confederate States of America.

War Department.

Official Business."

It was his call-up notice. He scanned the letter quickly. He was to present himself in Augusta on April 26th.

He looked at Drew. "Did you get your notice?"

"That's why I'm here." Drew spread his arms out on the back of the sofa. "It greeted me at my front door when I stumbled home an hour ago. Pretty quick, huh?"

"Yeah. I guess you're happy about that."

"I'm not thrilled about leaving home, Sid. But I do want to fight for the Cause."

"Oh, yes," Sid said, placing the letter on the mantel. "Good ole' Cause. Worth dying for, I guess. Especially since I have nothing to live for."

"Come on," Drew started.

"I'm sure you know what happened last night." Sid sat down on the armchair opposite the sofa. "You seem to communicate much better with Catherine than I ever did."

Drew was silent.

"Why'd you tell her I was going to propose?"

Drew turned his eyes to the window, avoiding Sid's gaze. "It seemed like a brash move on your part, since you'd only been back a few days. I thought a little warning might be apropos."

"It would have been brash. Did she tell you I didn't propose?"

"She said she stopped you."

Sid chuckled, shaking his head. "I should have known Catherine's pride would keep her from admitting I broke it off myself."

Drew finally met his eyes. "You?"

"We agreed to part ways—amicably."

"Oh," Drew said. "Look, I'm sorry about all this."

"I'll be fine," Sid said. "I still have your friendship, right?"

"Of course." Drew rose and went back to the window. "Did you see the newspaper this morning? There are riots in Baltimore."

"No," Sid said. "What about?"

"Maryland's still on the fence, you know. I guess no one warned them about some Union troops passing through on their way to Washington."

"I see."

"Four soldiers killed," Drew went on. "That's all the article said."

"Hmmm..." Maryland was far away.

"Some of the troops are from Pennsylvania."

Sid sat upright in his chair. "What?"

Drew chuckled. "You don't have any friends fighting for the Union, do you?"

Sid shook his head. "Not that I know of."

"I know I don't." Drew turned his steel grey eyes to Sid. "Anyway, we leave next Friday. Just wanted to see if you got your papers, too."

"Thanks," Sid said. "I guess it's really happening, isn't it?"

"Looks that way." Drew punched Sid's shoulder on the way out. "See you later."

For the next week, Sidney tried to think as little as possible of women or war. Instead, he wrapped up affairs at Tall Pine.

He sent for Mr. Pierson, the overseer Hattie and Lem had complained about. He joined Sidney in the drawing room and took the glass of sweet tea Chloe offered him.

"I wondered when you'd be calling for me," Pierson said, leaning back in the leather armchair.

"Is that right?" Sid asked. "Why?"

"Well, I thought you'd want to know how things have gone during your absence."

"I already know a bit," Sid said. "You might have noticed you're missing a few darkies."

Pierson shifted his weight. "About that… I couldn't keep those two rascals down. They was ornery from the first day I started."

"I don't want excuses," Sid said. "I don't know if you heard the news, but they're free now."

"I did hear some gossip to that end."

"And so are you." Sid looked him squarely in the eyes.

"Excuse me, sir?"

"You're free to go," Sid said. "I won't be needing your services anymore."

"Now just you wait a minute. You can't blame those escapes on me. It ain't my fault."

"Like hell it isn't," Sid said. "I hear how you've been treating the darkies. That's not how we do things here."

"I ain't mistreated no darky."

"You can go now," Sid said. "I don't want to see you on my property again."

"Yes, sir." Pierson slammed his half-empty glass down and stalked out the door.

Sid rested his head in his hands.

The next afternoon, he met with his father's attorney, Charles Cardwell.

"Are you sure this is what you want?" Mr. Cardwell asked. "I don't think your father would approve."

"My father isn't here to give us his opinion, so I must do what I think is best."

"And what if Chloe and George won't stay on for the pension you're suggesting?"

"I'll hire a few new hands. But I don't think it will be a problem."

"This is unprecedented—a young man leaving to fight for the Confederacy, and freeing his slaves first?"

"What can I say?" Sid asked. "My circumstances are not the same as others. I'm not leaving any womenfolk at the estate."

"Then sell the slaves and invest the money."

"I've made my decision, Mr. Cardwell."

Sidney had Attorney Cardwell's page deliver the papers to the slaves. He wanted no accolades. That evening after supper, Sid sat in his father's study upstairs, thumbing through the record book and making some notes of his own. Chloe came to him, her paper in her trembling hand.

"Mr. Sidney, I don't understand."

"You're free," Sid said.

"Haven't I always been a good servant, sir?"

"Of course! No one could ask for a better nurse—and the way you keep this house is impeccable."

"But I don't want to go!"

"I hoped you wouldn't. All the slaves are free to stay until they find better positions. And I want you and George to stay on here to take care of things."

"I see that. But I always been here taking care of things. You don't gotta pay me, sir."

"Yes, I do, Chloe." Sid leaned back in his father's chair, running his fingers through his hair. "You might not understand, but it's only right to pay you for your work. I've never thought of you as my property. I wish I had enough to reimburse you for your years of loyal service."

"Now, don't you talk nonsense, Mr. Sidney! This is the kindest thing any white folk ever done for me. You make me proud." Tears spilled over onto her cheeks. "Lord, you make me wish you was my own son."

Sid went and put his arms around her.

"Me and George'll take real good care of the place."

Sid slept better that night than he had since arriving in the South.

That Friday Sidney left for the war. Plenty of other boys from the Atlanta area had enlisted and were also leaving to become part of the Third and Fourth regiments of Georgia. They would rendezvous in Augusta and then go on to Richmond, Virginia to be organized. Chloe went with Sidney to the train station, but stayed at the carriage after giving him a tearful hug. He walked up onto the platform, weaving his way through the crowd until he found Drew.

"Hello." Drew's voice was flat.

"Good morning," Sid returned.

Catherine stood next to Drew, their hands twined together.

Sid's breath caught in his throat. He looked up and Catherine's eyes met his. Her face grew crimson. She took her hand out of Drew's and folded it with the other over the ivory handle of her parasol.

Sidney edged away from them, his heart racing. When it was time to board the train, he sat alone until Drew found him and sat beside him.

"I haven't seen much of you this week," Drew said.

"Looks like you've been a little busy."

"Did you really think she'd wait around for you all those months?" Drew asked.

"Why not?" Sid gritted his teeth.

"I'm not saying it's impossible," Drew admitted. "Plenty of girls wait for their beaux, but their beaux usually keep in touch a little better than you."

Sid stared hard at the floor boards, his ears burning with shame.

"She tried to resist me. She really did. But she had to give in eventually."

"I don't have to listen to this!" Sid started up.

"Take it easy, Sid!" Drew grabbed his arm and pulled him down onto the seat again. "You really had no idea?"

Sid was silent. He could have guessed if he'd wanted to.

Drew shook his head. "You'll find another girl—maybe several. I hear soldiers can have all they want."

"I don't want those kinds of girls," Sid said.

"It's amazing what a broken heart does to the best of men." Drew yawned.

"My heart isn't broken over Catherine," Sid said. "I told you I ended it myself."

"Well, you ought to be congratulating me then, I guess!"

"Forgive my rudeness," Sid scoffed. "Anyway, what makes you think she'll wait for you?"

"She has to." Drew smirked. "She's my wife."

Sid's jaw dropped in disbelief. "Since when?"

"Just last night. Sorry we didn't invite you, but we didn't think you'd come. And it was a small affair—just a few of us in Catherine's parlor."

Sid forced himself to breathe steadily. He got up and this time Drew let him sidle past. Sid sat by himself on the opposite side of the train car.

The regiments arrived in Augusta by evening and lodged in a camp at the edge of town. Sid wandered the tent rows until he saw a boy he didn't know stowing his belongings in one of the tents. He dropped his satchel on the ground in front of him. The boy looked up. He was pale, with flaxen hair.

"You have a tent-mate yet?" Sid asked.

The boy shook his head. Sidney introduced himself, offering his hand.

"Roger Williams," the boy replied, barely looking up as he shook it.

"Where're you from?" Sid asked.

"Marietta."

"I didn't think I'd seen you before. I'm from Roswell."

Sidney and Roger left their things in the tent and joined some other fellows at the campfire.

Drew was there, talking to Charlie McMichaels loudly as Sid walked up.

"Catherine and I tied the knot yesterday!" He glanced at Sid and lowered his voice.

A few of the other boys snickered.

"Guess he showed you, Sid," one of them said.

At the other end of the circle, Jimmy and Sam Richardson made room for Sid and introduced themselves to Roger.

"The jokes will stop if you don't pay them mind," Jimmy said to Sid.

The Richardson brothers told him that members of the regiment were stationed throughout the city. Once the whole regiment arrived and was accounted for, they would continue on their journey to Virginia. Sam took out a flask and offered it to Sid, then Roger.

"Blackjack, anyone?" Jimmy pulled out a deck of cards and began dealing them.

"Sure," Sid agreed.

The four of them played cards late into the evening.

The next morning, the men were assembled in a common area and a Captain William Musgrove announced that the governor had directed him to take command of the companies rendezvousing in Augusta. A few other officers assisted him in passing out uniforms. Each new soldier received a dark blue jacket and trousers, ankle-high boots and a kepi as well as a belt. Sid fingered the Georgia oval belt buckle for a moment. Then an officer thrust a weapon at him.

Sidney stood holding his uniform in a bundle under one arm and an Enfield Rifle Musket in the other hand. When the companies were dismissed, Jimmy and Sam walked back to camp with Sid and Roger.

"Can you believe this?" Jimmy exclaimed. "Our very own muskets!"

"You didn't think they'd send us to war without weapons, did you?" Sam shook his head.

"Don't pretend you're not excited," Jimmy shot back.

The four boys paused by Sid's and Roger's tent to examine their guns.

Sid put his finger inside the end of the barrel to feel the rifling.

"I heard talk of these," Roger said. "They'll shoot a target at 500 yards."

Jimmy let out a low whistle. "Fine weapon, if you ask me."

Nodding, Sid pulled the hammer back and put the gun to his shoulder. In spite of his distaste for the idea of fighting for the Confederacy, he found himself reluctant to stow his weapon. He lingered at the tent after he'd changed into his uniform, enjoying the feel of the smooth wooden gun in his hands.

He heard steps approaching and quickly put the musket aside before opening the tent flap. A darky stood in front of him, holding a basket. The aroma of fresh, hot cornbread wafted into the tent.

"Private Sidney Judson?" the Negro asked.

"Yes," Sid stepped out of the tent.

"A gift from the Misses Anderson." He handed the basket to Sidney.

"Thank you." Sid didn't know what to say.

"The ladies ask you to dine at their home this evening, if'n it suits you."

Sid thought the cornbread tasted as good as Chloe's. If courtesy hadn't demanded it, curiosity alone would have prompted him to attend the meal. He took Roger with him. A Negro maid showed them into the parlor, where two young women sat with their mother. All three of them rose to greet the boys.

"I am Mrs. Giles Anderson." The mother took their hands with a smile. Her graying brown hair was swept up into a bun. "I heard a company from Roswell arrived and I took the liberty of looking up your name, Sidney. I'm so glad to see you."

"And I you, ma'am," Sidney returned, still uncertain of their relationship.

"Your mother was my first cousin."

"Oh!" Sid took a deep breath. "Have we met before?"

"No, dear. Though I did send my condolences when I heard of my cousin's unfortunate passing."

"Yes," Sid said. "Thank you. I thought your name was familiar."

It was a lie, but he felt he must say something. The rest of the evening, however, conversation flowed easily. Only polite replies were required in response to her animated daughters, Elsie and Sadie. The food was delicious—everything from cream soup to prime rib, ending with a mixed berry cobbler. Elsie and Sadie peppered the boys with questions about life in the army, gushing with praise for their bravery. The girls' cheeks were rosy and their brown curls shone in the candlelight.

So far the war had meant only camaraderie and admiration for these boys. For the time being Sid was content to steer clear of Drew, playing cards and sipping whiskey in the evenings. In the mornings, the troops assembled for drills at Captain Musgrove's command. They were expected to learn to load and fire their weapons three times in one minute. Afternoons were free, and the boys often organized a game of rounders.

Sid found flirting with the Anderson girls a pleasant diversion. They turned out to watch the rounders games, cheering for Sid when he was at bat. Their mother invited Sid and Roger to dine with them often.

When Roger wrote home to his family, Sid wrote to Sarah and Daniel. He wrote to Tom. He thought of writing to Rachel, but didn't know how to finish the letter he had begun. He carried it in his satchel, waiting for the right words to come to him.

When Captain Musgrove collected his letters for the post, he glanced at the addresses. "Pennsylvania? What are you writing to Pennsylvania for?"

"Relatives, sir," Sidney explained.

"You have relatives in the North?" The Captain lowered his eyebrows and squinted at Sid.

"A few, sir." Sid flushed, scrambling for an explanation. "But I have relatives here, too. In Augusta. I don't need to write them because I see them every day now."

"You don't mind if we read these, then? Standard policy."

"Yes, Captain. I have nothing to hide."

Those were the only letters he sent North from Augusta. He didn't want to arouse any more suspicion.

In a matter of days they left for Richmond. A crowd of townspeople came to the depot to see them off. Elsie and Sadie stood with their mother on the platform, dabbing at their eyes with lace handkerchiefs. They kissed Sidney and promised to write to him. The soldiers boarded the train, shouldering their weapons. Every town through which they traveled turned out to cheer them on. As they passed out of Georgia, Sid observed a banner at a station that read, "God guard and bless our Southern boys." Turning to Roger, he saw tears running down his cheeks.

Roger brushed them away, apologizing. "It's my mama. I know she's missing me. I know she's praying."

Sid swallowed hard, fighting the lump in his throat as he thought of Aunt Sarah.

Then Drew stood up in the front of their rail car and boomed out, "Three cheers for our President, Jefferson Davis!"

The windows shook in their casings at their enthusiastic replies. Tears were forgotten and fear held at bay.

Before crossing the Virginia border, the boys discovered that the Governor had directed them to go to the Norfolk and Portsmouth area instead of Richmond. The Norfolk navy yard had been abandoned by the Federals towards the end of April, so the Confederates were free to move in. General Musgrove had not yet arrived. In the absence of orders the soldiers roamed the area, finding their own campsites. Sid and Roger pitched their tent in the navy yard, where most of the other boys were congregating. Then they ventured out to tour Norfolk with Jimmy and Sam.

As they headed away from the bay, they passed a group of ladies in front of a dress shop. Sidney nodded to them with a smile. None of them smiled in return. Rather, they turned away and the boys heard urgent whispering as they passed. They came upon a fish market and stopped to look for something they might cook for tea. The vendor, a weathered man with an uneven beard, glared at them over his pipe as they looked up and down the row of flounder, mackerel, and halibut. A middle-aged couple came along presently and began perusing the fish as well. Sid looked up just in time to see the woman poke her husband in the ribs and point to the boys.

"Oh, blast!" the man burst out. "Why don't you boys go back where you came from?"

The couple hurried down the street, leaving Sidney and his friends to look at each other in wonder.

"What the devil was that about?" Jimmy voiced the question they were all thinking.

The vendor spoke up. "You're not wanted here."

"But why?" Sam asked. "The people of Augusta loved us."

"You're not in Georgia anymore." He shook his head, removing his pipe from his mouth. "The Yanks deserted this town only a few days ago. They might come back anytime. We don't want any scuffles around Norfolk."

Their mood dampened, the boys returned to camp and quietly cooked some mackerel over the fire. Most of the soldiers kept to the navy yard after that.

In May, after Captain Musgrove had arrived, the soldiers elected officers. When the results were announced, Drew had been elected 2nd Lieutenant of their company. The boys settled into training. In addition to daily drills, they were put to work removing the many cannon the Yankees had left in the navy yard. They were crumbling with age and unfit to be used.

Later that month, Colonel Wright assembled the regiment and announced that they were to meet the enemy. A thrill went through the camp. Jimmy Richardson, standing next to Sid, murmured, "We'll kick their sorry asses!" Sid tried not to think about what they would face, he just followed orders as they set out on a short train ride to a nearby town with several companies of the Third Georgia. But they did not meet the enemy that day, or the next. A more thorough scouring of the area found that the report had been false and there were no Yankees there at all. Sidney hid his relief from his companions, nodding in agreement with their loud complaints.

A few days later, on May 23rd, Virginia voted for secession, cementing its place as a Confederate State. News of the war came faster. As the soldiers were breaking for their midday meal on Friday, a Confederate cavalryman rode into the camp. His horse was sweaty and foaming at the mouth from galloping. Colonel Wright, standing near Sid and Roger, stepped out and took the reins as the soldier slowed his horse to a stop.

"Where's the General?" the cavalryman panted.

"General Gwynn!" the Colonel shouted.

The General emerged from the officers' tent. "What news?"

"The Yankees invaded Virginia, sir," the soldier relayed. "Alexandria has been taken."

General Gwynn chewed on the end of his pipe. "Casualties?"

"Very few, sir. Only a few shots were fired." The cavalryman produced a sealed letter. "This is for you."

The General took the envelope and opened it, scanning the letter quickly. "All right," he nodded to the horseman. "We'll stand by for further orders."

That weekend, the boys were on edge, most hoping a real battle was in sight. Sidney was uncomfortable, and relieved when most of the excitement had subsided by Monday.

seventeen

THE next afternoon, Sidney overheard the Captain telling Drew that postal ties with the Union were to be cut off at the end of May. He took some paper with him to the camp-fire that evening, thinking he really ought to risk one last letter to Sarah and Daniel.

My Dear Aunt and Uncle,

I've missed you terribly these past few weeks. I would have written more often, but feared the officers' disapproval. I hardly know what to write as I've learned little of what war really is. We have yet to enter any battle. Virginia recently approved secession. Most of the boys were happy about that. At least we're officially camping in friendly territory now. It seems our country really is split in two.

Sidney stopped. He had been about to write that the Confederate capital was to be moved to Richmond, but that would surely get his letter confiscated. He instead shared some details of camp life, how the cooking was nothing like Sarah's and Rhoda's and he longed for a real bed.

Please give my regards to everyone in town and tell them I think of them often. I can only pray that this war won't keep us apart longer than I can bear.

Your loving nephew,

As Sid signed the letter, he became aware of Drew's eyes on him. He was sitting across the fire. All the others had retired for the night. Sid looked up.

"Who're you writing to?" Drew asked.

"My aunt and uncle," Sid answered.

"Ah—one more letter North, eh?"

"I lived there for a year. I think they might want to know how I'm doing."

"You know you're not supposed to talk about the relocation of the capitol?"

"I know."

"We hoped it would secure Virginia as a Confederate State," Drew spat towards the fire. "Seems we've succeeded."

"You say 'we' as though you were involved in the decision." Sid smirked as he folded the letter into its envelope.

Drew said. "You wish you'd been elected like me."

"No." Sid got up to leave. "I wouldn't be able to stand myself if I were like you."

Drew was silent as Sid went back to his tent.

In early June, General Gwynn gave orders for three companies of the Third Georgia to cross Hampton Roads Bay and march North. Colonel D.H. Hill of the First North Carolina had asked for reinforcements at Big Bethel. Sidney's company was among the troops chosen to come to their aid. Long before dawn on Saturday, June 8th, Captain Musgrove woke the soldiers. Sid and Roger grabbed their satchels and joined the other boys boarding rowboats at the water's edge. They marched into Colonel Hill's camp soon after the sun rose.

Hill immediately put the boys to work alongside his men, helping to build defenses against the enemy's anticipated attack.

Sid pushed his sleepiness aside and worked hard with the other soldiers. Sometime after the noon meal, two Confederate scouts galloped into the camp. Colonel Hill walked from the defenses to meet the scouts at his headquarters by the road.

Sidney set down his rock on top of the entrenchment and turned to Roger. "What do you think that's all about?"

Roger shrugged. "Maybe the Yanks are coming."

Drew, on the other side of the wall, stood up. "I hope we get to help rout 'em!"

Sid wiped his sleeve across his forehead and squinted at Colonel Hill, talking to the two riders.

"Let's go down there," Jimmy said. "Make sure we get in on this."

Most of the boys had stopped working now and were watching the Colonel, who had turned to talk to some of the other officers.

"No," Drew said. "Wait for orders. Being hotheaded won't make a good impression."

They watched for a few moments. Then Captain Musgrove detached himself from the group of officers and walked quickly up towards his company working on the hill. The boys gathered together as he approached.

"See? What did I say?" Drew said. "We're going to kill some Yankees today."

The boys straightened as the Captain arrived, pausing to catch his breath. "The Federals are advancing. We've been ordered to join with some of the other troops to pursue the enemy."

Sid's heart began to pound. He expected to hear cheers from the other boys, but when he stole a sideways glance at those closest to him, their eyes were as fearful as his own must be.

"We'll be under the command of Lieutenant-Colonel Lee, of the First North Carolina," the Captain went on. "So, get your muskets and assemble on the road by Colonel Hill's headquarters."

The boys scrambled for their guns and joined the other men meeting on the road. Major Randolph directed some soldiers rolling a howitzer cannon into place. Lieutenant-Colonel Lee rode up on his horse and motioned for them to follow him. They marched off at a quick pace, Lee and a few other officers circling them on horseback, Randolph's men pushing the cannon. Sid's musket kept slipping in his sweaty palm. He adjusted it as they marched. After a while, Major Randolph rode to the back of the troops to report to Lieutenant-Colonel Lee. Moments later, Lee commanded them to halt and assume the formation.

Sid, toward the front of the assembly, found himself in a line of men. Lee called out the command to load their weapons. Sid opened a cartridge and poured the gunpowder down the barrel as he'd practiced so many times during drills. He was trembling, but he drew the rammer and finished loading as fast as he could. Then he saw them in the distance—Union blue uniforms, advancing towards them down the road.

"Fire at will!" Lee commanded.

The air was suddenly filled with the sound of gunfire. The Union party stopped their advance and attempted forming a line. Sidney fired and reloaded as if controlled by some other force. The canon boomed out from behind him. Suddenly the Yanks were retreating. A river of blue streamed away from the steady rebel line.

"Charge!" Lee cried.

The boys began running, muskets ready, chasing the Federals down the road. They didn't stop until the Yankees had run across New Market Bridge, miles north of Bethel.

As he caught his breath on the march back to camp, Sidney reflected on the fact that his first skirmish had lasted the better part of a minute. He was glad it was over. Now he knew he could fight if called upon, and yet he dreaded the next time even more.

As they continued building entrenchments later in the afternoon, a scout reported another marauding party of Yankees just a mile away. This time, other companies were called upon to chase them back into their own territory.

That evening, Colonel Magruder arrived at Bethel and assumed command of the troops. Drew stopped by their campfire later and related a conversation among the officers to Sam, Jimmy, Roger and Sid. He told how Hill had described their day to Magruder.

"He told him about the Yanks," Drew said. "He was pretty proud of us, too. He called this last attack 'the second race on the same day over the New Market course, in both of which the Yankees reached the goal first.'"

The boys laughed.

Monday morning, Colonel Magruder woke the camp early, while it was still dark. The boys were to advance on the enemy. Sidney fell into line, next to Roger. Jimmy and Sam were right behind him; Drew somewhere ahead, with the other officers in their company. To their left marched another company. A man Sidney didn't recognize looked up and smiled brightly.

"Hello," Sid said. "Sidney Judson."

"I'm Henry Wyatt," the man said. "First North Carolina."

"Ah," Sid nodded. "We're from Georgia. Came up from Norfolk the other day."

"The colonel pulled troops from all over, I guess," Wyatt said. Turning to the man marching beyond him, he added, "This is John Thorpe."

"Pleased to meet you," Sid nodded.

"Excited about the battle today?" John asked.

Roger jumped in, "I hope it's a real battle. Enough with the skirmishes and false alarms."

"Can't argue with you there," Wyatt agreed. "I guess we'll just do the best we can for our country, whatever lies ahead."

The men marched together, remarking to each other now and then. A few miles up the road, plans abruptly changed. Magruder ordered the men to fall back. They turned and picked up their pace, hurrying back towards the entrenchments.

"You've gotta be kidding me," Sam grumbled to Jimmy. "Are we ever going to get to fight in this war?"

Word spread through the troops that they indeed would get to fight that day. Magruder had stopped their advance only because the Federals were advancing themselves.

"Colonel Magruder knows what he's doing," Wyatt said. "If the Yanks are marching, prepared for a battle, it's better to fight them from our own ground, where we have protection."

"I suppose," Sid agreed.

They reached the entrenchments soon after sunup. Sid's company, along with Wyatt's, was sent to take their post towards the front of the troops. They stationed themselves to the left of the road in a damp, wooded area. Roger dropped his pack, sitting on a large rock, his musket laid across his knees. Sid sat next to him, rummaging in his own satchel for some hard tack. He offered some to Wyatt, who was standing near them.

Wyatt shook his head. "Don't get too comfortable. We don't know that the Yanks were far behind us."

"If they come at all," Roger grunted.

"They'll come." Wyatt looked out towards an open field beyond the woods. "Unfortunately that field is the perfect place for their deployment when they arrive."

"Hmmph." Jimmy sat against a tree close by. "I'm with Roger. We'll be lucky if we fight today." Then he sprang up from the ground. "Damn, this place is a swamp. My trousers are wet!"

Wyatt finally sat down on a fallen log next to Thorpe, but kept his head up, watching the field and the road. Captain Bridgers, from their company, soon came by, along with Captain Musgrove.

"Stay alert, boys," Bridgers said. "The enemy will be here before we know it."

"They're strong, too," Musgrove added. "They have more troops than we do, but I doubt they have as much heart."

The Captains moved on to organize the rest of their troops. After a while, they circled back around, telling the boys to find good spots for cover and ready themselves for battle, listening for the signal to fire. Roger and Sid set up behind the rock they had been sitting on, while Wyatt and Thorpe found cover behind their log. Jimmy had gone off to find Sam and Drew. Sid didn't know any of the other men around them. He watched them take cover behind trees and stumps. He felt the dampness of the earth seeping through the knees of his trousers, but there was no help for it.

"Psst!" Wyatt whispered. "Here they come!"

Sidney looked towards the road. Beyond the field, a faint shadow moved and sparkled. The sunlight reflecting on guns and bayonets.

"I'll be damned," Roger breathed. "We are going to shoot some Yankees today."

Sidney glanced over at him. Roger was down on one knee, with the other leg bent—and unmistakably trembling. Sid settled himself and turned his eyes to the steadily growing shadow. His gun was ready to fire. He could easily take aim. He could almost hear them now. Soft scraping of boots on the worn dirt road, idle chatter fluctuating, a drum and a fife. Had they any idea they were about to die? Sidney was ready. He could see the blue of their coats and hats. It seemed an eternity before they were close enough to make out individuals. Sid looked into the sea of faces approaching, noticed a boy with blond hair sticking out from under his cap, saw him pick up his chin and laugh.

"Fire!" Captain Bridgers cried.

"Fire!" Captain Musgrove echoed.

Shots rang out. The Union regiment suddenly came alive and sprang into action. Several companies tried to deploy in the field as Wyatt had feared. The Confederate men worked as one. Sidney closed his eyes briefly each time he pulled the trigger to protect his eyes from the gunpowder. It filled his nostrils with its pungent odor. A Yankee fell to the ground in the field. Sid heard a shout to his right. He looked over to see a North Carolina boy clutching his arm. Sid glanced around as he ripped open the next cartridge with his teeth. No one else seemed to be wounded. Wyatt and Thorpe were focused on the fight. Sid finished loading and raised his gun to fire. He only managed to get off a few more shots before he realized the Federals were withdrawing into the woods beyond the field. The enemy troops scattered in different directions, hiding among the trees.

"What do you think they're doing?" he asked Roger, reaching for his canteen.

"Maybe they're giving up," Roger said.

"Naw! They have lots more men than we do," Sid said. "They wouldn't give up so fast."

Wyatt called over, "They're probably trying a different strategy, falling back into the woods for cover. Then they'll attack somewhere else."

"But we drove them back," Roger said. "We drove them back this time!"

"I don't think our day is finished yet," Sid said.

"Damn! That powder makes me thirsty." Roger lifted his canteen.

"Sure does." Sid took another swig from his own.

The injured boy was wrapping a handkerchief around his arm with some help from another soldier.

"You all right over there?" Sid called to them.

"It's just a scratch," the boy called back. "I'll be fine, thanks."

Sid nodded.

Drew came walking through the woods then.

"Everyone all right?"

"Sure," Sid answered. "Fellow over there was grazed by a bullet, but other than that we're not hit."

"Good," Drew nodded. "Our company fought well. Stand by for orders. Captain Bridgers hasn't received any yet, so we'll be staying here until we find out where the enemy's headed next."

The boys checked their muskets, watching every direction around them, unsure where the Yanks might reappear.

Before long, Drew came again, almost running this time. "Get moving! We've been recalled to occupy the entrenchment across the river. Let's go!"

The boys strapped on their packs and shouldered their muskets as they hurried after Drew. The woods seem to come alive with

Rebels, rushing towards the bridge over the river.

"Ready, charge!" Captain Bridgers yelled.

Clumsily, Sid fixed his bayonet and put the butt of his musket against his shoulder, running along with the other boys. As they neared the bridge, Sid realized it was being fired upon from the very fort they had been sent to occupy. Musket balls landed in the water and ripped chunks of wood from the bridge as they thundered across. But they continued running, up towards the entrenchment.

"Fire at will!" Bridgers called from the front of the troops.

Sid stopped briefly to load his gun. The first Rebels reaching the fort fired shots. Sidney followed the rest of the boys as they crested the walls, firing at the enemy. He aimed at the Federal mass and pulled the trigger. He took cover to reload and fired again. Suddenly the Yankees were retreating, pouring out of the other end of the entrenchment, streaming towards the woods. When the last of them had disappeared into the woods, the boys broke into cheers.

"Did you see them run?" Sam Richardson was right behind Sid.

"We sent those New York bastards packing!" Drew cried, lifting his fist in victory.

"Good job, men," Captain Bridgers said. "Now, let's get organized. This battle is far from over."

Following orders, the boys lined the wall. Sid found himself between Roger and Jimmy. Sam took the spot to the right of his brother and the two kept murmuring excitedly to one another. Jimmy flashed a grin at Sid.

"Exciting, right?" he said. "We haven't lost one man and we're still beating them."

Roger jumped in. "And we're far outnumbered, too!"

Sid nodded. His heart was slowing to a normal rate at last, but he was still on edge, waiting for the next development. He could hardly believe they'd taken back the entrenchment without so much as a scratch. He glanced around and caught sight of Drew, crouched down talking with Captain Musgrove. Wyatt and

Thorpe were just a few yards away against the wall. Everyone was jubilant, but expectant. With the rush of adrenaline ebbing away, Sidney felt empty.

A commotion drew their attention in the direction of the bridge again. Trees obstructed the view of the bridge, but Sid could see Confederate uniforms rushing through the woods and he could hear shots being fired. Bridgers and Musgrove stood to observe the action.

"It's Colonel Stuart," Bridgers said. "He must have been recalled to the entrenchments as well."

Stuart and his troops rushed up the hill and stormed into the work to join the Rebels already there. Bridgers shook hands with the Colonel, who was still panting with exertion.

"I think the Yanks are angry!" Colonel Stuart said. "They don't like being beaten!"

"They'd best get used to it," Captain Bridgers smiled.

The new troops organized alongside Bridgers' and Musgrove's men. Their excitement slowly quieted. The boys soon heard shouting across the field to their left. Sid carefully peeked over the wall to see the Federals crossing the creek. They had white bands around their caps.

"Don't fire!" they shouted. "Don't fire!"

"Are they surrendering?" Roger looked at Sid.

Sid shrugged.

"Maybe they've had enough!" Jimmy smiled.

Colonel Stuart called out, "Stand by. Hold your fire."

Sidney watched as the whole column of Yankees crossed the creek and formed on the field. Some of them took cover behind a farmhouse.

"That house doesn't help us," Sam said.

The Yankees started cheering then, and suddenly the officers realized their intent.

"Fire!" Called Captain Bridgers. "Fire at will!"

"Fire at will!" echoed Captain Musgrove.

The boys complied. Sidney took aim at the rushing column of Federals and fired his musket. He reloaded and fired again. Every misgiving was forced from his mind as he fired and reloaded repeatedly. All he knew was the velvet barrel of his musket in his palm, the sharp scent of powder stinging his eyes. After what could have been minutes or hours, Sidney realized the Yankees had stopped charging. They weren't falling back and they were still firing, but the Rebels had stopped their advance. Still firing, Sidney heard Bridgers address his company.

"We need to set fire to that house," he said. "It's providing the Yankees with too much cover."

"I'll do it!" Sid glanced over to see Wyatt jump up.

"You'll be under heavy fire," Bridgers said. "We need more than one."

"I'll go, too," Thorpe stood next to Wyatt.

Two other boys joined them.

"You're brave men," Bridgers told them. "Go ahead. As soon as you're ready."

Sidney fired again and turned to watch as Wyatt and his friends jumped the wall and charged towards the farmhouse. Musket balls landed around them, ripping into the earth. Sidney could barely breathe. He couldn't take his eyes off Wyatt, running ahead of the others. He was only thirty yards away when he was stopped mid-stride by a musket ball. He fell to his knees.

Sid rose, starting to call out, "Wy—" But his voice caught in his throat. Wyatt lay on the ground. Sidney could do nothing. He stared at his fallen body and let his own musket drop. The other three were down, as well. Sidney hadn't seen them fall. Perhaps they were only wounded—or frightened. But Sidney knew Wyatt had been shot and that bright smile of his was gone.

The farmhouse erupted in flames. What Wyatt had set out to do was accomplished with the firing of a howitzer. As the house burned, the Yankees retreated. Thorpe got up and went over to Wyatt. Sid left his musket and sprinted out to them. Thorpe was already pulling Wyatt by the armpits, so Sid picked up his feet and the two of them rushed back to the fort with him. As they dropped him behind the wall, Thorpe fell to his knees next to the body.

"Oh my God! No!" Thorpe grabbed Wyatt's bloody face and screamed, "Damn it, Henry!"

Sid sat down on the earth, leaning against the wall. A few boys gathered around Wyatt's body. Another North Carolina boy took Thorpe's arm, trying to pull him away. Thorpe shook him off and kept screaming at Wyatt. Bridgers commanded someone to check on the wounded. Sid just sat against the entrenchment, staring at Wyatt's bloodied head. At Thorpe's angry outbursts. He couldn't hear him anymore. All he could hear was the rush of his own blood in his ears. Two minutes ago Henry Wyatt had been alive as Sidney Judson. He pressed his hands to his forehead, felt the beads of perspiration—cool on his fingers. Became aware of the pulse throbbing in his temples.

Captain Bridgers squatted by Wyatt and put his hand on Thorpe's shoulder. Thorpe suddenly stopped his railing and collapsed into sobs. Bridgers was talking, his voice a soothing baritone.

"No one will ever forget how brave he was. He was a loyal soldier. I haven't seen a man more committed to his country. And willing to risk his life for it. Just as you did, John. You were right there with him, running out into the field, into danger."

Thorpe sniffed, rubbing his stained face. "I was scared."

"We were all afraid, John," Bridgers went on. "Courage is not lack of fear. Lack of fear is foolishness. We are courageous when in spite of our fear we do the right thing—for country, for family, for God. That's what Henry did. And I know you'll carry on for him. You'll keep his memory alive, won't you?"

Thorpe nodded.

"Take your time here," the Captain said. "Say your goodbyes to Henry."

Captain Bridgers stepped away. Sid rose, bowed his head, held his hat briefly to his heart. Then he left them alone.

He walked along the wall to where his musket had fallen, shouldered it, and went back to his tent. Camp was deserted for the time being—his company hadn't returned from the battlefield yet. Sidney quickly packed his few belongings and set off into the woods with his satchel and musket. He knew what he had to do with a clarity he'd never felt before. He was afraid, but he would not turn back.

eighteen

Dearest Rachel,

I have much news to share with you. Sometimes, as I lie alone in the dawn, trying to fall asleep, I wish I had never left Pennsylvania. If I hadn't, though, I wouldn't have learned who I truly am. I wouldn't have discovered for myself that I was fighting for a cause I didn't believe in.

I am a true Yankee now, to the bone. I always knew what was right—or at least I realized very soon after I came to live with my aunt and uncle. But I fought it. I held onto my past and now I don't know why. It was the only way I knew. Even though my life had been only seventeen years so far, it was still my whole life, and it was hard to look back at it and see that it had been lived with a false perception. It was hard to shake it off and move on to something different, even if different was so much better.

Sidney stopped writing. Another letter he wouldn't send. He never seemed to be able to put the words down quite right. He stashed the letter with the growing stack in his satchel and turned back to the skinned rabbit, roasting over the fire on his bayonet.

He'd begun marking the days on the back of one of those letters. It was Saturday evening, June 22nd. Twelve days since he'd walked out of camp. Now he shuddered to think he'd been so brash. He could be shot for desertion. At the very least, he would be made an example by ongoing public humiliation in front of his regiment—forced to wear a ball and chain or paraded around wearing a desertion placard. But he knew if he faced the decision again, he'd do the same thing.

After he finished eating, he began walking. He'd stick to the woods until after dark. In plainclothes, with his musket, he could easily pass himself off as a hunter. Each day, as he put more distance between Big Bethel and himself, he breathed a little easier. Just before dawn that morning, he'd traveled through the outlying villages of Baltimore. Tonight he reckoned he'd be crossing into Pennsylvania, but he wouldn't know for sure until he reached the Susquehanna River. Even then, it was still a long way to Wilkes-Barre. He wasn't sure whether to follow the river the rest of the way or continue guessing the best route North, as he'd been doing. So far, he'd followed the drinking gourd and the moss on the trees as Hattie and Lem had. When they shared their stories with him in Uncle Daniel's and Aunt Sarah's kitchen, he'd found their tale interesting, never realizing he would need to use their expertise as a guide himself.

To pass the time as he hiked, Sid let his imagination take over. He pictured his arrival in town, the look of joy on Tom's face, Aunt Sarah's excitement and the tears she would surely shed. In his mind, all the townspeople turned out for his homecoming. His first meeting with Rachel could happen any number of ways. But he always stumbled over this, realizing how self-gratifying his musings were.

Sid looked up and stopped. A horse stood just a few paces ahead of him in the path. A man sat on its back, observing Sidney. Sid met his eyes.

"Evening, sir," he said.

"Evening," the man answered. "Mind if I ask what brings you here?"

"Not at all." Sid thought as fast as he could. "I think I may have lost my way. I've been out hunting this evening and now that I'm heading home, I can't remember the way very well. These woods are new to me."

"I should hope so," the man said. "These are my woods!"

"Oh, I'm terribly sorry," Sid tried to sound sincere. "I had no idea."

"I'm Leslie Evans," the man said. "And you are?"

"Jim," Sid lied. "Jim Rogers. I'm new to the area."

"You must be from Freeland if you're headed this way," Leslie said.

"That's right," Sid said, grateful for the information. "Just set up house in Freeland a few weeks ago. Am I heading the right direction then?"

"Yes sir," he said. "But a few paces up, you'll find another path and that will take you out to the road. I live in Manchester—guess that's why I don't recognize you. Nice country up there in Freeland. But in these parts, we keep to our own property. We don't hunt other men's woods."

"My apologies, sir," Sid said. "I'm from the city. I didn't know."

"Of course," Leslie smiled. "Don't mention it."

"As you see, I didn't find anything worth shooting anyway," Sidney said.

Leslie nodded. "Have a good night. Hope you get home before dark."

"Thank you," Sid walked on.

He was almost surprised Leslie hadn't heard his heart pounding. He was shocked that he'd been able to fool him. After a while, he took a furtive glance over his shoulder. Leslie and his horse were continuing down the path in the direction from which Sidney had come. He would have to be more alert. What if it had been a Home Guard? No one should be able to sneak up on him like that. When

Sidney reached the path Leslie had mentioned, he forged across it and headed deeper into the woods, away from any footpaths—he hoped. Then he had another terrifying thought. What if Leslie came across the fire Sidney had burned that evening? Sid had put out the flames, but there were surely a few smoldering embers. If Leslie followed the path long enough, he might smell smoke. That would very well blow his cover. The thought made Sidney's heart race faster. Sid broke out in a sweat and began jogging, then he ran. He kept going deeper into the woods, yet roughly heading northward.

Sidney kept on that way all night—running or jogging, only slowing to a walk if he had to climb over rocks or a fallen tree. Every snapping twig made his heart pound harder and added urgency to his step. As dawn neared, he came out of the woods onto a deserted road. His eyes, accustomed to the darkness of the night, couldn't make out any living being as far as he could see. He looked up at the sky, checking the drinking gourd to see that he was traveling in the right direction. He would follow the road for a while, then head back into the woods for his daytime snooze, though he doubted he'd be able to sleep today. But he had to be close to Pennsylvania by now. The Home Guards would not be a concern once he crossed into Union territory.

After he'd been walking for some time, he stopped and cocked his head, listening. Water running. Perhaps it was the Susquehanna! No, it wasn't loud enough. Maybe a creek. The first rays of sunshine were turning the edge of the sky from black to blue. A farmhouse stood a hundred yards down the road on the right.

"If I cut through these fields towards the woods, I could follow that creek," Sid said under his breath. "It might be a tributary of the Susquehanna."

As he left the road, he stayed on the cut grass close to the farmhouse. If he trampled the taller grass in the hayfields, someone might notice and follow his trail. He glanced towards the house as he passed. There was only one light inside, probably the farmer getting up early to milk his cows. Then he noticed another light, closer to the road. Sid stopped short. The light was held by a very small figure. Small enough to be a child or... Sid's heart started pounding. He turned away from the woods and started towards the light. Hope and fear surged in him at once. What if it was a trap? He reached the road again and there in front of him was a statue—a tiny black stable boy holding a lighted lantern.

Sid forced his trembling legs to walk to the front door. He knocked quietly. Whispers inside, a chair scraping the floor, then a hand at the latch and the door was open. Sidney looked into the face of a middle-aged woman, graying hair pulled back from her soft, pale face. Over her shoulder, he saw a man in work clothes, sitting at the kitchen table.

"Can I help you?" the woman asked.

Sid's breath was short. He tried to quiet it as he spoke. "I know it's early. I'm sorry to disturb you, but I saw the light at the road."

"Yes," the woman said. "We were expecting..."

"A shipment?" Sid said. "Is the wind blowing from the South?"

The woman just looked at Sid. Her husband stood up. "Why don't you come in, son?"

Sid stepped inside and the woman shut the door behind him.

"We aren't looking for trouble," the farmer said.

"Neither am I." Sid shook his head. "Just a meal and a place to sleep. Then tell me where to head next."

"You sound like a Southerner," he said.

"No." Sid shook his head again. "I was a Southerner, but not anymore. I'm going North, to my aunt and uncle in Wilkes-Barre."

"What's your name, boy?"

"Sidney Judson."

The farmer's eyes sparked. "What's your uncle's name?"

"Daniel Judson. His wife is Sarah. Do you know them?"

"Yes—then your father is David?"

"David was my father—he's gone now. Daniel's the only family I have left."

"Any family of Daniel Judson is a friend of ours." The man reached for Sid's hand. "I'm Gary Elwater. Welcome to our home." He turned to his wife. "Edna, get this boy some breakfast."

"Surely!" she said, turning to the stove. "After you've eaten and had some rest, you'll have to tell us all the news of Sarah and Daniel."

Soon she had Sidney seated at the table before a stack of hot cakes and mounds of sausages and fried potatoes.

"Mind if I ask how you know my family, ma'am?" Sidney said.

"I grew up in Wilkes-Barre." Mrs. Elwater smiled at Sid. "Sarah was one of my dearest friends."

A lump rose in Sidney's throat. For the first time in twelve hours, his heart rate had slowed to normal. He was among friends.

"We'll talk more later on, before you head off," Mr. Elwater said. "I need to milk the cows now. You eat up and then get some rest."

Surviving on what he could hunt and forage, Sidney hadn't realized how hungry he was. He made short work of the ample breakfast in front of him. Mrs. Elwater then showed him to a small room behind the kitchen. Sidney stretched out on the cot there and soon drifted off to the peaceful country sounds of cows lowing and sheep bleating.

He awoke in the early afternoon, looking around the simple room, at the plank walls and the burlap curtain separating it from the kitchen. He roused himself, rubbed his eyes and walked out to the kitchen where Mrs. Elwater was at the stove again.

"You're awake," she said. "You slept all morning. We've been to church and back and had the noon meal already. Did you get some good rest?"

"Yes, ma'am," Sid answered. "Best I've slept in two weeks."

"Good," she said. "You can have your bath now. Take this tub into the back room."

Sid dragged the tin tub over the rough wooden floorboards into the room where he'd been sleeping. Then he helped her carry water from the stove to the tub until it was half-full.

"Here are some clean clothes for you, Sidney." Mrs. Elwater handed him a stack of freshly smelling clothing along with a cake of soap. "You get washed up now. Then I'll get you something more to eat and we can all chat."

"Thank you, ma'am," Sid said.

Sid felt like a new man. He sat at the table, clean and dry, eating a bowl of okra soup when Mr. Elwater came in from his chores.

Sidney stood up. "I don't know how to thank you, sir."

"No need." Gary sat down across from him. "Please, sit down. I'd like to know how things are going with your aunt and uncle. And how you came to be traveling North in this manner."

Sid paused and took a long breath. "My aunt and uncle are well as far as I know. Did you grow up in Wilkes-Barre as well?"

"No." Gary shook his head. "Edna lived there until she was in secondary school. Then her father, a minister, was transferred down here to Freedom, where I lived."

"Excuse me," Sidney said. "Freedom? Is that where I am?"

"Yes," Gary said. "Freedom, Pennsylvania."

Sidney smiled. "I'm in Pennsylvania then!"

"That's right," Gary said.

"You have no idea how happy that makes me," Sidney said. "Please, go on. Finish your story."

"After Edna and I married, we took a few trips North to visit Edna's acquaintances, especially Sarah. Daniel and I got along well together from the moment we met. We don't see them much, what with the distance and all, but since we're both involved in the Railroad, we keep in touch."

"I see," Sid said. "I really haven't had much recent news from my aunt and uncle. As far as I know, all is well. After my parents died, I lived with them for almost a year." Sid told them that he went South again when the war began and he'd deserted the army almost two weeks ago. After he finished speaking, the two men sat in silence for a moment.

Then Mr. Elwater spoke. "So you are a Confederate soldier."

"No, sir," Sidney said. "I was one."

Mr. Elwater cleared his throat. "Technically, you still are."

Sid swallowed hard. "Sir, I cannot express to you how certain I am of my decision. I will never fight for the Confederacy again. I am not a true Southerner. I believe slavery is a horrid institution. I lived with my aunt and uncle for almost a year and never turned them in for their dealings with the Railroad."

Sid looked across the table into Gary's quiet brown eyes, searching for something to tell him, to convince him that he was trustworthy. Then, in the back of his mind, flickering like a small flame, came Rhoda's words to him when the war started. "You're from the South, but you ain't a Southerner!" He relayed the story to Mr. Elwater.

Gary smiled. "I believe you, Sid. I can tell you're an honest boy. But I can't jeopardize the entire Pennsylvania Underground Railroad for you. So, I'm not going to send you to any other stations. But I will tell you the best way home from here. And send you off with a pack full of food. You're smart. I have no doubt you'll be safely home again within another week."

That evening, after filling his pack with provisions, the Elwaters walked him to their gate. Mr. Elwater handed him some bills.

"No, sir." Sid tried to give them back. "You've already done too much for me!"

Mr. Elwater pushed his hand away. "When the food we've given you runs out, you'll need to buy some."

Sid hesitated. "Well, I'm going to reimburse you. Once I get home, I'll send you the money."

"Pshaw!" Gary said. "You'd better get started on your way."

"You take care of yourself now," Mrs. Elwater said.

Sid shook their hands. "I don't know how I can ever thank you enough."

"We're here to help, Sidney," Mrs. Elwater said. "We don't expect our thanks in this life."

"No, of course you don't," Sidney said. "But thank you just the same. I'll never forget your kindness to me."

"Give our love to your aunt and uncle," Mr. Elwater said.

Sidney set out to cross the Susquehanna and continue North to Lancaster and beyond. It turned out Mr. Elwater was right. The following Saturday morning, Sidney arrived in Wilkes-Barre, walking up River Street. He paused on the River Common, looking across the street at the house through the early morning mist. He could faintly smell ham frying. Sarah and Rhoda must be making breakfast. He was surprised to find his stomach in knots. He wanted nothing more than to go into the house, but he wished he'd never been away. He hoped everything was the same as he'd left it. There was nothing to do but find out.

He crossed the street and mounted the steps to the front porch. When he stepped inside the door, Rhoda came out of the kitchen into the dining room and stopped short. She stared at him.

"Rhoda!" Sid laughed. "It's me!"

"Mr. Sidney! You plum scared me out of my mind!" Then she stomped her foot. "You's home, Mr. Sidney!"

"Well, you said I'd be back when I came to my senses."

"Took you long enough." A warm smile crept onto her lips. She pushed the door to the kitchen open. "Missus! You better get out here!" Then Rhoda came out to the foyer, wiping her hands on her apron.

"Glad to see you back in one piece," she said.

Aunt Sarah came out to the foyer, crying, "Sidney! You're here! You're really here and safe!" She rushed into his arms and he lifted her from the floor.

"Daniel!" Aunt Sarah shouted in the direction of the stairs. "Sidney's home!"

Daniel came to the top of the stairs, shaving brush in hand, white foam clinging around his beard. He wiped his face with a towel as he descended.

"Well, I'll be..." Uncle Daniel's face wrinkled as he gave Sid a hug. "Welcome back!"

Aunt Sarah put her hand to Sid's cheek. "I prayed you'd come home, Sidney."

"We're just about to sit down to breakfast," Rhoda said. "I have to poach the eggs and when I come back, you tell us all about everything."

"He's just come in the door," Daniel said. "Let him catch his breath."

"Oh, you're right, sir," Rhoda said. "I don't mean to rush you, Mr. Sidney."

Sarah led them into the dining room. She set a place for Sidney while Rhoda went into the kitchen.

"You look well," Sarah said. "A bit thin, but we'll soon fatten you up."

"I'm fine," Sid stood behind his chair. "Thanks to your friends, the Elwaters, I've been eating all right since last Sunday."

Aunt Sarah's eyes went wide. Uncle Daniel's mouth dropped open.

"The Elwaters?" Daniel said. "How did you happen to meet them?"

"I haven't seen Edna in ages!" Sarah clasped her hands. "Are they well?"

"Yes, very well," Sid said. "They asked me to give you their best."

Rhoda came into the dining room with platters of food—ham, poached eggs, and bread. "We've a feast for you, Mr. Sidney. Now, don't you go telling all the news with me in the other room!"

"Sorry, Rhoda." Sid chuckled. "You haven't missed much."

"I don't want to miss anything!"

They took their seats. Rhoda's eyes fixed on Sid.

"Well now... I don't know that there's much to tell," Sid stammered. "I mean, it's hard to know where to begin."

"Take your time," Rhoda handed him the platter of eggs and bread. "You need to eat. Don't feel no pressure to talk."

"Well, the short of it is that I deserted the Confederate Army." Sid slid two eggs and some bread onto his plate.

Daniel nodded. He took the platter from Sidney.

"And good for you!" Rhoda said, pouring the coffee. "Make sure you get some ham."

Sidney complied, taking a bite. "And I walked here. When I got into Pennsylvania, I found the Elwaters' farm. I knew they were in the Railroad because they had a lawn jockey with a lighted lantern."

Sarah smiled. "Oh, how wonderful! Then you've been eating well at Railroad stops!"

"Well, not exactly," Sid said. He explained Mr. Elwater's dilemma.

"But you would never betray the Railroad!" Sarah put down her fork.

"I understand his predicament, Aunt Sarah. And, really, I wouldn't want to cause any problems."

Daniel nodded. "Gary has a responsibility to protect the Railroad. He can't put it at risk."

"Exactly," Sid said. "They were both so kind to me. They gave me food and money to take with me. It would have taken me much longer to get home if they hadn't given me directions and loaded me with provisions."

For the remainder of breakfast, Sid answered their questions about the South, the War, and his long walk North. As he finished his last forkful of ham, he looked around the table at the faces he'd missed so much. Tears were running down Sarah's soft cheeks.

"Oh, don't mind me!" She waved her napkin at him, shaking her head. "I cry when you leave. I cry when you come home. I'm just thinking that this is exactly how it should be. Your chair isn't empty now!"

Sid smiled. "You're right. It is exactly as it should be."

"You need to get some rest, though," Sarah said. "We can talk more after you sleep."

"Yes, ma'am." Sid rose. "I could certainly use a good nap in my own bed."

But Sidney couldn't sleep. He tossed back and forth on his bed, unable to quiet his mind. He was finally home—and Rachel must be nearby. He could try, unsuccessfully, to get the rest he needed, or he could visit Rachel and find out if her feelings for him were any different than they had been.

Aunt Sarah was in her sewing room, hemming one of Uncle Daniel's shirts.

"You're up already?" she asked.

"I couldn't get to sleep." Sid stood in the doorway. "I think I'll get washed up."

"All right," Aunt Sarah said. "But you must be tired from your journey. You haven't had a decent night's sleep in... how long? Weeks?"

"I'll catch up eventually," Sid said.

After he had bathed and dressed, Aunt Sarah came into the kitchen and got him a big glass of iced tea.

"I don't want to rush you to talk about everything," she said. "But whenever you're ready, I'd like to hear more of what happened when you went back to Roswell."

Sid sat at the kitchen table and the words came. He poured out the whole story to her as he sipped the tea—all about Catherine and Drew, enlisting in the army, the Battle of Big Bethel, and Henry losing his life.

"I don't know if I can explain it," he said. "I knew we could die, but it didn't hit me until Henry... all I could think was that if I died in battle like him, I was fighting for the wrong side. I'd known it all along, but it took Henry's death to make me do something about it."

"So you deserted." Sarah filled his glass again from the tin pitcher on the table. "And traveled all that way by foot."

Sid nodded. "It sounds harder than it was. I was scared at first. I was afraid the officers might come after me—maybe Drew would hunt me down. Then I was afraid the Home Guard would find me. But once I realized I had crossed into Pennsylvania—Well, I may have technically been a Confederate, but I felt I was finally on friendly soil."

Sarah smiled. "You were. You will always have a home here."

"I never thought twice about that."

"Good." Sarah wiped the pitcher with a terry cloth towel.

"The best part was traveling in the dark," Sid went on. "I did a lot of the walking at night, so I wouldn't get caught." He had felt safer in the dark, under the great expanse of the heavens. It had been easier to feel close to God, and to remember why he was making this journey.

He did not tell Sarah his heartache over Rachel. It seemed too private to put into words. But again he grew anxious to see her as he stared at the beads of perspiration forming on the tin pitcher. One of them grew large enough to slide down to the table, leaving a streak in its path. More drops were quick to join it, landing in a small puddle on the tabletop.

Sarah took his glass. "Well, if you can't sleep, what are you going to do this morning?"

"I'd love to go right back to work at the store," Sidney said. "But I imagine Uncle Daniel has found an employee."

"Yes," Aunt Sarah said. "He hired Caleb Mahoney when school let out, actually. But I'm sure he won't be able to continue come fall."

"Who knows what the fall will bring," Sidney said. "I might be fighting for the Union by then."

"Don't rush things, Sidney." Aunt Sarah shook her head.

"I think I'll go for a walk," he said. "It's been so long since I've seen everyone."

The sooner he saw Rachel, the sooner he could stop worrying about the first awkward meeting.

"Just remember," Sarah sighed. "It's been a long time for them, too."

nineteen

THE walk down River Street to the White farm was as familiar as though he'd done it yesterday. Sid stood on their front porch. His heart pounded so hard he couldn't think. He willed himself to raise his fist and knock on the front door. Maybe no one would be home.

But the door swung open and a surprised Hattie greeted him with a basket of laundry.

"Mr. Sidney!" she said. "You're back!"

"Yes, Hattie. Keep it down. I'd like to surprise the others."

"Oh, sir, no one's in the house. You sure surprised me!"

"Where is everyone?"

"All gone into town, 'cept Miss Rachel. She's in the barn, feeding the animals."

"I... I'll go see her, then," Sidney faltered.

"Well, all right," Hattie said. "How's things in Roswell?"

"All is well," Sid nodded. He tried to quiet his breathing and answer Hattie politely. "Mr. Pierson is gone. The other slaves are free. Chloe and George are paid servants at Tall Pine now."

"Mr. Sidney," Hattie whispered, her voice trembling. "You are a good man."

"I did what I thought was right." Sid shrugged, his face flushed. "I'd better go."

"Can I offer you anything to eat?" Hattie followed him out onto the porch.

"No, thank you." Sid shook his head. "Rhoda's stuffed me to the brim already."

As Hattie headed for the clothesline, Sidney set off towards the large, white barn next to the road beyond the house. The barn was meticulous inside and out. Rough hewn wooden stalls stood on both sides of a wide center aisle. Sid walked quietly to the door of the grain room at the end of the aisle. He rubbed his clammy palms on his trouser legs. Rachel stood with her back to him, reaching down to scoop oats, then straightening up. He wished he could just stand and watch her, unknowing, forever. The solid sound of oats on metal met his ears. Rachel's chestnut hair caught the sunlight from the window beyond her as she moved. Suddenly she turned. And stopped.

"Sidney?" her voice was a whisper.

For a moment he couldn't answer. He only nodded. Then his voice came to him. "It's me."

"What are you doing here?"

"I came to see you."

"I thought you were in the war."

"I was. For a while. But now I'm back."

"But why would you come back here?" Rachel stood stock still, clutching the bucket by its handle. "Don't you have a wife to go back to? I thought you'd be married to Catherine."

"No, I..." Sid shook his head. "Catherine married Drew."

"I'm sorry."

"It's all right." Sid shifted his weight. "You know, it turned out I was right. I didn't think she still cared about me."

"Oh," Rachel said. She carried the bucket out of the grain room and went to the stall on Sid's left.

"Can I help you?" he asked.

"No." She shook her head as she maneuvered the big, iron lock and opened the door. "I'm almost done."

When she came out of the stall, Sid closed and locked the door for her.

"I'm sorry about Catherine," she said.

"Why?" he asked. "I told you I didn't care about her anymore."

"I don't really believe that."

"Well, you're not entirely wrong," Sid admitted. "I mean, I wasn't in love with her, but since you'd turned me down cold, I thought maybe I could care about her again—at first. So, it was pretty rotten to find out she'd taken up with Drew while I was gone, but it didn't hurt nearly as much as..." He broke off and swallowed, thinking of that day with Rachel on the River Common.

"Did you fight, Sid?" Rachel asked. "What was it like? You didn't get hurt, did you?"

Sid sat down on a bench against one of the stalls opposite Rachel. "Not exactly."

"Are you all right?"

"Yes, I'm all right," he said. "What happened in battle was awful, but that's not what I'm talking about."

Rachel stood looking at him. She seemed further away than she had on his long journey home. He had to say something. The distance was unbearable.

"Damn it, Rachel, you broke my heart," Sid's voice shook.

Sidney stared into her green eyes. Her gaze shifted.

"I told you to write to me," she said.

"I couldn't."

"I wish you had."

"I didn't know what to say," Sid said. "I was an idiot. I know I shouldn't have expected you to wait for me while I went home to Catherine. But if you had, then I wouldn't have..."

"What?" Rachel asked. "What did you do? You think you would have resisted her if I'd said yes? Don't fool yourself!"

"Rachel, listen to me. Even though you said no, I still realized within a few days that I could never be with her."

"Because of Drew."

"No. It was before I knew about her and Drew. I broke it off myself."

Rachel sniffed. "Oh."

"I don't blame you for saying no. I was cocky and stupid. I didn't deserve you then. I don't deserve you now."

"Sid, please stop." Rachel set the empty bucket down on the plank floor.

Sid looked up at her again. "Why?"

She finally looked into his eyes. "Have you seen Tom?"

"No." Her eyes and nose were slightly red. But she was still the most beautiful thing he'd ever seen.

"We've become close," Rachel said, her voice flat.

Sid gripped the bench with both hands. "That is not amusing."

"I don't mean it to be."

"Are you engaged?"

Rachel shook her head with a smile. "No, we're not engaged. Not yet."

Sid got up. "I need to go." He started walking towards the door of the barn.

"Sid, wait," Rachel said. "Don't go."

Sid stopped and turned around. His jaw was clenched so tightly, he could feel a muscle twitching in his face.

"You have no right to be angry," she said.

Sid spun around and stalked out of the barn. If he stood there talking to Rachel any longer he would have to either put a hole in the barn wall or take her in his arms and kiss her. He didn't look back and he didn't stop walking till he got home. At the front door he changed his mind, crossed the street and went down to the riverbank.

He skipped rocks for a while, pacing back and forth in the pebbles at the waters edge. But the anger was not dissipating, and he had a fleeting thought that if it did, he might have to face even more unwelcome feelings. He headed back towards the house, unsure of what to do next. When he got to the Common, Rachel was just reaching the front porch. She saw him and crossed the street to where he stood.

"It's pretty bold of you to come over here," Sid said. "Don't you think your beau would mind?"

Then he saw that her eyes were even more red. He softened. "What's wrong?"

"I just wanted to tell you I never meant to hurt you." She stopped and glanced around the street. A woman with a baby was walking up the other side. "Can we go down to the river?"

Sid turned and led the way down the steep bank, holding Rachel's arm tentatively.

When they reached the big rock, close to the water, Rachel leaned against it and looked at Sid, waiting.

Sid scuffed his shoes on the pebbles. Finally, he said, "You don't belong with him, Rachel."

"You don't know that."

"I know you. And I know Tom."

"What right do you have to tell me I don't belong with him?" Rachel's voice rose. "You left and you didn't write to me! I didn't hear from you for two months."

"Why didn't you ask my aunt about me?"

"Why didn't I ask your aunt if you'd married Catherine?"

Sid started walking back towards Rachel.

"I don't know, Sid." Rachel crossed her arms. "Why didn't I think of that?"

"Why didn't you?" Sid leaned on the rock next to Rachel.

"You bastard!" Rachel turned her eyes towards him and tears spilled down her cheeks.

Sidney couldn't muster an ounce of anger now. "You made it very clear you didn't care about me."

"You waited until the day before you left to say anything." Rachel sniffed, wiping at her tears with the edge of her sleeve.

Sid reached for Rachel's hand and pressed his body against hers, breathing in her aroma—wholesome, like bread baking.

"I hate you!" she said.

"No, you don't." He chuckled as he realized she was clinging to him as hard as he was holding her.

He bent his head and kissed her neck.

"No!" She pushed him back. "Stop. I have to think of Tom."

Sid kept holding her hands. "What kind of understanding do you have?"

"We have no understanding. He just started spending more and more time with me... and I didn't stop him."

"Because you missed me." Sid smiled.

"You say it as though you're happy about it." Rachel slumped, her back against the rock.

"I am happy that you missed me." Sid stood in front of her, his arms resting on the rock, his body as close to hers as it could be without touching. With each breath she took, her breasts just grazed his chest. He went on, trying to keep his heart from racing. "All this time I thought you didn't care about me. And for the past thirty minutes, I thought maybe you were in love with Tom."

"Well, you may be happy, but I'm miserable. I've been miserable since you left—and now that you're back it's even worse because of Tom," Rachel said.

"But if you had no understanding—"

"Sid, he cares for me," she said. "I don't want to hurt him."

"I'm in love with you. That didn't stop you from hurting me."

"That's different," she said. "You're a cad."

"True enough," Sid said. "What happened with Tom and Eliza?"

"Oh, I don't know," Rachel said. "She must hate me now."

"I thought Tom was interested in her, too."

"Maybe you wanted to think that."

"Only because he told me he wasn't interested in you."

"He did?" Rachel asked.

"It was a long time ago," Sid said.

"I wish it were still true."

Sid brought her hand to his lips. "Rachel, I loved you long before I said anything. I tried to stop after you turned me down, but I couldn't."

"I'm going to talk to Tom—today. Right now," Rachel said. "It would hurt him more if I let him go on thinking I might love him."

Sid nodded, rubbing the back of her hand with his thumb. "Can you come over to the house after you talk to him?"

"All right," Rachel said.

Sid smirked. "I'd like to see you again."

"You would?" Rachel raised her eyebrows and smiled slowly.

"I wrote to Tom," Sid said. "He could have told you I didn't marry Catherine."

"We never talked about you," Rachel said.

"Why not?" Sid's brow furrowed. "You were my closest friends."

Rachel shrugged. "I never stopped thinking about you, but I couldn't bring it up. Every time I wanted to ask if he'd heard from you, something would stop me. I think he must know."

"That's wishful thinking," Sid said.

"I can't help it," Rachel said. "But Tom and I—I know it could never have gone anywhere, even if you didn't walk into my barn today."

Sid drew her close to him and buried his face in her neck. She let him for a moment, then pulled away again. "I need to get it over with."

They climbed the bank together, but she let go of his hand as they reached the Common.

"This will ruin your friendship," she said.

"Maybe not."

"I'll come to your house as soon as I can, but I don't know what his reaction will be. I want to break it to him gently—if I can."

"All right," Sid nodded. "Just promise me you won't go over there and change your mind."

"No." Rachel shook her head. "I'll see you soon."

She continued onto River Street. Sid watched until she turned down Union Street. He tried not to think about the scene inside the Mahoney's house, but he couldn't help wondering how it would play out.

When he went into the kitchen, Rhoda was at the stove, stirring the celery sauce for dinner.

Sarah sat at the table, shelling peas. "How was your walk?"

"Fine," Sid said.

"Why don't you try to rest for a while?" Sarah suggested. "I'll come get you when dinner's ready."

"I won't be able to sleep, Aunt Sarah," Sid said.

He left the kitchen and went up the stairs to his room. Things with Tom would never be the same. What kind of man steals his friend's girl? Men like Drew. Sid's satchel still lay on the floor where he had left it earlier that afternoon. He picked it up and took it to the ladder-back chair against the wall. Aunt Sarah's journal was near the bottom of the bag, as he hadn't looked at it in quite some time. He sat on the chair and flipped through it, searching for some kind of comfort.

18 August, 1839

Daniel and I had an argument this morning. We don't argue often, but when we do, it's quite upsetting...

Sid flipped the pages again.

We went to the Independence Day celebration and had ice cream...

He turned towards the back of the book, hungrily searching the entries. There it was.

3 October, 1840

Melinda and I took tea together this afternoon. She's made up her mind to marry Atticus White. I hate to write this about my friend, but I hope she can be worthy of such a fine man. Although it's been two years, I can see that she's never recovered from losing David. She didn't tell me what happened, and I would never ask, but I can use my brain. After the rumors died off, I began to believe them. I can understand it would be hard to move on after something like that. I just hope she's told Atticus. I tried to tell her how to know if you should be with someone forever. I explained how I knew about Daniel, that even though we each have our faults, deep down in our hearts we knew we could make it through tough times together. Our love was so strong that we didn't want to be apart.

Melinda just kept repeating that Atticus is a good man from a respectable family and he would have a fine income from the farm. I even went so far as to ask if she loves him. She said, "Of course" and changed the subject. I know people get married all the time because it's a good situation and maybe they're fine. Perhaps they even grow to love each other. I just don't see Melinda having that kind of character. Even when she was with David, I wasn't sure she had what it took to make a marriage joyful throughout the years. If she doesn't have a strong love for Atticus now, I'm afraid she will never be happy. I pray I am wrong.

Sid jumped as Aunt Sarah poked her head into his room. He slammed the book shut and looked up.

She laughed. "Sidney, I gave you the journal. You don't have to read it in secret anymore."

"Oh, I know... you startled me, though."

"What part were you reading?" Aunt Sarah asked. "If you don't mind my asking."

Sid's face grew warm. "It was... about when Mr. and Mrs. White were engaged."

Sarah's forehead wrinkled, then cleared. "I was worried about them, wasn't I? But they're all right I suppose."

"I think you made some good points," Sid said. "I think you were right."

"Let me see," Sarah reached for the book.

Sid opened it back up to where he'd been reading and handed the journal to Sarah. She read for a moment, then looked up. "You think I was right?"

"She isn't happy," Sid said.

Sarah paused for a moment. "Do you think she would have been happy if she'd married your father?"

"I don't know," Sid said.

"Melinda could be happy if she chose to be," Sarah said. "She has a wonderful husband who's loved her enough for both of them. She has five beautiful children she should be proud of... I love her because she's been my friend since David was courting her, but I can recognize her bitterness and it didn't come from marrying Atticus."

"I think I understand that," Sid said. "But if two people love each other the way you and Uncle Daniel do, then they should do everything they can to be together, shouldn't they?"

"I would think so... as long as they go about it morally."

"What if it will hurt someone else?"

Aunt Sarah sighed. "You mean Tom?"

Sid stared at the pine floorboards and nodded, his ears burning.

"You know as well as I do that Rachel can't marry Tom."

Sid looked up to see the corners of Sarah's lips twitching upward into a smile. Then there was a knock on the front door. Sid left the room and bounded down the stairs. There was Rachel, her face ashen. Sid stepped out onto the porch with her.

"Are you all right?" he asked.

She shook her head. "No... Yes... I'm so relieved. I feel better than I have in weeks—months, really. But I feel awful at the same time."

"What can I do?" Sid looked at her, feeling helpless.

She reached out and took the edge of his shirtsleeve. "Just, hold me?"

Sid pulled her into his arms and finally they pressed against each other. He put his lips to hers and she didn't pull away.

Some time later, Aunt Sarah came out onto the porch to find the two wrapped in each other's gaze, sitting on the porch swing. Rachel quickly rose, fishing in her purse for a handkerchief.

"Oh, Mrs. Judson, I'm so sorry," Rachel said. "I didn't mean to be rude."

Sarah hid a smile. "You could never be rude, Rachel dear."

"I was just… we were, um…"

"Catching up," Sid stood up behind Rachel and put his arms around her waist.

"Sid—" Rachel protested.

"Well, it's about time," Sarah said. "I've had enough of your dillydallying."

The three of them burst into laughter. Aunt Sarah reached out and hugged them both. "So I'm not the only woman happy to have Sidney home?"

"No." Rachel smiled, blushing. "I can't even begin to tell you how much I missed him."

"I can't say I'm surprised," Sarah said. "Won't you join us for dinner?"

It was already dark when Sidney walked Rachel home that evening. Though it was June, the air was chilly. Sid kept his arm wrapped tightly around Rachel.

"I've never been happier," Rachel said. "And yet, I feel so guilty."

Sid pulled her closer.

"Tom was so cold," she said. "I wish he'd been angry with me, but he just shut down. He said he knew it couldn't last. And then he told me to leave."

Sid sighed. "I wish I could do something. But I'm sure he wouldn't want to see me. Was he alone at the house?"

"No," Rachel said. "I saw Mrs. Mahoney when I arrived and then I thought I heard her talking to Caleb."

"He has them, Rachel. He'll be all right."

"I hope so."

"He may never speak to us again, but he'll get over it."

"We were such good friends—the three of us. I just feel awful about it."

When they arrived at the Whites' house, Rachel's mother was out on the porch, wrapped in a shawl.

"Mother," Rachel ran up the walk. "I thought you and the girls were at Ruth's for the day."

"I came home right after tea and I've been worried sick ever since." Mrs. White's voice was crisp.

"I'm sorry," Rachel said. "I should have left a note."

Sid walked up to the porch. Mrs. White turned to him and stiffened in recognition. "Mr. Judson." She looked sharply at Rachel. "Where's Tom?"

Rachel sighed. "I was over at the Judson's, Mother. Sidney's home."

"I see that," she said.

"Why don't you and I go inside, Mother? I'll explain everything." Rachel turned to Sid. "My Father's still off on some Railroad business."

"You're telling that to this Southerner?" Melinda White spat the words under her breath, but Sid heard them.

He climbed the steps and faced her. "I may be a Southerner, Mrs. White. But I'm not a Confederate. Not anymore."

"I could never trust a born Southerner," she said. "I'll see you inside, Rachel." She stepped inside the house, closing the door quickly behind her.

Sid couldn't read Rachel's face in the dim light from the window. "I'll stay until your father gets home," he said.

"Don't be silly. He won't be home until midnight."

"But she's angry already. What will she do when you tell her?"

"She won't be happy," she said. "But I can't make her happy—even when I try."

Sid drew her close and kissed her. "You've made me beyond happy, just by being Rachel White."

She pressed her face against his neck. "Walk me to church tomorrow."

"All right," Sid said. "I'll be here."

She went inside then, to face her mother. Sid stayed on the porch, listening, but he could hear only their muffled voices. He sat on the top step until the house grew silent. Someone put out the light. He could do nothing more for Rachel at present.

Early the next morning Sidney went down to the river to fish. Later, Sunday morning activities would take over, but for now he would commune with God in his own way. He had been standing in the water only half an hour when he heard a voice from behind him.

"Nothing biting this morning?"

Sid turned around to see Tom sitting on the rock at the river's edge.

"How long have you been there?" Sid asked.

"A while, I guess," Tom answered. "Didn't you want a fishing partner?"

"I—" Sid broke off

Tom slid off the rock and gently landed on the damp earth. Sid waded back to shore and stood beside him.

"How come you didn't come to see me when you got into town yesterday?" Tom asked.

"Well, I went to see Rachel first," Sid said. "And after that I really didn't think you'd want to see me."

"Oh," Tom met his gaze.

"Am I right?" Sid asked.

"That depends," Tom said. "I'd want to see my old friend. But I wouldn't want to see the fellow who stole my girl."

Sid swallowed. "I'm sorry, Tom."

"No you're not," Tom said.

"I'm sorry it had to be this way."

Tom narrowed his eyes at Sid. "I'm not stupid. I had a feeling she cared about you all along."

"Were you truly in love with her?"

"I was headed that way."

"What happened with Eliza?" Sid pressed. "I thought you had feelings for her."

"Maybe I did, but after you left, things with Rachel happened so fast." Tom shook his head. "It seemed like it was meant to be."

Sid was silent.

"I don't know what you expect, Sid. What do you want me to say? That it's okay. We can still be pals, just like before?"

"Only if it's the truth."

"Well, I can't say that… I knew she was in love with you. Even before you left I knew. But I guess I thought you were gone for good and maybe she could fall for me. Maybe she would have."

Sid shook his head. "No, Tom."

"We'll never know, will we?" Tom said. "But it's better this way. I wouldn't want to be second best anyway. That's not enough for me."

Sid did not know what to say.

"I have to go," Tom said suddenly. "I missed you at first, Sid. But now I wish you never came back."

"I understand." Sid's stomach churned. He reached out to shake Tom's hand.

Tom turned away and walked up the bank to the Common.

Sid watched him go. Then he climbed up on the rock himself and sat gazing at the murky water running swiftly on its course. He tried to slow his breathing. Of course Tom was spiteful. Sid knew his pain. He hated the thought that he'd brought on his brother what he himself had experienced—only perhaps worse, and he couldn't take it away. Only time would do that.

And Rachel loved him—Sidney Judson, the born Southerner.

His mind wandered back to the first time he had sat there more than a year ago, after overhearing his uncle and William Gildersleeve talking at the store. He'd been so determined to stop their Railroad plans. Sid shook his head. What a difference a year can make. Now he sat on the same riverbank, a changed man. It had been a long road with a few casualties along the way. But at last he was exactly where he was meant to be.

Acknowledgements

It's impossible to include the name of every person who has contributed to this work in some way. Still, I must try to list the most important.

First, my mother, Susan Burnett Roskos, who not only passed on to me her love of the written word but also read and critiqued many of the early drafts of this novel and offered her support of my vocation in countless ways. My writing group and dear friends Demery Bader-Saye, Pauline Palko, and Linda Steier, patiently read chapter after chapter as the book evolved. Their advice was invaluable during the long revision stage. Jesse Ergott supplied me with fly-fishing information, while the Fish Commission revealed the types of fish that lived in the Susquehanna River in 1860. Bruce Leach offered his extensive Civil War knowledge to answer questions my research failed to satisfy. Sherman Wooden shared his knowledge of the Underground Railroad and the capture of runaway slaves. My sister, Anne Roskos, gave me her insight regarding the depiction of African Americans in the novel.

My brother, Steven Roskos, shared his expert medical advice concerning battle wounds that were ultimately edited out of the story. My friend, Susan Currier, encouraged me to pursue publication with Avventura Press. I found the Luzerne County Historical Society to be a wonderful resource, especially for viewing copies of the Luzerne Union newspaper. Friends generously answered my pleas for advice as I entered the publishing process: Patricia Souder, Nancy Famolari, Leslee Clapp, Marsha Hubler, and Kelly Schneider. My father, Donald Roskos, was invaluable as a copyeditor with his eye for detail. To those who cared for my children while I wrote, I can never thank you enough: Edward and Violet Treat, Donald and Susan Roskos, Elizabeth Treat, Natalie Treat and Olivia Treat. This book would be far from complete if I did not have the precious quiet time your generosity afforded me.

My husband, Todd, supported me in every way—something that can perhaps only be understood by other spouses of artists. My children, Camilla and Adrian, are my greatest works. My little family has enriched my life in ways that have only improved my writing. I thank God for them and for guiding me along the path to realizing my dream of seeing this book in print. He has been with me every step of the way.

A number of books proved indispensible in my research. The following are a few of them.

Galloway, Tammy Harden, ed. *Dear Old Roswell: The Civil War Letters of the King Family of Roswell, Georgia.* Macon, GA: Mercer University Press, 2003

Long, E.B. with Barbara Long. *The Civil War: Day by Day.* New York: Da Capo Press, 1971

McClane, A.J., ed. *McClane's New Standard Fishing Encyclopedia and International Angling Guide.* New York: Hold, Rinehart and Winston, 1965

Wooden, Sherman F. *The Place I Call Home: How Abolition and the Underground Railroad Shaped the Communities of Northeastern Pennsylvania.* Montrose, PA: The Center for Anti-Slavery Studies, 2009

Historical Note

This book is a work of fiction. I have done my best to give an accurate depiction of the Civil War, the Underground Railroad and the town of Wilkes-Barre as it was in 1860 and 1861. While Sidney and his family and most of his friends did not actually exist, a few of the characters were real people.

William Camp Gildersleeve was one of the foremost figures in the abolitionist movement in Northeastern Pennsylvania. Originally from Georgia, he lived on North Franklin Street in Wilkes-Barre and used his home as a refuge for runaway slaves. He was one of only a handful of abolitionists in Wilkes-Barre and made many night trips to Abington and Providence (now a section of Scranton) with runaway slaves. From there, the slaves would journey on to Montrose, one of the most active stations on the Underground Railroad. As portrayed in the novel, most of Wilkes-Barre's residents had southern sympathies and the abolitionists living there met with great resistance and sometimes violence. The disturbance mentioned in Aunt Sarah's journal, with a mob breaking up an anti-slavery meeting at the courthouse, actually happened just as she described it. The following day, a false message was sent to lure Gildersleeve to the Pheonix Hotel. A mob fell on him there and attempted to make him promise to cease his activity in the anti-slavery movement. When he refused to do so they threw hatter's dye on him, concluding that he ought to look like the African Americans he loved so much. After this, they mounted him on a fifteen-foot pole and carried him down the street planning to end up at a tavern and funnel whiskey down his throat, as he was also a teetotaler. One of Gildersleeve's daughters stopped the proceedings with the help of a young man.

Marshal Jacob Yost was a real U.S. Marshal in 1860. The account of the fugitive slave shot in the street near the courthouse is fictional, but a similarly upsetting incident occurred seven years earlier when marshals attempted to arrest fugitive slave William Thomas. They tackled him in the dining room of the hotel, beating him and attempting to handcuff him. Thomas was strong and fought back, preventing the officers from taking him. Bloodied, he ran into the river. The marshals fired their revolvers into the air to frighten him, but he pressed on, following the riverbank to escape. The gathered mob, surprisingly, took Thomas' side and prevented the agents from pursuing him any further.

Sidney's regiment, the Third Georgia, existed. I took much of his experience as a soldier in the Confederate Army from accounts of army life by soldiers in this regiment. Most of the events occurred similarly to the way they are described, from the rendezvous in Augusta, to the train ride to Norfolk and the soldiers' duties in the Norfolk navy yard. Even the banner, reading "God guard and bless our Southern boys" comes from an account by a member of the Third Georgia. I took a large liberty with history when I put Sid's company in the Battle of Big Bethel. The Third Georgia was not a part of this battle, but as a writer, I thought it feasible that a few companies could have been recruited to help fight.

The Battle of Big Bethel took place on June 10, 1861. When relating the story of the skirmishes two days before the Battle of Big Bethel, Colonel D.H. Hill called the second attack "the second race on the same day over the New Market course, in both of which the Yankees reached the goal first" just as Drew relates in the novel.

Henry L. Wyatt was an actual soldier. He is generally regarded to be the first enlisted Confederate soldier killed in action during the Civil War. His friend, John Thorpe, and the officers involved in the Battle (aside from Drew) were also real people.

When it comes to information about the Underground Railroad, it is sometimes difficult to distinguish fact from fiction. Since those involved had much at stake if they were found out, it was important to keep information secret. I have included in the novel some devices that may have been used to help slaves escape to the north. The use of the Drinking Gourd (also known as the Big Dipper) as a guide is generally accepted as accurate. Also, it is believed by some historians that a lighted lantern or a flag in the hand of a lawn jockey may have been used to signify a safe house. Some historians have speculated on the use of quilts to guide slaves on their journey. Upon further research, I found the majority of sources think this unlikely. In all of my references to fictional journeys of runaway slaves to the north and in the story of Sidney's own journey, I hope I have conveyed the message that those who escaped slavery faced great danger and hardship. I am awed by the immeasurable courage it took them to follow their hearts in the hopes of finding freedom as well as the courage of those who helped them along the way. I hope that their courage will inspire my readers to pursue freedom in their own lives and to take a stand for the persecuted and oppressed today.

For Further Reading:

Adleman, Debra. *Waiting for the Lord: 19th Century Black Communities in Susquehanna County,* Pennsylvania. Rockland, ME: Picton Press, 1998

Bradford, Sarah. *Harriet Tubman: The Moses of her People.* Mineola, NY: Dover, 2004

Hendrick, George and Willene Hendrick. *Fleeing for Freedom: Stories of the Underground Railroad, as Told by Levi Coffin and William Still.* Chicago: Ivan R. Dee, 2004

Jacobs, Harriet Ann. *Incidents in the Life of a Slave Girl Written by Herself.* Simon & Brown, 2012

Jones, Gordon L. "Turning Point: The American Civil War" *Atlanta History: A Journal of Georgia and the South.* Spring-Summer 1996

Kashatus, William C. "In Immortal Splendor: Wilkes-Barre's Fugitive Slave Case of 1853." *Pennsylvania Heritage.* Spring 2008

Spear, Sheldon. *Chapters in Wyoming Valley History.* Shavertown, PA: Jemags & Co., 1989

Spear, Sheldon. *Wyoming Valley History Revisited.* Shavertown, PA: Jemags & Co., 1994

Stowe, Harriet Beecher. *Uncle Tom's Cabin.* Dover Thrift Editions, 2005

Wooden, Sherman F. *The Place I Call Home: How Abolition and the Underground Railroad Shaped the Communities of Northeastern Pennsylvania.* Montrose, PA: The Center for Anti-Slavery Studies, 2009

Internet Sources:

http://www.civilwarhome.com

http://www.3gvi.org/ga3history.html

http://wbwilliamcgildersleeve.blogspot.com

CPSIA information can be obtained
at www.ICGtesting.com
Printed in the USA
BVHW042154130622
639714BV00005B/31